A highly acclaimed author, she has twice won a prestigious Crime Writers Association Dagger for her short stories. She has also won Stonewall Writer of the Year twice. A co-director of the Fun Palaces campaign for greater access to culture for all she was awarded an OBE for services to the Arts in 2016. Her website is www.stelladuffy.wordpress.com

'Fast and bold and thrilling, *The Hidden Room* is an audacious take on the psychological thriller that turns the genre inside out'
Christobel Kent, author of *The Loving Husband*

'Wonderfully gothic and sinuous, Duffy's *The Hidden Room* is a top-notch psychological thriller filled with crazed cults, strange occurrences and creepiness galore. A superbly original, highly tense and often moving crime novel'
Stav Sherez, author of *The Intrusions*

'A dazzling, gripping novel – the kind of book you can't put down even as the tension rises to almost unbearable levels'
William Ryan, author of *The Constant Soldier*

'What a novel – dark, devious and shocking: chillingly nuanced, and with a remarkable candour about it, too. We never stop rooting for Laurie and Martha'
Andrew Taylor, author of *The Ashes of London*

'A stunner . . . a psychological thriller of depth, intelligence and emotion'
The Times

THE HIDDEN ROOM

THE HIDDEN ROOM

STELLA DUFFY

virago

VIRAGO

First published in Great Britain in 2017 by Virago Press
This paperback edition published in 2018

1 3 5 7 9 10 8 6 4 2

A CIP catalogue record for this book
is available from the British Library.

ISBN 978-0-349-00790-8

Typeset in Bembo by M Rules
Printed and bound in Great Britain by
Clays Ltd, St Ives plc

Papers used by Virago are from well-managed forests
and other responsible sources.

MIX
Paper from
responsible sources
FSC® C104740

Virago Press
An imprint of
Little, Brown Book Group
Carmelite House
50 Victoria Embankment
London EC4Y 0DZ

An Hachette UK Company
www.hachette.co.uk

www.virago.co.uk

For my fellow crime writers, with huge thanks for
welcoming me back – after 12 years – to crime.
The warmest, kindest group of writers.

For the first thing we saw were their blankets, blankets
... and ... before after 30 years ... all that
... he wanted, kitchen sink of water ...

Acknowledgements

My thanks to Antonia Hodgson, Lennie Goodings, Zoë Hood, Olivia Hutchings and all at Virago, and to Stephanie Cabot and Ellen Goodson Coughtrey at The Gernert Company – I am hugely fortunate to have publishers and agents who greet my (frequent) changes of writing direction with positivity and support. My love and gratitude, as ever, to Shelley Silas. Special thanks to Rose Barnecut and to my Duffy cousins for the sheep.

Acknowledgements

One

Laurie grew up in two places.

Her adopted parents were wonderful, they are her true family, as is the family she has created and lives in, loves in, now.

Laurie lived in a community when she was a child.

Some people called that community a cult, and she was taken away when she was nine years old.

She didn't stay in touch with anyone from there.

She never went back.

Nothing remains from that time in her life.

Laurie keeps secrets.

Two

Martha drove along the country lane back to their home, the land lay ahead reaching towards the sea she knew was there, distant and tempting, Martha loved to swim, in any weather, any water. The grey of the morning mist was gone, leaving the wide flat land green and soft. Their three teenagers were all in school, she could keep on, ignore the hidden turn-off to their house, go to the sea, but that her deadline was looming, and this was an otherwise uninterrupted afternoon to work. Martha was driving too fast, as she always did along this stretch. When they first moved out here she'd been a timid city driver, scared of narrow roads and sharp bends, hedge-rows that hid sight of oncoming traffic, now it was second nature to her and she drove without thinking about the road. Swim or work, swim or work, swim. She sailed past the turn-off and on, another forty minutes to the cold, grey sea.

After her swim, sitting on the shingle beach, Martha wrapped herself in the old towel she kept in the back of the car, feeling strong, vibrant, alive. Now that her thoughts had been sluiced clear of confusion by the shock of the cold, she found she could admit it, she was a little bit infatuated, a bit sixteen and fluttery when she thought of him. And she was enjoying the feeling. Happily married, happily mothering, Martha knew she would do nothing about it, that it would not develop into anything more, that this was just a feeling, but it was a good feeling, an exciting one, and Martha was hungry for excitement.

Until the last year, Martha and Laurie had always shared childcare reasonably evenly, certainly more so than the majority of their friends. Both freelance, once the babies were off the breast and on to the bottle, they had simply allocated jobs according to whoever had the most pressing deadline, aware that the scale could shift with a single phone call. They'd screwed up a few times, impossible client demands for both of them coinciding with a sick child or a plumbing emergency, childcare and housework a burden for a week or so, rather than simply part of daily life, but generally it had worked well.

Since Laurie's unexpected success eighteen months ago things had been different. For almost two decades Laurie had happily carried on with the unsung, under-paid work she loved, designing small community spaces, helping tiny housing associations make the most of limited resources and increasing cuts, creating careful extensions to schools or to simple public buildings. The architecture she practised had very little to do with the massive glass and concrete edifices that usually won awards, and far more in common with the people that used them. It was not fashionable, and the students who took her courses at the two universities where she taught part-time, loved her for her interest in the way communities worked, as much as the spaces she helped them imagine.

Over twenty years of practice, Laurie had built up a port-folio of clients, who commissioned regularly even if they didn't pay well, allowing her to keep people as her central focus. She pushed both students and clients towards dreams that were rooted in a hopeful but solid reality, which meant that she was never going to win the big prizes. Until eighteen months ago and the ceremony where she did win the prize, the biggest one, stumbling up to collect the chunk of etched glass and the certificate and the cheque, mumbling 'Hell fuck damn sorry wow thank you damn' in shock, grateful for the time delay on the radio broadcast and the fact that the news team hadn't expected her to win either, so they didn't have a camera pointing in her direction, at least until she'd realised she was meant to smile and look grateful. Laurie was grateful, she was also the most surprised person in the room.

Martha was not surprised, Martha had always believed in her wife and in her vision of building for people, for com-munities. Martha was thrilled for Laurie when the prize led to more work, more commissions, more lecture offers. Even now, a year and a half later, when the requests still showed no signs of abating, Martha remained delighted, but she also had her own work designing websites, and they had three children. Martha had become the prime carer by default, which had never been the plan, and had almost grown into a problem – until Martha had something else to occupy her thoughts, someone else. Someone to think about when she was increasingly the only parent picking the kids up from a late practice or date, the only parent around to enforce Sunday-night homework. Someone to make her feel a bit sixteen again, and a lot less thirty-nine. A lot less almost forty.

She drove home fast, she got to work, finished a tricky section for an even trickier client, and made dinner, knowing the twins would come home starving from swimming practice, Hope hungry after dance class, and Laurie would be grateful. She played old music as she cooked, songs from her teens, indulging the thought of him – interested in her, talking directly to her, not about this or that, but about her life, her thoughts, her dreams. It was like being in love without the messy lust part. Nothing to worry about. Nothing much, Martha was smart enough to know that part of the thrill of thinking about him was that Laurie didn't know about him, and when everything else was a little mundane, a secret was a fine thing.

Three

Back when they first met, the main thing Martha noticed about Laurie was that she was dauntingly beautiful and while she was small and fine there was nothing delicate about her, nothing fey. Five years older and apparently so much more worldly, Laurie already had style, sharp and strong. Years later, Martha would despair, trying to find something to please Laurie's specific and discerning taste for a gift, but when they were in their twenties, Laurie's style was a badge of distinction. They'd had no more than three conversations when Martha decided that Laurie was wiser, braver, tougher than she'd ever be, more secretive too. Laurie answered questions in short, staccato sentences, she began conversations as if she was about to leave the room. Laurie's waiting, the holding back that she later explained as shyness, as fear, appeared to Martha as mystery and depth. Martha wanted a lot more of Laurie, from their first introduction, and always after. Martha always wanted more of Laurie.

*

They met to make a new piece of work. Martha was in her third year as a fine-arts student – a three-year waste of time according to her farmer father who just wanted his daughter to come home and work with him, take over the farm eventually, and a longer waste of talent according to her teacher mother, 'By the time you unlearn all the rubbish they teach you, you'll have spent five years screwed up by their bollocks'. Alongside their coursework, the students were given three months to work cross-arts. Each student was assigned another art form, something their tutors decided would benefit their own work. Martha drew everyone's short straw when she was sent to assist a new firm of young architects, with a specialist line in making ancient work accessible to the general public. The site was a Roman mosaic uncovered during building works, studied now to see if it had to be left where it was, or might be lifted and transferred, surveyors and developers looking on anxiously, time as money ticking away in shards of broken pottery, excavated lives.

Martha had been working on massive canvases, end-of-terrace walls, hoardings. She turned up at the site on her first morning as agreed, prepared to do the work, get her hands dirty if need be, but not really interested. Ahead of her she had three months on site, plenty of time in the spring evenings to keep on with the vast canvas stretched out in her landlord's empty garage, and then she'd deliver the last of her coursework and be a fully-fledged artist, with the piece of paper to prove it. Martha was twenty-one and the first person from her family to choose the arts as work. She still believed that a piece of paper could make a difference.

Very quickly she discovered that she found the detail, the intricacy, fascinating. Working now on something that had once been made by hand, brand new, so long ago, interested her much more than she had thought. There was a whole architecture for which this mosaic had been made, and now here were the tiles, exposed to the light of a bright April day for the first time in close to two thousand years, uncovering a story piece by piece. By the third week Martha was looking forward to going to work every morning. Then Laurie came back from her holiday with family in the States and rejoined the team of people who had been telling Martha that she needed to be careful of Laurie, to make sure Laurie didn't think she was only there for the credit. Laurie, built up as a tartar, who turned out to be quietly spoken and patient and so much else. Laurie who was watching Martha.

Martha, who liked being watched by Laurie.

'My name is Laurie.'

She was guiding Martha's hand as Martha unsteadily dusted a tiny area of precious tile, Laurie made her student's fingers lighter, softer, slower.

'See? It takes longer this way, but the dirt lifts better, you can begin to see what you're looking at.'

Laurie smiled when Martha turned to her, they both knew what they were looking at.

That night, in bed, Laurie stretched over Martha, watching for her reaction.

'That's quite a tattoo,' Martha said finally, her eyes tracing the lines on Laurie's skin that ran from her left collarbone, over her left breast, twisting to the right side of her ribcage.

'Isn't it?'

'When did you . . . ?'

'I will tell you, but it's not a story for tonight.'

'What is the story for tonight?'

'This.'

Laurie kissed Martha's lips.

'And this.'

She kissed her left breast.

'And this.'

She kissed her right breast.

Martha lay back and let Laurie tell her a story. She believed every word.

Two years later, Martha gave birth to their daughter Hope, and not two years after that, they bought the house in the fens.

'It's twins,' the doctor had said. 'You're having twins.' She pointed to the screen with her free hand, the other rolling the imager back and forth over Laurie's just-there belly.

Laurie closed her eyes, Martha blinked, trying to make sense of the blobs on the screen, while jiggling a fractious twenty-month-old Hope on her lap.

'Twins,' Martha said, because she couldn't think of anything else to say, because she had no idea what reaction she was supposed to give, no idea what she thought yet. Or rather, because she was thinking too much. They loved their little flat, Hope had only just moved into the box room, not that she slept there most nights, but they called it Hope's room, and so did she. No one would have called their half-house spacious, they had part of the garden, sharing with an upstairs neighbour, they were close to shops and the Tube, had friends and a park nearby. It was easy for both women to get to work, and they'd thought they could hold on there a little longer, keep the new baby in with them, spend longer saving towards a bigger flat. Laurie had no intention of moving out of London as so many of the parents at Hope's nursery seemed to do, once they had a second and a third child – property prices they'd say, or fresh air, or better for the kids to have a big garden.

While Martha sometimes spoke longingly of country air or green views studded with hills, she also remembered being a bored teenager and her horror at the darker aspects of farming, so much of that life given over to long hours and bad weather and blood and dirt. Only city people thought farms were pretty. She'd helped with docking lambs' tails from the age of five, done bloodier things too, when she had to. She'd holidayed with her father's brother, the younger brother who became a butcher when Martha's father inherited the farm. From her uncle and his wife she'd learned slaughtering, skinning, butchering. Even at fourteen Martha understood it was a real skill, something of use, much as she hated the blood, the way it stayed in the cracks of her fingernails, the smell in her nostrils. Her father had thought it would help her in future when she took on the farm, but Martha had never wanted the farm, the country was dirty and smelly and damn hard work. Neither Laurie nor Martha had any intention of leaving central London and moving to the suburbs, or worse, one of those sleeper villages just beyond the M25. And yet.

'Twins,' Laurie repeated, her eyes wide.

That night they sat up in bed and looked at properties, those nearby to get a sense of prices, and those further afield that they could afford. Their flat went on the market the next month and, for all the reasons they had loved it themselves, they found a buyer almost immediately. No chain, cash purchase, all they had to do was find somewhere to live.

Martha found the house online, it was the one she kept going back to, it was the one she loved on sight, and it was totally impractical.

'It's falling apart.'

Laurie wasn't exaggerating, the estate agent's blurb had opted for unusual candour: *Needs restoration and love. Lots of love.*

'We can fix it. You're an architect.'

'I'm not a builder and this is no hidden treasure.'

'You don't know that yet.'

'And you do?'

Martha shrugged, 'It has a stream.'

The stream meant her mind was made up. Martha loved water, the sea, a lake, a pool, bath, shower. The twins loved it too, when they were little they'd play in their paddling pool for hours, by the time they were in their teens they were both happy to exhaust themselves swimming length after length after length in the local pool, purely in the hope of cutting one tenth of a second off their times. Hope and Laurie went along to their competitions, but Martha was more enthused about being a swim-team mum. Laurie was happy to play many mother roles but, unlike many of the girls she'd gone to high school with, back in the States, she was no soccer mom.

The children did call her Mom though. Laurie was Mom and Martha was Mum.

It was how they shut up Martha's cousin when she was first

11

pregnant with Hope and the cousin asked, 'But won't your baby get confused?'

Laurie laid her light brown arm against Martha's pale, freckled skin, 'Different skin, different eyes, different hair colour, different height, different names. Probably not.'

'I can see it has a stream,' Laurie was saying, looking at the page, 'it also says the stream has been rubbish-logged for some time and needs clearing.'

'It has an attic, and land. We'll make it gorgeous. You'll make it gorgeous. And it has loads of space, a garage, a conservatory, two sheds, and an outhouse lean-to. What do you think that is?'

'Probably the bathroom.'

It was the bathroom, but only in the way Laurie used the word. The outhouse lean-to was the only toilet for their first year in the house.

Hope was grizzling and she wasn't going to get herself back to sleep, Laurie got out of bed and tried one last thing, knowing it was already too late,

'Martha, I don't want to live in the country.'

'I know, I love London too, but we can't afford it.'

'This house isn't even in a village.'

'We couldn't afford it if it were in a village.'

'It's in the middle of nowhere.'

'Yes, way better than a village, if it were in a village we'd have to make friends with new people.'

'It's miles from anywhere.'

'A forty-minute commute to the city,' Martha quoted.

'Capital-C?' Laurie asked.

'Obviously not.'

'Right, some local city, small city.'

Hope's grizzles had turned to proper wails.

'Coming baby,' Laurie called out to her.

When Hope was finally sleeping again, Laurie carefully got into bed, it was just starting to turn from autumn to winter and she was shivering. Martha rolled over.

'You're still awake?'

'It has a stream,' Martha said, 'the house has its own stream.'

They booked to see it that weekend and Martha persuaded Laurie that they should put in an offer the following week. They were terrified when it was accepted within two days. Terrified and thrilled. And, because it made Martha happy, Laurie put aside her fears of living in a place with no neighbours, no lights in the distance at night, a place that scared her because it was so far from anywhere else.

Now, after fifteen years of slow renovations, the house was both old and startlingly new. They made the new parts bright and light and open, and restored the oldest rooms, making them the warm heart of the house. Their work was especially successful where the kitchen became a big, bright room easily holding all five of them alongside assorted friends, Martha's parents for Christmas dinner, and most of Laurie's huge family of adopted siblings every second Thanksgiving. Martha loved the views as much as the place itself, from every one of the upstairs windows there was a different view of the fens, flat and open stretching out to the sky and the sea, and even Laurie found she was able to look out at the distant nothing and see it was beautiful, though she still missed the rush and noise of the city. Now that the twins were teenagers,

Laurie sometimes talked about moving back, how it would be when they were just two of them, and the house and big garden took too much upkeep. Martha had had a hard time in her mother's last few years, her mother too ill to cope with the farmhouse, her father too busy caring for her mother to look after the farm properly, and both of them leaning heavily on their only child. It was only after his wife's death that Martha's father had agreed to sell the farm, though he kept the old house, selling off the land around it. Laurie suggested he come and live with them, but he was having none of it. He told them both not to be daft, that he was fine by himself, thinking about his wife and the land, but he must have been lonely, sometimes, often. Martha sometimes worried what would happen, when the children were grown, if Laurie went first and she was there, with only the house for company. Laurie promised it would never happen, that she was never going anywhere without Martha.

'Although a lovely little flat right in the centre of town, when the kids are all grown up, that wouldn't be so bad, would it?'

'If it hasn't got a stream, I'm not going,' was Martha's answer.

And so they stayed in their rambling old-new home with the astonishing views in the low land, beneath a high sky, and the children grew and it was all, more or less, just fine. Even their secrets.

Four

'I hate you, don't you dare come over here, I hate you, fuck off!'

A door slammed shut, the house shook, there was silence for a moment, then something thudded heavily against a wall, followed by a muffled shatter and a low groan. There was a brief, all too lovely moment of silence, and then the wailing began, sobbing, shouting and wailing.

Martha looked at Laurie, 'Your turn.'

'I can't do this one, I only ever met him once.'

Martha bit her tongue to stop herself pointing out that Laurie hadn't been home enough to get to know their daughter's boyfriend. Ex-boyfriend. She smiled instead and said, 'But she is your daughter.'

They both laughed.

When people looked at Hope, saw Laurie's brown skin, her almond eyes, her high cheekbones, delicate build, they often said, 'So Hope must be your daughter?'

They were right, but not in the way they'd assumed. Hope grew from Laurie's egg and their donor's sperm, but

Martha carried her, just as Laurie carried the twins grown from Martha's eggs and the same donor sperm. To those who didn't know them well, the who-gave-birth-to-whom question seemed to really matter. If either mother, if any of the children, could be bothered telling them that their guess was wrong, then the whose-egg-was-it question seemed to matter almost as much. Martha often wondered if people were quite so crude about adopted children, and how anyone fell in love with a stranger if biology really mattered so much to them.

It had mattered at first. When they were trying to get pregnant, they'd thought that swapping eggs would help them trust that they were both the mothers. The minute the midwife placed Hope in Laurie's arms, the moment Martha first held the twins, they realised they were both mothers to all three children, then and always, in love with each of the babies, and biology had nothing to do with it.

'Even if I knew what to say about him,' Laurie said, 'you're way more patient than me, especially about things like this. You'll only get annoyed when I tell her to stop screaming after five minutes.'

'You could try not doing that?'

'I could, but it'll be on the tip of my tongue anyway. You go, you're nicer than me,' Laurie was nudging Martha with her foot.

'That's true.'

Laurie grinned and Martha knew she'd lost, 'What are you going to do?' she asked.

'Make dinner.'

'I doubt Hope wants to eat.'

'She'll be starving after this. And wanting a new phone if that crash was as bad as it sounded.'

'You think?'

'I do. And if she thinks we'll just buy her another one . . .'

'Yeah, you're right. I am nicer than you.'

'It was an expensive phone.'

'Four years ago. It's my old one. Just because you had a childhood of deprivation, doesn't mean—'

Laurie had heard it before, 'Whatever. The twins'll be home soon, they'll be hungry even if Hope isn't. You deal with her now and we might even be able to manage a peaceful meal, then we can settle down and watch TV like everyone else.'

'Hope's been dumped, the week before her school dance, by an idiot who's just discovered he fancies her best friend more than her. I don't think we're going to be spending the night cuddled up on the sofa watching *The Sound of Music*.'

'Good, I hate that cheesy crap.'

Hope's furious cries increased and Martha downed the last mouthful of wine in her glass as she got up, 'What's for dinner?'

'Mac-and-cheesy crap.'

Mac and cheese. Laurie stirred the sauce, and her hands were Dot's hands, grating cheese, stirring sauce, waiting for it to thicken, not too much, not too little, just right. She made their meal, thinking of Dot and Henry, the people she called Mom and Dad, the people who were her mom and dad, who had raised her, saved her, taken her in along with their other adopted children, bringing them up, black, white, brown alongside their own mixed bag of birth kids. Henry white, Dot black.

17

Dot had often said, 'White folks are always so surprised that our babies don't just turn out regular coffee colour.'

To which Henry would always add, 'Bad coffee at that.'

People were also surprised by the children that Dot and Henry took in. They started with one, added another, and another. Hippy hangovers who'd rolled into the seventies planning to teach the world to sing, Henry and Dot believed good old-fashioned love could fix everything. It turned out that neither love nor common sense could fully save Laurie and the other adopted siblings from what they'd seen, been through, from memories that lurked in nightmares and snatches of song, but Dot and Henry persisted, and, in the end, love was more or less enough.

Laurie was persisting too, even though success brought its own difficulties, even though she knew she was leaving too much for Martha to do and that Martha's stoic martyrdom on the altar of motherhood couldn't go on for ever, Laurie persisted with their own version of happy families. Every now and then she thought she was just about on top of it, thinking we're OK at this, the kids in their teens and none of them were too fucked up, not yet.

Laurie stirred, nodding, we didn't screw it up yet.

I didn't screw it up yet.

I didn't run away, I didn't run back. Not yet.

The sauce was done, Dot's hands on the wooden spoon, Dot guiding Laurie's hands. She was nine years old, in third grade though she'd only gone to school for the first time that year. Dot teaching her the feel, the resistance that said the sauce was ready, teaching that we don't always cook by recipes and measures and timing, or even by look, sometimes we do it by touch.

Adult Laurie cooked and remembered that Dot had taught her how to feel, while, in another room, Martha held their daughter who was now feeling all too much.

Laurie poured the sauce over the still-steaming macaroni, and as she put it in the oven she finally heard Hope break. She had been shouting all that time, screaming at Martha as if it was all her fault, and finally she was crying, quietly. Laurie pictured Hope in Martha's arms, their beautiful girl, thinking her world was over because some stupid boy had dumped her. It was true, Jon was good-looking, Laurie had to give him that, but sixteen, and stupid. He had to be stupid if he'd dumped their gorgeous girl. Then she heard Martha's voice, soft and low, reassuring.

Laurie set the oven timer, nodding to herself, Martha was good at reassuring, holding, making better. The safety of Martha's embrace was definitely a part of their love, she could imagine her treading just the right line between placating and letting Hope moan. Laurie knew that she would have been more likely to tell Hope to get up and get on, even when she was trying to be kind, gentle, she'd find herself saying the wrong thing, too brusque, too hasty. She usually put it down to not having had Dot's mothering, any mothering, until she was nine years old. And that was true, but Laurie also knew she was far more impatient than Martha, even more so since Hope became a teenager, they were too sharp with each other, too likely to hurt, accidentally, and sometimes intentionally. Where once Laurie had been able to shrug off her spats with Hope because they were just too similar, now she often found herself on the receiving end of Hope's 'You don't understand me, it's all your fault'.

She had felt the same at Hope's age, even Dot and Henry's embrace eventually became stifling. Not that she blamed them to their faces back then. She blamed the Chinese mother and father, or maybe just the mother, the one who had let her go, let her be shipped to America, the birth mother was an easy target for ire, whatever the poor woman's reasons might have been. Laurie also blamed the system that had allowed the desert community to buy a baby, twisting rules and circumventing laws to bring in new blood, purchasing the progeny of a brighter future, the community who had made her theirs. Once she was pulled out of there and safely with Dot and Henry, Laurie trained herself not to think about the time before, and within two years of living in the crammed house with all the other kids, she had convinced herself she remembered nothing of the old life at all. By the time she was fifteen, it was almost true. Sometimes she found herself lapsing into a particular rhythm as she walked, or recoiling at the scent of rose oil, but mostly she chose to ignore the missing years before Dot and Henry. Their love, their home, their open arms became her place of safety. As an adult she recognised that she had everything to thank them for, even the voice with which she now spoke, the voice she found only after she had been living with them for six months, her own voice that returned when she was allowed to make her own choices. Eventually. And the mac and cheese, Laurie definitely had them to thank for the gift of comfort food.

A car pulled up outside, the kitchen ceiling lit by bright head-lights. People always drove with their headlights on full out here, the better to see along the narrow, winding road that led to their house, lined with big, dark trees on either side.

Car doors slammed, Laurie heard Jack and Ana, laughing, running over the gravel, waving goodbye to their friends, the back door opened, slammed shut, and they were home. All home, all five, safe and sound. Laurie resisted the temptation to lock the door.

Later, after the twins had eaten and Hope had pushed food around her plate, after a run-down of swim times and races won and lost, after Jack had prodded and poked and finally, gently, teased a smile from his older sister, just one, then it was time to wash dishes, gather papers and books, prepare for a new week. Sunday-night blues turning into Monday-morning rush.

Before Laurie and Martha went to bed, they looked in on their children. They had done it at first, as every parent does, revelling in the blissful moment when the little one was perfect and easy, tiny chest rising and falling. Then there were the times they looked in to make sure the lights were off and they were actually sleeping, that bit between seven and twelve when their children's growing pains showed up in small rebellions, books read long after lights-out, phone sneaked to call friends, snacks eaten in a bed made itchy with crumbs. Now they would look in and more often than not the twins were already sleeping, they both trained so hard, three times a week after school as well as four mornings, that they fell asleep the minute they got to bed, barely shifting in their dreams. Hope was different, often still at her desk, working, reading, drawing. At seventeen it was hard to insist she went to bed, she was finding her own rhythms, their baby girl, nearly woman, the best they could do was suggest; maybe it's time to turn out the light, maybe it's time to try to sleep. Laurie and Hope shared the insomniac's fear of the dark room, the boredom and the loneliness of another night awake. The mothers stood at Hope's door, whispered good-night, then went up to their own bedroom.

Soon after, Martha was sleeping easily as Laurie lay listening to the night, assuring herself that the doors were locked and their babies were safe. Eventually she would sleep, but rarely well, rarely for more than a few hours at a time. In her childhood, in the years before she was taken to Dot and Henry, she had been trained to be alert for the quietest call, the faintest light, the lightest touch. So many of her childhood nights were full of broken sleep, leading to the damaged selves which, like a bone that mended badly, must be broken again to be reset, re-made. Laurie had re-made herself, but even so, sleep was a broken promise.

Five

There were no broken promises in the community. Abraham's dream was the confirmed prophesy, their lives in the desert were his vision made real, and every promise was offered in the knowledge that no break was possible, no rescinding countenanced.

Laurie was seven years old when she was covenanted to Abraham's youngest son Samuel, who was nearly nine. They were brought before the whole community, more than sixty people gathered in the big hall, waiting while the children were dressed for the moment, readied for the promise. The room was silent during the waiting, silent when the outside door opened and Samuel was led to the dais where Abraham sat, ready to receive him.

Samuel knelt, 'Father.'

Abraham was his father and he was the father of the community, he had built it on his own prophesy, with his wife Ingrid by his side, at his back, at his beck and call. Ingrid was the first of her husband's acolytes, and his most beloved. Abraham often said that it was her faith in his vision that allowed him to found the community. Even so, Ingrid received no special treatment on the compound, no special favours from the father of her three sons. If anything, some noted that Abraham was tougher on Ingrid and the boys, expected more from them – more obedience, more whole-hearted giving, more surrender to the needs of many rather than the preferences of just one. Abraham had given up the possibility of an easy family life in order to create this sanctu-ary in the desert, renouncing the comfort of the blind world in order to open all of their eyes to the searing beauty of real life in true community – the least his immediate family could do in return was to live as fully a part of the whole as possible. To give themselves to the land as Abraham had done.

Abraham nodded when Samuel called him father, 'To all of you, yes,' he replied, and many in the room felt a moment of pride that Abraham truly did consider them as important as his own flesh and blood, a moment that was quickly checked when Abraham looked around the big hall and asked, 'And who of you felt special, chosen, when you heard me say I am father to all?'

There was silence, and then half a dozen right hands were raised, half a dozen more, another ten, twenty, each one accompanied by a left hand to the breast and the words, 'I accuse myself'.

More silence, more waiting, right hands remained raised, left hands on beating chests, Samuel kneeling still, his knees pressing into the wooden floor.

Outside in the centre of the compound, standing alone on the land where they heard Abraham's revelations, Laurie waited. She wore the thin white cotton dress of all the covenanting girls. She hadn't seen Samuel before he was taken inside, but she knew he would be wearing a white shirt, white trousers, that's what the boys wore for the promising. She had seen them before now, her friends from the children's group, up at the front of the big hall, kneeling before Abraham, being special, being loved. The wind lifted and Laurie shut her eyes tight against the stinging dust. Shut her eyes too, against what it might do to her dress. It was hard to stay clean in white clothes, the wind whirled dust around the compound every day, on the rare occasions it rained the whole place became mud. Abraham had helped them understand that to be untidy, to be messy or dirty, was a failure, not just of cleanliness, but of respect for the whole community. Anyone who did not take care with his or her appearance was showing a disregard for their brothers and sisters, insulting the whole. Laurie squinted down at her dress, the wind had missed her, mostly, she shuffled even though she had been told not to move at all, the dust lifted, shifted, she was clean. She waited.

Inside the big hall, they also waited. Abraham looking from one person to another, noting whose hand was raised and whose was not. Some of those with their hands carefully clasped before them wondered if they should have raised their hand. If it might have been better to admit to a fault they had not committed than to risk Abraham calling them out now, asking why they did not have the courage to admit failure. There was always a chance that Abraham would challenge one who failed to accuse themselves. Everyone craved Abraham's attention, the glance of the father that became the loving look, the embrace, the kiss on the forehead. Craved it, and feared it, his attention was also a laser beam and it went straight to the heart, searching out forgotten failings, mistaken intentions. Sometimes it was better to hold up a hand, anyway. Sometimes it was safer.

Then he smiled. He looked around the room and his arms were wide open and he was laughing, 'My beloveds, my perfect community of beloveds. So generous in your care for each other, for my spirit in each of you, so willing to offer your truths, your wickedness, your failures.'

He left the dais then, walked right past Samuel whose head was bowed as required, whose knees were now burning with waiting, kneeling, the room of people behind him now in joyous uproar as Abraham, his father – their father – went to each and every one of the community and kissed them, hugged them, held them, loved them.

Samuel knelt and waited, and outside, Laurie wished that they would call her in, that she might be covenanted with Samuel, that it might all happen soon, before the dark clouds came closer, before her dress was ruined, her promise broken before it was made. Laurie stood alone in her pure white dress and wished to be a good girl, no matter how wicked it made her – wishes were wicked, prayer was permitted, only obedience to the rule of the community showed true commitment, and surrender to the whole was the one real obedience. Like many of the children, Laurie wasn't quite sure what the big words meant, but it didn't matter, because she knew what they were in action. And, as Abraham often explained, willing compliance was the one true prayer.

Later, Abraham anointed first Samuel and then Laurie, touching their foreheads with the rose oil he wore on his own skin. He held the cup to their lips and they each took a sip of the pure rainwater, preserved for these occasions. Abraham bound their right hands and their left hands with a long thin strip of old red cloth, whispering to the two children the promise of their future lives, and then Samuel and Laurie led the community in their dance that night. They led stumbling, unsure, it was difficult to make the steps with their hands crossed and bound to each other, but they led anyway. Exactly as Abraham often explained, they led because the others followed – he had dreamed the community into being, and it was a community only because they all surrendered to the dream. The dream and the promise, all tied together in a long, thin strip of tired red cotton.

It was hard to sleep that night, it had been exciting to stand out, to lead the dance, Laurie tried to coax herself into sleep with the pattern – breathe in, hold, breathe out, hold. Sometimes she wondered how long she could hold the breath for. In the days that followed, the darker nights after the covenanting, when she discovered what else she had promised when she was bound with the red cloth, what else was expected of her, when the scent of rose oil on Abraham's skin became suffocating, she tried to hold her breath for longer and longer, tried to find that held moment, that not-really moment. That night she held and let go, held and let go, until she felt the holding lower her into sleep.

Six

The moment before the in-breath, when she was only empty, only waiting. The held moment where there was nothing and − then. There was again. Air, breath, life, breathe. In out, in out. Laurie had learned many things in the community, before she was taken to Dot and Henry, this was one of the few she had held on to. How to be in that place in-between, how to breathe and not breathe, how to be, waiting. It was a technique she still practised, when she was alone, private, in a place she kept apart from her family.

Laurie found the room one day when she was alone in the house. Martha had taken Hope, four, and the twins, just two, to visit her parents − it was Mother's Day and Martha's mother was already ill. Martha made the journey to build memories for herself, if not their too-small children. Laurie was meant to be working, she had a brief to deliver for a client who professed to care about the local neighbourhood, and as Laurie sat at her desk, stalling, she acknowledged that she was not going to deliver what the client wanted, and he was not going to commission her.

They were using the small attic as an office, a place to store their designs and dreams for the house, far from inquisitive little fingers, and Laurie was up there, under the eaves, tiny shards of sunlight pushing through cracked tiles, singularly failing to get on with what she knew was a pointless task. She turned away from the desk, looked around, imagining what had been there before.

The chimney stack rose crooked from below, smoke stains reached upwards where bricks had crumbled over years, soot lines dripped like sad mascara from the leaks around the chimney. The tiny attic window, definitely not original, but not recent either, its glass thick to the point of opacity, showing only outlines of trees outside, was bent as much from the waves in the glass as decades of wind speeding across the land. The floorboards were sanded, not by machine, but by the boxes of junk and old carpets pushed and pulled across the floor over the years, as lives were put away and reclaimed or thrown out. The centre of the room was the smoothest, the edges were still rough, as Hope had discovered early on, struggling upstairs by herself and collecting a centuries-old splinter deep in her fat little knuckle. After Laurie had carefully pulled it away and rinsed and washed and kissed the sore point – memories of other hurts to her own skin, her own body, pushing at the edge of her mind and just as quickly pushed away as she concentrated on Hope's sticky, tear-stained face. After she had covered the entry point with antiseptic and a plaster and kisses, Hope looked at the offend-ing part of the floor, the little nook usually hidden behind the open door to the attic, and said, 'Bad room, bad floor.'

Now Laurie stared at the point behind the door, the corner Hope had been exploring when the floor stabbed her, the corner they never looked at properly because they always left the door to the attic open, three small children made the silence and privacy of closed doors a rare luxury. The corner behind the door where a narrow bookcase had once been built to measure, now the shelves were gone and the space was used for nothing more useful than storing ironing boards. Three ironing boards. Two metal, one wooden, as if the occupants of the past hundred years wanted a mausoleum for their dead ironing boards. While neither Laurie nor Martha ironed anything if they could help it, they hadn't yet got around to throwing out the boards. There they stood, slotted into the gap left by the frame of an old bookshelf. The shelf must have been built into the corner behind the door, and – now that Laurie really paid attention to it, anything to avoid getting back to work, the empty frame, a bookshelf hidden behind an open door – it looked all wrong.

She stood up, unlike Martha, Laurie didn't have to worry about smacking her head on the low beams of the attic or the old central rooms of the house. She stood so she was directly opposite the crack in the door. And then it was absurdly obvious, the thing she'd missed while all their attention had been in carving a home out of this house, taking care of the babies, working to earn whenever they could. There was a space where there should not have been, a gap, three or even four feet wide judging by the depth of the wall alongside the staircase twisting up to the attic, there was a space behind the bookshelf behind the ironing boards.

Laurie heard the car roll up outside, she heard the brakes

squeak, the door open and shut and then Martha's call, time to go down and help her bring in the babies.

Laurie never knew why she didn't tell Martha about the space straight away, ask her to come and see, explore. The moment before the in-breath. Laurie waited, she made a choice, she went downstairs.

It was another two weeks before Laurie was alone in the house again. Martha was taking Ana, Jack and Hope to a play at the twins' group in the closest big town, a good thirty minutes' drive away. Laurie always said that Martha was the braver mother, easier with unknown parents, more comfortable in the playgroup chat, and it was true that Martha was easier with strangers, but that wasn't Laurie's reason for staying behind this time. The minute the car was out of the drive, Laurie was up to the attic with a claw hammer, a mallet and a drill. She had just over three hours to get through to the other side and find out what was hidden by the bookcase, and she was hoping for something other than cobwebs and spiders.

It was a room. Narrow, wide enough for a single bed with a very little space to move alongside, and just over six feet long. It was definitely a part of the house, and it had once been a room, the bookcase had been nailed and drilled into place against what had been a door frame. Now, although the door was missing, the original hinges were still there, rusted into the frame. There was a window too, almost half the length of the end wall. It was covered by ropey branches of the ancient wisteria that smothered this corner of the house, vines twisting into each other, so that the tiny amount of light that came through was diffuse, the branches nested against the streaked

31

glass. The old vines must have been why they hadn't noticed the window from outside. Laurie had wanted to remove the wisteria since they moved in, she didn't trust it not to bring the house down around their ears, but Martha loved it, made her promise to keep it. The roofers cut away much of the excess in the main part of the house, and promised that the chimneys were not at risk from curling colonisation. They made it through the long first winter of new babies and outside toilet and the brutal north wind sweeping across the frozen flat land they had chosen as home. Then came a long, slow spring in the cramped oldest part of the house, the two women huddled together with the twins and toddling, stumbling Hope, weeks with intermittent hot water as the ancient boiler died a lingering death, finally coming to the point where neither of them had a brave face left to put on. It was exactly then that the old wisteria opened up, washing the house in late-spring lilac, mauve, purple in evening light, and even Laurie had to admit it was stunning. So the wisteria stayed for the beauty of just four weeks of blossom, and the other forty-eight weeks of the year Laurie whispered threats to it,

'Don't you dare twist into my roof, don't you dare curl round my chimneys, don't you dare break my house. Don't you dare.'

It hadn't broken the house, not yet, but it had hidden a whole tiny room. This side of the house faced east, and the light coming through that window in the morning, before the wisteria had grown so high, so dense, must have been glorious. It must have been intended. Someone had built this tiny room specifically for the morning light.

*

Laurie loved the morning. There was a time in her childhood, after the covenanting, when waiting for morning was
the best she could do. Daylight, sunlight, was her friend.
Martha thought that was why Laurie found English winters
so hard, lingering into March in the weak light, direct sunlight withheld on all but the coldest, sharpest of days. Laurie
was an early riser, not just to be away from the dark of her
sleep-scarce nights, but to welcome the day, get going with
the day. So when she found the little room behind the bookcase she saw it as a gift. She didn't think Martha would have
minded if she'd said she wanted a space, for her work, or even
just to think. But it wasn't only a room that Laurie wanted,
she wanted a secret, something of her own.

She created a new routine, meditating in the room, in the
mornings when she was awake long before Martha, she
would head upstairs and as the dawn broke through the vines,
she would breathe out, hold, breathe in, hold. The room
white-painted, the wisteria branches pushed back, ever such a
little, to not give away from outside what was hidden within,
if Martha ever looked up. She never did, never had. Martha
paid attention to the wisteria four weeks a year, her vision
blurred by the purple mist, the rest of the time she was intent
on her work, on Laurie, on the children. Rarely in that order.

The early-morning light filtered green through soft leaves.
These days it was harder for Laurie to find a time to be in
the room alone, especially now that the twins were up early
for swimming training, even more so since her own success
meant she was away from home so much. Often she didn't
open the door to her room for weeks at a time, but when she

could no longer close her mind to the sound of blood pulsing in her ears, to the shadow of her memories, she would find a reason to be alone in the house, alone in the room. It was not often enough to make it better, but enough to get by, getting through on breaking morning and solitude.

Martha had the all-new, hi-tech shed office at the end of the long back garden, and Laurie had this space, under the eaves. They had a dream of a proper office space for Laurie, she'd even drawn up the plans, picked a spot beneath the crumbling old tumble-down garden shed, long unused, had started marking out foundations but, as yet, had got no further. Martha never came up to Laurie's office unless it was to bring her coffee and a kiss, the children were far too immersed in their own lives to care about Laurie's workspace, and so Laurie had the hidden room, for her secrets, for the memories she chose not to have, for the nightmares she could not control.

Breathe out. Hold. Wait.

Seven

'Breathe.'

'I am breathing.'

'So can you look at me now?'

'No,' Martha winced, her eyes half-shut, her head down, she shook her head.

He waited a moment more, another, almost a minute before he spoke, 'I'll still be here when you look up.'

He spoke quietly, and it hit home. He wasn't going anywhere, she was stuck sitting opposite him, she was going to have to open her eyes eventually. Martha took a deep breath. It was excruciating, this embarrassment, exquisitely sharp, edging towards deep shame, and yet, she had to admit, found it hard to admit, it was also exciting, there was something very appealing about being asked to be this honest. Martha hadn't felt like this in years, this exposed, this heard. Even while she knew she was blushing, her fists clenched, her stomach tight, Martha acknowledged she was enjoying this, the way he encouraged her to put words to her truth. She was a designer, she liked to work alone and in silence turning others people's ideas into beautiful pages, filling screens with stories that told themselves in a myriad of user-friendly ways. Martha was good at creating narratives out of disjointed possibilities for other people, she had very little practice in telling her own story.

She tried again, tried to look up at the man asking her to consider her place in her own story, and the acute discomfort of meeting his eyes meant that she looked instead around the nondescript rented office they were sitting in. She noted the dull picture on the wall – a vase, some flowers, insipid blues and greens – the fake leather of the chairs, his matching hers. She looked anywhere but at him.

'You are going to have to look at me eventually,' he said, quietly again, but more insistent now.

'I don't know,' she said, her eyes firmly on the low table between them, 'I could just get up and leave, I could not look back at all.'

'Without saying goodbye?' he asked and Martha could hear that he was smiling.

'No, I couldn't do that, I'm too well-behaved.'

'I wouldn't let you anyway.'

'You wouldn't let me?' she laughed, and the laugh helped her to look up, to look directly at him.

He was tall and Martha thought he was maybe a full decade older than her, possibly as close to fifty as she was to forty, but his shaved head did away with any possibility of grey as an indicator and he was strong, toned, his body very much that of an ex-dancer. So yes, he probably could stop her if she tried to leave, but the idea of this softly spoken man stepping up and physically blocking her way was absurd.

'You'd bar the door?' she asked.

He shook his head, 'We're not here to talk about what I'd do.'

'Nice deflection.'

'Thank you,' he nodded, allowing her a momentary win in their status tussle, 'So maybe now you can answer the question?'

She took the plunge, 'I don't know why I find it so hard, talking about what I want . . .'

'Yeah, you do,' he pushed.

'It feels so . . .' she looked away again.

'Say it,' when she sighed he spoke more urgently, 'Martha, say it.'

'Self-indulgent?' she asked.

'You tell me.'

'OK, yes, it feels self-indulgent and self-absorbed and selfish. And just a bit bloody stupid, when I have a perfectly happy life, to be having a crisis about . . .'

She faltered and he prodded again, 'About?'

'My work.'

'Really? It's just about your work?'

'Yes . . . no.'

'Then what?'

'You don't let up, do you?' she said.

'No.'

'Well, then, my work and . . . me. A crisis about me.'

He smiled, satisfied with her answer and she relaxed as he began to speak, Martha was happier listening to him, it was far less exposing.

'It would be difficult to have a crisis about anyone else, wouldn't it?' he asked.

Martha shrugged, thinking he obviously didn't have teen-age children, but she let it go.

'You're all you've got,' he said, 'you've become a part-time carer for your father, you said that Laurie's very busy with work, more so than before, that she's away a lot of the time, that means you're doing more of the childcare ...'

'They're teenagers, they wouldn't thank you for calling them children.'

He raised an eyebrow, 'No, you're not going to get away from the subject by starting a semantic discussion. Stop intel-lectualising it, Martha. Feel it a bit more. It makes sense for you to ask "What about me?", you're allowed to think about yourself. You're allowed to think for yourself. After all, you are nearly forty – and isn't that part of the problem? So if not now, if you're not going to address your problems now, then when?'

She laughed out loud then, at his cheek, it was a long time since anyone had pushed her like that. She liked it.

That had been her first session, goading her to feel the frustra-tions she had been pushing aside, ignoring. Of course Martha knew that many of the choices she made were best for them as a family, for each of the children, for Laurie, for her father, that fewer of them were best for Martha. She'd nodded when he had suggested that perhaps she often did what she thought was expected of her, needed from her, rather than what she really wanted. Not that she minded, not really, her parents' relationship had been enviable, right up until her mother's slow death, and Martha took their generous care of each other, their selflessness as parents, as a template for a long and successful marriage, for her own happy family. But recently she had begun to wonder if being so intricately tied to just one other person was sensible, in the end. Her father's ravaged mourning, his inability to make even the most basic choices without his wife to counsel him, the burden he believed he had become to Martha – all of it suggested that he might have been stronger in his grief if he'd had more of a life apart from her mother, if he had been as much an individual as he was one half of a couple.

When Hope's dance teacher had first suggested a coaching session, Martha hadn't known what to say. New to town, he had taken over the classes when Hope's teacher of the past four years had suddenly decided she was giving it all up to go travelling, sick of small-town life, sick of not doing what she had dreamed. Which was fine for the teacher, Martha understood the feeling very well, but it had caused some grumbles among the parents and students. It only took a few classes for Hope to decide things had changed for the better. After initially moaning that their classes were being taken over by 'some stupid American bloke who doesn't even teach ballet', Hope quickly became his most passionate advocate – both of the work they did in classes and of the man himself. A passion made most obvious when he extended the advanced group's two standard classes a week to ninety-minute classes on three days, with a full morning every Saturday and there was not one grumble from Hope.

Martha had met him one evening, her turn to drive the girls home after their dance class, interested in this man who could get Hope and her friends to commit to so many hours of training every week without complaint. She was not surprised that he was good-looking, she'd been a teenage girl herself, she knew that the chances of them following an ugly man quite so avidly were slim. She was surprised when he asked her if she wanted a coaching session with him.

'For free, the first session is free. To see if it works.'

'Er ... why?'

He grinned, a little shy, Martha thought, maybe more used to being questioned by young people than adults, if he was questioned at all.

'I'm retraining. I love dance, always have, but it's getting harder to make a living, and sometimes parents think it's weird for a man to be teaching, especially when so many more girls than boys want to dance, even now, and I'll need another career eventually. My students tell me I'm good at encouraging them, coaching their motivation as well as their technique, so I thought ...'

'You'd retrain. Makes sense,' Martha nodded, 'but the girls think you're great, they'd hate you to stop, it was bad enough when their last teacher left.'

'Not yet,' he said, 'I'm only in my second year, that's why I need clients. I need the practice.'

'And I'll be good practice?'

He looked right at Martha then, the hint of bashfulness entirely gone, 'That would be up to you.'

She had said yes because she often said yes and then worked out what it was she'd said yes to, a trait that had become stronger as she grew older. In response to Laurie's marked reticence to try anything new, Martha had determined to be different so that their children had role models for both yes and no. The yes to coaching was one of her good choices. It was useful to have someone outside the family to talk with about her father, his all-consuming grief, the grief she felt for her mother but had to put aside to care for his. It was very useful to have someone to help her consider how to manage their family life now that Laurie was away so much, how to find time for her own work, even though that work felt mundane compared to Laurie's new-found love of her own. Martha kept on with the sessions because it was useful to talk to someone about these things, because he put her on the spot and she found that she liked it, she liked being pushed to think about what she really wanted, in the same way that Hope and her friends liked being pushed in their dance class, pushed to do better, be better, pushed to excel.

Martha also kept going back because there was something particular about being with him, an edge of something else, nothing as obvious as a romance or even a flirtation, but there was definitely something. Martha kept seeing him because in those sessions she felt awake.

Eight

Laurie had called just two places home. Not her birthplace, that Chinese town of which she had no recollection, nor her years in the desert community, which she pushed from her memory if she could. The first home was the ramshackle old house where she had lived with Dot and Henry and her adopted family, the second was the house that she and Martha had raised their children. Between these two were student dorms that morphed into shared apartments in the States, followed by shared flats in London, shifting words from roommates to flatmates. There were rooms in cold blocks, rooms in damp houses, bedrooms with lovers, the few women and the fewer men who came before Martha, but none of those places was home, not even the flat they had shared before they moved out here. They'd loved the flat for the location, not for itself. They loved the house because they made it together.

Their once-lonely old house was now home because they had marked it as theirs, labelled it with living. The scuff marks on the walls and the trainers in the hall, the fine cracks of plaster from too-often slammed doors, the heights inscribed on the kitchen door frame as the children grew, these were the scars of a full family life.

Laurie had loved Dot and Henry's home, where they took her in and held her with a suggestion of touch instead of actual holding, back when she still flinched at the possibility of another person's skin on hers, when she made herself nests of cushions and barricades of chairs to hide behind. Dot and Henry coaxed her from silence into speaking, into singing even, and when she finally let them reach her, they held her into being a child again, their child, one of their many.

'When I was eleven years old I came home from school to find a garden dug over by the back fence, because the night before my brother Gary had said he'd like to grow some vegetables, so Henry just went right ahead and made a wish into reality.'

Laurie told Martha about it as she dug into the ground at the furthest end of their uneven garden space, carved out of farmland that had long ago been drained, clawed back from the wetlands that always threatened to seep back. She was finally making a start on the garden office she'd been planning to build herself for years. The rubble of the old shed had been shifted to one side and Laurie was determined to dig out the foundations, eventually. Doing every bit of it herself would be harder work, take longer, it would also give her more time before she left the office upstairs that gave her access to the hidden room. Laurie knew it was time to stop having secrets, especially now that she was away so much, now that people had suddenly become interested in her work, and she could feel Martha's dissatisfaction, wanting more of Laurie's time, her energy. Beginning the dig for the office was a statement

43

of their future – Laurie would finally get around to building her garden office, at the corner of Martha's, the two of them making their own work, side by side. The unexpected success had jolted Laurie forward, it was time to let go of her upstairs room. Even so, she was pacing herself.

'Gary was sick of gardening before the end of the season, but Henry took it over and like every time we moved on to new things, he just shrugged. Dot and Henry were fine with us moving on, they prided themselves on helping us do it. And in no time, that new garden felt like it had always been there. The potato patch gave the sweetest, earthiest potatoes I've ever tasted.'

'So that's why our kids have half a dozen passions at once?' Martha asked, watching a single cloud in the wide sky, slowly gaining strength in the early spring air.

'Sure. Kids are supposed to have passions and when the passion fades, we just turn that basketball hoop, volleyball net, trampoline . . .'

'Quilting kit, wood carving, lino-cuts, bicycles . . .' Martha added to the list.

'Unicycle, yes, we just turn it into our lives.'

'Our kids are so lucky.'

'Sure,' Laurie said, 'but it's all second-hand. Kids are meant to have passions and they're meant to pass. You've seen Dot and Henry's home, it was no tidier when I was a kid than they keep it now, it was rarely clean, and it was never quiet. I love that ours is the same.'

Martha didn't reply and Laurie turned to her, worried by her non-response, 'What?'

'Nothing. I'm just . . .'

'I know,' Laurie reached out and held Martha to her.

Martha let herself be drawn into her wife's embrace and stay there for a moment, shutting out her restlessness, her confusion, the part of her that wondered where she could make her own mark in all of this family life, where she could be just Martha, not mother, wife, always there, always reliable Martha.

She leaned into Laurie and whispered, 'I love you.' She meant it.

'I know. So will you get me a beer?'

Martha laughed, 'It's not even midday.'

'There's a time limit on beer?'

'Not for you, my love.'

Martha got up, went into the house and Laurie kept digging. She knew her wife wouldn't come back with just one beer, there would be a bottle each, and a bowl of nuts maybe, or a sandwich. The twins were off at swim training and Hope at her dance class, there was time to dig some more, to eat and drink together, time to be together in the sun. All good. Laurie dug deeper in gratitude and pushed away the nagging thought that such ease could not last.

Dot and Henry Patterson, high-school sweethearts, were not able to have children. They tried and failed and tried and failed. It was harder to adopt back then, without children of their own, so they became foster parents, and they fell in love with so many of the babies and care-worn children and heartbroken, life-broken teenagers that were sent to them, that they decided they'd just try harder with the adopting. Once they'd made their decision, they kept on putting in application after application, never taking no for an answer and, as Dot said, 'Something just shifted inside one of us, both of us.'

It was just a few weeks after they had been offered six-month-old twin girls to adopt that Dot found out she was pregnant, which was why Laurie's three big sisters went through school as a trio, nearly-triplets.

'You cut your parenting teeth on three babies at once and it'll break you or make you want more,' was another of Dot's sayings, and she said it proudly as they took on other children, welcoming what became Laurie's family into their messy, noisy home. They had two more birth babies, then a foster boy, older than the first three, who ended up staying and staying until he might as well have been adopted – as he was, finally, just two months before his sixteenth birthday. There was another adopted baby, a boy, and then there was nine-year-old Laurie, brought right across the country to the one couple a trail of social workers thought might be able to help. Seven children already, and they were brought a cold, staring mute, a child other foster parents had been too frightened to try.

'Baby, I agreed the moment they showed me the photo,' Dot told Laurie, 'though Henry knew I'd said yes before I even got off the phone.'

Dot never did tell Laurie what she said when she heard the full story.

Dot and Henry's house was always warm, even though there was never enough money to heat it properly through the damp coastal winter. It was always welcoming, despite Henry's slim wages as a gardener and odd-job man, supplemented with Dot's pay from her three cleaning jobs that went every week on food, every cent. Even so, the door was always open and the house welcoming, the bargain-bin cookie jar free for all. With so many children and teenagers and adults trooping in and out, Dot made sure there was always somewhere to be quiet, to curl up with a book and hide in a different story. Laurie wanted that for her children, for their family. She wanted both the welcome for any of their friends, neighbours, and she wanted her children to have peace and quiet when they needed it, privacy, a door to close and a space of their own, no matter how small, but all their own. And so she made it for them, because she had been brought up to understand that sometimes a hiding place was all that was left.

Nine

A hiding place on the compound. Newly covenanted, newly aware of what being covenanted meant, at least to the young girls, Laurie looked for hiding places. Sometimes hiding happened in plain sight, merging into a group of girls hard at their chores, bending deeper into the garden where they were weeding so she would not be seen, singled out. Sometimes it meant misbehaving, doing something against the rules to ensure she would be punished, put away in the dark place, as if she were hidden by those in charge. At night it might mean pretending to be sleeping too deeply to be woken without causing a fuss – Abraham hated fuss – so that they went on to another girl, also covenanted, also called. Or it meant faking a bad dream, screaming just as she heard them come into the room, coming to find a girl. Girls who were sweaty and tear-stained were not wanted, not as first choice anyway.

Laurie became adept at hiding, and when she could not hide, when she was found, chosen, offered up, she schooled herself in holding, waiting, knowing that time would pass, that she would breathe again.

Ten

Laurie and Martha expected Hope's upset to go on for a while, but two months later they were surprised that nothing appeared to have shifted, she seemed even more stuck in her fugue state of loss. Hope dug into her bedroom and refused to come out other than for dance classes, school, and the occasional meal.

'I don't know what to do,' Martha said, both of them whispering, even though the old walls were thick and their room far from Hope's.

'Neither do I,' Laurie said, 'I didn't think she even liked him that much.'

'She doesn't like him at all now, I found a voodoo doll of him under her bed.'

'You looked under her bed?'

'I was taking Cat for her jabs—'

'She's called Mittens,' Laurie interrupted.

'No, you and Jack call her Mittens, the girls and I have always known that's a stupid name.'

'She's got little white paws.'

49

'She's a cat – and that's not the point, she jumped out of the basket just as I got her in. I chased her all the way up the stairs and then she scrambled under Hope's bed. Anyway, there was this figure, he's carved out of something, not wood, more like an extra-tough potato or something.'

'How did you know it was Jon?'

'It says *JON* in red ink on the forehead.'

'Not blood?'

'Not blood.'

'Small mercies.'

'Judging by the number of pins stuck all over it, Hope's not feeling very merciful.'

'Did you put it back?' Laurie asked.

'Yeah, after I'd dragged Cat out, I returned her homemade icon to the den of fluff balls and discarded homework that live happily beneath our firstborn's bed.'

'He wasn't even that special.'

'Jon? He's pretty. Teenage girls like pretty in boys, they're safer that way.'

'Or not.'

'Maybe, but Jon doesn't look so pretty now with half a dozen pins to his groin.'

Laurie frowned, 'Really? Do you think they were having sex?'

She was half hoping that Martha didn't have knowledge that she didn't, and half hoping that at least one of them knew what was going on with their daughter.

Martha shook her head, 'I don't think so. I think Hope would be upset if they'd been screwing, she's only angry.'

'Only? She's furious.'

'Sure, but that's embarrassed anger, not sexual shame.'

Laurie nodded in the dark, 'You're right. I think so too. That kind of shame looks different, feels different.'

Laurie slipped her arm around Martha's back, pulling her in, and she felt that old flip that seemed incredible after so long together. In one moment they were best friends chatting late at night, friends who'd seen each other at their worst, who understood that all these years of love had little to do with the physical, not in these busy days of ordinary life – and then the click happened, as it had done for so many years, the slip slide from everyday friends into extraordinary lovers, the place where the connection was only physical, all physical.

They were two, Laurie and Martha, two in sex, in love. Neither woman believed in the cliché of not knowing where the other stopped. Laurie's pale brown skin, Martha's ivory white, they knew they were apart and together, happy to be both. Martha knew that Laurie's skin was softer than hers, smoother, how could she ever not want to know which was Laurie and which was herself? It was Laurie's flesh she kissed, Laurie's flesh she wanted. She did not desire her own flesh. They were happy to be together, apart.

Afterwards, as Martha was drifting into soft-limbed sleep, Laurie thought about how it was when they were fucking, how the children didn't matter and it was as if they were back before the babies, before the house, they were all body, only body, just skin, flesh, touch, taste.

And then Martha muttered from her half-sleep, 'Hope needs something to take her mind off him. That potato thing, it's not good.'

'It's not good,' Laurie agreed, eyes open in the dark.

*

'There's a casserole in the oven, bread in the cupboard, salad in the fridge, help yourselves.'

Three pairs of feet clattered over each other up the hall, Jack's the loudest, heaviest as ever.

'Jack, trainers off!' Martha shouted and 'Ana, don't forget you have that French coursework to do,' and 'Hope, there's a letter for you on the worktop.'

Laurie kicked her, 'Why did you tell her?'

'Because there's a letter on the worktop and it's addressed to her.'

'But now she's going to get all upset again—'

'He might be declaring undying love, handwritten. It's very old fashioned. Sweet. You think I should have hidden it?'

'Until she'd had dinner, maybe.'

'As if Mum would ever do anything sneaky,' Ana said, walking into the sitting room, her skin still flushed from the hundred lengths and the dozen timed races she'd completed that evening.

'You weren't supposed to hear.'

'The walls have ears, isn't that what you said when we were little?'

'Yeah,' Martha answered, 'I liked you when you were gullible.'

'Fair enough, I believed Mom about the eyes-in-the-back-of-her-head thing too.'

'That one's true,' Laurie said, not looking up from the pile of papers she was sifting through before her lecture the next day.

Ana nodded, 'Weird. Anyway, Hope won't be worried about a letter from Jon.'

Now Laurie looked up, 'Why not?'

'She's all about her dance teacher now, like half the girls at school.'

'Jack thinks she's still upset about Jon,' Martha said.

Jack and Hope had a special connection, Ana had been so self-sufficient, right from the start, she didn't leave a lot for Hope to look after, to play big sister, but Jack was very happy for Hope to baby him when he was a baby, run after him when he was a toddler, bring him extra snacks when they were at school together, and attend his swimming competitions as chief cheerleader once he started doing well. Or she had been, until this big heartbreak sent her into herself.

'I did, she was,' Jack added to the conversation, coming into the room with a plate so laden Laurie couldn't imagine he'd left anything for his sisters, and straddling one of the old armchairs that had been perfectly passable before their son became a giant, 'Only it shifted a couple of weeks ago. Ana's right, she is all about the teacher now.'

'All the dance girls are,' Ana said.

'And the gay boys,' Jack mumbled, his mouth full.

'There are gay boys in your class?' Laurie asked, paying attention now.

'It's a dance class, Mom,' Jack responded, lisping the 'dance' just to piss her off, 'What do you think?'

'I think,' Laurie answered, getting off the sofa and heading for the kitchen, lightly rapping Jack on the head with her knuckles as she passed, 'that young men who talk with their mouth full don't get pie for dessert.'

'You made pie? When did you get time to make pie?' Jack was six years old again.

'You'll never know,' she said, and left the room humming.

Later, with the TV news in the background, over shop-bought pie and ice-cream – Jack was right, Laurie hadn't had time, but she had found a good bakery on her way home – they all laughed at Jon's ham-fisted attempt at a reconciliation letter, in which, as well as insisting Hope was the only girl he'd ever truly fancied, he also suggested that he keep on with the new girl, and that he and Hope 'hang out anyway, in case it doesn't work'.

'Poor thing, he's trying,' Martha said, but Hope was having none of it.

'Mum, I'm an idiot for missing him still, a bit, but he's way more of an idiot to think I want him when he's officially going out with someone else.'

'Sure, but it's obvious he's having second thoughts.'

'Let him have them,' said Hope.

'I admire his guts,' said Jack, 'you have to hand it to him, he's had you in the palm of his hand – as it were – for long enough, and now he has Jocasta Brewster in the same place.'

Martha winced at the 'palm of his hand' line, and Ana, who always glowed bright red with any minor embarrassment and was horrified that Jack was intimating sexual activity between Hope and Jon, knew she was making it worse by her own blushes. She was spared further embarrassment by the look of horror on Hope's face.

'Shit,' said Jack.

'You are such an idiot,' said Ana, glaring at her brother.

'Jocasta Brewster?' said Hope, 'Jocasta fucking Brewster?'

Hope threw down her bowl and ran from the room, Laurie just managed to save the carpet from a fat squidge of cherry filling, Ana ran after her sister, and Jack shook his head, 'I thought she knew.'

Hope's bedroom door slammed, walls shook, and the voodoo doll took another stabbing.

Eleven

Hope got over Jon, and then she got over Jon and Jocasta, mostly because they got over each other. She got over and she got on. Laurie continued to struggle with her increased profile and the accompanying workload, Martha continued with her own work, finding it ever so slightly dull with none of the shine that Laurie's had taken on, the twins went to swimming competitions, Hope had dance classes and there were mocks and actual exams and all the attendant upset – Hope's fear of failure, Ana's apparent disregard for her results, good or bad, though they were always good, alongside Jack's determination to do as little revision as possible, whatever the outcome. Laurie found herself thinking about how it was to be a teenager, the day-to-day of school that felt so important to them now, each high or low so vital, and yet, in the long run, would have almost nothing to do with the people that her children became.

Laurie was nine, almost ten when she first went to school. Dot and Henry had expected her to find it hard, but for all the wrong reasons. Laurie had been raised in patterns and rhythms, the rules of school should at least have given her a sense of security, but while she had been used to a much more rigid hierarchy and a much tougher system in the community, those rules had made sense in a greater scheme of things where Laurie was a small but vital cog in a wider orchestration, where everyone was needed, but no one mattered more than the whole. Conversely, the rules at the school twenty minutes' bus ride from Dot and Henry's seemed to be made one day and broken the next, tried out and discarded on the whim of the principal. It had taken her a while to understand that both teachers and children genuinely cared about things Laurie found utterly petty. Even now, she still found it hard to put on a concerned face for the teacher worried about Jack's lack of homework or when another parent was upset that Ana and his own daughter were texting too late at night. The rules that Laurie had grown up with in the community were about the core of herself, her very being. Sometimes she thought that all of the training she had endured was the only thing enabling her to be the mother of teenagers, to act as if she cared at all about Jack's exam results or the subjects Hope would choose next year, as if she thought anything mattered other than that Ana understood that she was loved, no matter what. Nothing else mattered to Laurie, nothing but that her children were at ease in their own skin, and she had Martha's love. The world she was now in demanded that she act as if exam results also mattered, she didn't have to believe it as well.

Spring had finally, fully arrived, the wisteria proved it so, and summer was hinting at an early start, when Laurie came downstairs after a late night of work and an early morning of the same. Martha had already taken the twins and a couple of team-mates to their competition in east London.

'You're still here?' Laurie stopped at the kitchen door, surprised to see Hope at home this time on a Saturday morning.

Hope smiled, 'We have a later start today, I'm on my way now.'

'I could give you a lift. I can do the shopping while you're in class, we can go for hot chocolate afterwards?'

'I'm OK to go by myself, Mom. I have to run, I don't want to miss the bus.'

'What about tonight, shall I get pizza? The twins have a swim-team thing, we could share a couple of pizzas between us three?'

'I'm fine, honest, I'll probably go for sushi after our class with some of the others, I won't be home too late. I'll text, don't worry.'

Hope kissed Laurie goodbye, slung another shapeless jumper over the one she was already wearing and left the house, hurrying to the bus, hurrying up the driveway as if her class was all there was in the world. Laurie watched her from the kitchen window, their bus service wasn't great, but they were safely driven and usually on time. Hope had twenty minutes to get to a bus stop that was a ten-minute dawdle away, and her eagerness to be gone started something in Laurie, reminded her of herself at sixteen, seventeen. It was not a good memory.

'There's something going on.'

'With who? What?'

Martha was stuffing her mouth with pizza – once Laurie

58

had suggested it, despite Hope turning her down, it was all she wanted to eat, so she ordered in for the two of them, took it out to Martha's shed office on a tray with the half bottle of wine they hadn't finished the night before. Martha had come straight in from her day ferrying swimmers and gone out to work, but while she made a weak protest about needing to keep going, once Laurie was at the door with wine and pizza, she gave up. Martha had a Pavlovian response to the shape of a pizza box, the pop of a cork. Every now and then she'd try to deny herself, worried about drinking too much, eating too many bad foods, but she had no skill in holding back. Laurie loved that about her, the way Martha threw herself into everything, quietly, with no fuss, but fully. Including her half of the pizza.

'Do not eat that, don't you dare!'

Martha held the crust to her lips, took a tiny nibble, and then, when Laurie laughed, relaxed, waiting for her to hand it over, she bit off a huge chunk.

'You'll choke.'

'It'll serve me right,' Martha said, her mouth full and grinning.

'Damn straight.'

'What's going on with who?'

'Hope.'

'Because she didn't want you to take her to the class? Because she has sushi friends now?' Martha paused, 'How the hell did sushi become a thing way out here?'

'It's small-town sushi, babe, lumpy rice and the only flavour from too much soy. And Hope – it wasn't that she didn't want a lift, it was more how she was.'

'How?'

Laurie didn't know how to explain to Martha what she'd seen in Hope, a suppressed excitement, and more, something darker, a sly secrecy. She didn't want to think she had seen it and she had no intention of explaining to Martha why she'd recognised it, what it meant to her, how much it reminded her of herself at Hope's age.

'I don't know, she's growing up, maybe it's just that, maybe I'm just freaked by the ageing thing.'

'Yours or the kids'?' Martha asked, smiling over her wineglass.

'Ours.'

Martha poured the last of the wine and lifted the pizza box from her desk to her already-littered office floor. Much as Laurie had tried, over the years, Martha had taken on none of her virtues of tidiness and cleanliness. Laurie picked up the box along with other detritus and made a careful pile beside the door, ready to take when she left Martha to her work.

Martha nodded approvingly as Laurie tidied up and said, 'Maybe she's seeing someone new. Given what a disaster that last thing was, maybe she just doesn't want us to know about it yet.'

'It's only a few weeks since she last stabbed voodoo Jon through the eye.'

'Well over two months, coming up three. It'd make sense. She's been going to school earlier, getting back later.'

'I didn't know.'

'You've been at work, you've been home later than them for ages now.'

Laurie frowned, Martha was right, 'Sorry, I know I'm leaving so much more to you, but if I don't follow up on all that's being offered now, I . . . '

'I'm not complaining,' Martha said, holding out her empty glass for Laurie to add to her pile.

'I just felt like something else was going on.'

'She's growing up, she needs to have secrets, it's normal,' Martha said, 'more wine?'

'You're working.'

'That's mean.'

'You'll thank me when it's all done later. I'll put a bottle in the fridge for when you come in. Don't be too long.'

Laurie went inside and wandered through the house. She put on the dishwasher, picked up shoes from the hall, and hung up dropped towels in the bathroom. She straightened cushions in the sitting room, and opened the curtains in Jack's room, he preferred his bedroom dark and his screens bright. She went up to her attic office and stared at her desk, not touching a thing. She had a big presentation still awaiting the final touches, but she was agitated and uncomfortable and couldn't get Hope's covert half-smile out of her mind. Finally, she gave in and pulled back the bookcase that covered the hidden space. She went inside and sat in the green-infused evening light that was sliding through the wisteria leaves. Laurie set a timer. She was always careful to set a timer, she didn't want to be disturbed by Martha coming into the house and looking for her. It had never happened yet, the tiny space remained unfound. And even though she used it rarely, it was precious to her. Martha knew quite a lot of Laurie's story, more than Laurie had ever expected to share with anyone, but she didn't know it all.

*

Breathe in, hold, breathe out, hold. And again, and again. Just breath, only breath. Laurie concentrated on the breath as she'd been taught when they took her to Dot and Henry, a thin, fragile child, afraid to take a step out of line, afraid to say a word, saying no words at all. The silent little girl that no one had known how to help, until Dot and Henry made her a safe place in a corner, somewhere that none of the other children were allowed to enter, and then Henry, that big man, folded himself up and sat alongside Laurie in her safe corner – alongside, not coming in, leaving her a space all of her own. He taught her to be still and quiet inside of herself, no matter what raucous noises the other children were making, no matter what fears were panicking her. A place to be still and let the memories be. Henry, who dealt with his Vietnam nightmares in the same way, showed Laurie that the past did not have to stay with her, in this house she was here and she was now and that was enough.

Laurie also set the timer to be sure she would be called back to the present. She'd gone back to her past once, and once was too much.

Twelve

Going back.

Five thirty-nine. Laurie was washed, dressed and plaiting her hair. All done in nine minutes flat. She had become slow, not up to the standard she'd been when they had stormed into the compound in the middle of the night and lifted out over half of the children. Grabbed them from their beds in a blur of shouting and torchlight and guns. They were small children, taken by the legitimate authorities in a raid that had felt like a kidnapping. Not all of the children were removed, those who were Abraham's own family and those who were the birth children of community members were left behind. The authorities could not take away those who had birth parents in the compound, not in that county, that state, at that time, a discretionary legality that literally meant the parent owned the child.

As he had done before, as he would do again if he had to, Abraham simply started over. He named those who remained his chosen family and they were thrilled to hear it. The community was skilled in the auspices of new beginnings, hadn't each of them come out here to create their own new beginning, singly and communally? They followed Abraham, a discipline of disciples, and if the missing children were mourned, it was not done so openly. The community accepted no public upset unless it was about a problem that could be reckoned, redeemed, righted. The law had taken away the adopted children, love might yet bring them back.

Laurie had returned. Prodigal daughter, home after many years away in the wilderness, Abraham announced she had made her trek following an inner compass that placed the community as her true north, Abraham her lode star. In truth, she was drawn by the letters Samuel had been sending for eighteen months, his phone calls in the night, whispering her back. He had made her his secret quest, seeking his covenanted helpmeet in stolen records, dead-end leads, a painstakingly slow search with one certain goal. When Samuel's first letter arrived Laurie was almost shocked back into silence, by the time the third came she was ready to respond. Samuel was deliciously persuasive and eventually the child who had been taken in the middle of the night came home, a young woman ready to take her place in the community.

Nine minutes to wash, dress, twist and pin up her hair. The community washed properly just twice a week, all of the men in the bathhouse, a quick turnaround, then all of the women afterwards. The other days it was cold water on the face, the pits, the bits – fast and sharp as the lick of the whip. Laurie had never understood why they called it a licking. The whip cut, it stabbed, it severed, it did not lick. It was not Abraham's whip, he had never personally beaten anyone, his gift was only love. They knew this because he said so.

Nine minutes.

Abraham says: When a young woman does not have to think about what to wear, it is easy to dress, and at speed. To be always ready.

When a young woman wears one of two dresses for six days out of seven, one day worn, one day washed, and worn wet or damp if it is not dry, if it could not dry in the bitter cold winter, when that is the case, and there is no vanity, no primping, speed is possible, readiness is all. The third dress, her best, was kept for the seventh day, and that dress matched the pure starched white of every other woman and girl on the land. Hand-made, three-quarter sleeves, a modest length to the knee, modest cut to the bodice, simple and pure and woe betide any girl whose dress was marred by a stain or a crease.

Without choice then, washing, dressing, hairdressing, was fast. As it had to be, lateness was disrespectful of the whole community, it could not be tolerated. Everything must be done for the good of the community, and done to perfection in the process.

Abraham says: Whatever we give, we must give at our peak, anything less is disrespect.

Five forty-five and Laurie was on her way to the kitchen. She was serving. The young men set out the tables; old wooden trestles, up for every meal, down again to make space for all of the other activities in the big hall. Three times a day they put up those tables and folded them down. Trestles made of rough wood, the table tops scrubbed over years of use to a smooth, silken finish, the undersides and leg-frames still brutal, rarely a meal where a young man wouldn't be biting at a knuckle, sucking at a palm, to release a painful splinter. Surreptitiously picking at the wound, of course, no point being seen to be hurt, no point being seen to be at fault. How can it be the furniture's fault?

Abraham says: If a person is in pain, then they must be at fault – their mistake, theirs to suffer.

Being at fault was the cost of being alive. Acknowledging fault was the method for attaining truth. And truth, to oneself and the community was the only real salvation.

The young men lifted, carried; the young girls served; the mothers cooked; the fathers farmed and gardened, built and drove. There were no people older than twenty-five who were not parents. Even the little children had tasks, helping with cooking, peeling, grating, kneading until they were old enough, at six, to join the boy and girl divide, the girls continued in the kitchen, the boys went out to the gardens and the fields. Work was not allocated on either preference or aptitude, but on age and gender. A fairer system according to Abraham, one that paid no attention to assumed talent or wealth, luck or contacts, was merely decided by the accident of birth.

For the three years that she was six, seven, eight, Laurie had been up even earlier than the general call, roused at four thirty, to bake the bread they had kneaded the evening before. When girls grew a little older, there was another division. Some of the young women were deemed comely enough to serve, others as homely and better for the kitchen, the laundry, the home garden, where the community grew vegetables, herbs, fruit. A young woman was either given one of the out-of-the-way jobs better suited to less attractive women, or she was not. There was pain in realising you had been judged a less attractive young woman. There was also pain in being judged beautiful.

Not that the men had it any easier. The best-looking of the young men were always on parade, expected to be both groomed and rugged, elegant and manly. Not a hair out of place, not a shirt unbuttoned, nor a hand uncalloused either. It was impossible, that land so dusty, grime in everyone's fingernails, grit always in the wind, in their eyes, skin, scalps, and yet the young men of the community were meant also to be sharp, handsome. Some of them especially so, for a year or two, that time when they could make a difference, or so they were told in public, and so Abraham told them again, the beautiful young women and the handsome young men, in the long, private conversations that left the special ones both glowing and scared. The pleasure, the terror, of a private conversation with Abraham, who was their all.

Abraham says: It is not in my words that you will find your path, it is through my words. Follow the words and they will lead you home to the dream.

For the time that they were most beautiful, right on that edge between youth and adulthood, the loveliest of the young men and young women were sent from the community into the world. These were the special ones, sent to return with salvageable souls who would join the vision made real, the covenanted dream. The other young men, plain or lumpen, those with bad skin or ungainly gait, went straight on to the land. They had no choice, they were ranch-hands and cowboys and, on the few fields where the old dry river very occasionally helped arid nature, they were ploughmen.

Those who were lovely, male and female, were trained to make a difference, sent to make a difference.

Six in the morning and the panicked rush of the last half hour suddenly ceased. Silence. Waiting. Silence until Abraham arrived, a silence that was all held breath and fear. Years later, Laurie swore she could still smell that silence, the fear in the stillness. Was the table cleaned well enough, the bread placed just so, the butter soft but not too soft? That damned butter. Their own, of course, made of the milk from the small dairy herd they kept to serve the community, on land that was freezing in winter and burning hot from just before first light in summer, simply getting milk from the poor beasts was hard enough. How could they ever win with the butter? They never won with the butter, never. Someone always disappointed. And disappointing meant reporting oneself, knowing oneself to have failed. Giving oneself up for reckoning.

I am at fault.

Once, naïve and childish, four or five, when playing was still permissible, encouraged – total freedom until six years of age and then the training began – Laurie had asked, 'If we have to be perfect at six in the morning, why don't we get up earlier? Why don't we just make it better the night before? Why must it all happen between waking and First Gathering?'

There was silence when she asked it, silence and what she

later understood to be fear for her, an outspoken little girl with a tongue that would no doubt need curbing in time. She waited for an answer, and because she was a child, not yet held accountable for her actions, the community awaited Abraham's reaction, his lead.

When he laughed, they laughed, carefully, waiting to see which way his laughter would go. It went to warmth, to a tousled head for the child, and relief all round. Even at her tender age, Laurie understood the value of his touch, that which was prized more highly for being so uncommon.

Abraham says: Suffer little children.

Abraham said it was a good question, a valid one, and went on to explain the value of discipline, that discipline made the disciple. He didn't explain that the rush, the panic, the fear of transgression was also the point, or that because he said so was all the reason he needed. He didn't need to, she learned soon enough.

Six o'clock, a chime, five more, everyone at attention, at their places, ready to go, ready for action, called already and ready to be called.

And they would wait.

And wait.

Six ten.

Six twenty.

The butter melting in its perfectly placed dish as forty-eight adults, fifteen children, stood waiting for his arrival and the toddlers played on in their corral, oblivious to the growing tension.

Some days Abraham was there at six, on the dot.

Some days he was there when they arrived, waiting for

them, helping out, making himself useful – making them nervous with his solicitous assistance.

Then there was no butter problem, or if there was, it was due to an awful accident.

Other days he might come in at six thirty, seven, seven thirty.

There was one morning of hard waiting. Laurie had not long returned, it was the dead heat of mid-summer, sweltering even before they had cooked the breakfast, the regulation breakfast that they all ate because Abraham ate it – eggs, grits, beans, bread. Butter for Abraham only. It was hard to stand for so long, the clock had chimed nine before he arrived. They had been waiting for three hours, waiting to attention, watching the eggs congeal on his plate, the butter turn to oil, the bread – just the one slice cut, half an inch thick, no more, no less, ready for him – watching that slice turn stale and dry.

They waited that morning, sure that there would be fearful punishment. And no one moved, no one stretched an arm out to help Maude, Abraham's own mother who had followed them out to the community when his father died. His own mother but treated the same as all of them, treated the same to show them that his love was impartial, not particular, all giving.

Abraham says: Woman, behold your son. Son, behold your mother.

Not one of them helped Maude when she fell and then lay there, two full hours, on the old wooden floor. The little children and babies were in their corral five hundred yards away, they could hear them playing, calling, laughing at the absurdity of those grown people, waiting, waiting. Later the parents in the big hall heard the babies when the laughter and chatter turned to cries, sobs, hunger, fear. The parents could not go, knew they had to trust their babies to five-year-old boys and girls, big brothers and sisters preparing to come to the adult tables, readying themselves to be like the adults who waited, in pain, in their own frailty, ignoring an old woman as she slobbered on the scrubbed, still gritty, always dusty floor.

When Abraham arrived he ran straight to Maude and then, crying in thankfulness, in astonished gratitude, he praised the whole community. He thanked each one of them by name, and each one was ashamed at the joy they felt, and revelled in it anyway.

Abraham knows me, he knows my name.

He thanked them for not breaking the rule, and he held his mother, reverse pietà for all to revere.

Maude, in turn, praised him, her son. Thanked him in broken words that stank of the vomit they'd left her lying in, spoke from a parched throat her gratitude that Abraham would hold her, the unworthy mother in his perfect embrace.

After Maude had been taken to the sick-house, after Abraham had eaten his meal – congealed eggs and stale bread and melted butter and praised each mouthful as he ate – after all of that, when they were finally allowed to sit and eat their own cold, congealed meals, he turned to them and he said,

'You see the joy you bring when you obey the rule, when we all obey for the greater love of community?'

He left the room, kissing each one of them on the head, as he went.

He kissed Laurie on the head too, and lightly, quietly, ran a fingertip across the back of her neck as he did so.

Her time away had given her both a wariness of Abraham and, she realised as she felt herself shift towards his touch, a yearning to be near him. She was frightened by Abraham's presence, and she wished for so much more.

Thirteen

Martha stood in the kitchen and listened to their children ready themselves for school, for friends, for swimming training and dance class, so much to do, so many places to be. She had been desperate to be busy herself as a teenager, her strongest passion was her desire to get away from the farm, to move to a city, any city, the bigger and busier the better. She had craved everything the city promised, everything the farm denied.

'I don't know why you wouldn't want all this,' her father had said, looking out across the wind-swept hills, he paused to whistle in the two dogs that were rounding up the ewes and their lambs, 'We'd love you to take the farm on.'

Martha's father was a man ahead of his time, happy for a girl to take on the land, and his girl was a natural. She could birth a breach lamb and had no qualms about tailing and tagging that lamb a day or two later. When it came to slaughtering a ram too old or a lamb broken in birthing and never going to survive, Martha was faster than her father, her hands more sure with a knife, her cut deeper, quicker, cleaner.

'I know you would, Dad,' Martha said, looking down at her hands, 'but I don't ...'

The past weeks had been busy with lambing, sorting the ram lambs for castration and those for meat, Martha's hands were soft with lanolin, ingrained with dirt and blood.

'You don't like it,' he said, quietly, his eyes on the dogs.

'I don't like the blood and the dirt, I don't like how it stays with me, stays on me, how I can smell it at night. I want to be surrounded by people.'

Her father, his eyes clear beneath a weathered forehead, looked along a line of hills that extended four miles south. He frowned, shook his head, and then whistled in the elder of the two sheepdogs, who soon had the younger keeping pace, 'Your choice, love.'

Jack yelled for Ana from the front door, bringing Martha back to now, and she looked around at the mess of breakfast, plates, mugs, cutlery and crumbs littering the room, marking Jack's zigzag trajectory from toaster to table to cupboard to sink, one hand to add butter, jam, peanut butter to his four slices of toast, the other to text. Her choice. She watched the twins rush off to catch their bus to training, Jack all force and passion while Ana was straight as a dart, just as they were in their swimming. To outsiders the twins were hugely different, only Laurie and Martha saw the little quirks that gave away their nine months holding each other tight, their matching little toes curving slightly inward. Even now they still mirrored each other in sleep, Jack on his right, left arm thrown behind, Ana on her left, right arm back, as if they might reach through bedroom walls, through years of walking as two and be back in utero, holding hands, ever-twinned. Even now they still shared secrets, silly things, whispered things, that neither mother nor Hope could get from them. Hope was different in her way too, far more easily thrown off course than her siblings, derailed by a text from an unhappy friend or excited mate that needed an immediate response, a long and intricate reply of empathy and inspiration. Where the twins looked in to each other for ballast, Hope had always turned to her mates, and had too often been hurt and surprised when her friends were not as steadfast as she was herself.

Since Hope's break-up with Jon, she had become the go-to girl for advice on dealing with heart-breaking boys. The most obvious manifestation of her new role was the way her breakfast cereal was now decanted into a cup and held carefully all the way on the bus, into class, and beyond.

'Hope,' Martha said, 'sit down and eat, at least finish those last few mouthfuls before you get on the bus.'

'Can't. Saira needs me,' Hope responded, adding a little more cereal to her cup, a drop more milk.

'Saira was rubbish when you were weeping about Jon.'

'I wasn't weeping, I was angry. Sadness is directionless, anger has focus and power.'

'OK,' Martha nodded, knowing that Hope was quoting her dance teacher, he'd said something very similar to Martha in a recent coaching session; 'Martha, you say that you're sad about seeing less of Laurie, with her being so busy right now. But isn't it possible that you're also angry? Anger is far more useful, it has actual power to it.'

The words had stayed with her, left her wondering what she really was feeling. She didn't want to be reminded of it right now.

She tried again, 'Saira was a hopeless friend, and here you are, bending over backwards for her.'

Hope stopped in her texting, thumbs poised over the keys, 'Because she was unreliable, you think I should be too?'

Martha knew she was defeated, 'I just think you should think about yourself sometimes too, you know, like eating your breakfast undisturbed by your friends.'

Hope picked up her cup of cereal and kissed Martha.

'It's not all about the self, Mother,' she said, 'in dance, in an ensemble, the individual is just one part of the whole. You maintain a successful whole by taking care of each other.'

'I know how groups work, Hope, I grew up on a sheep farm.'

'Good, then you'll be glad to hear that you only truly achieve by working at your peak in every area possible. Which is why I'm meeting Saira to work on her history project.'

Hope bowed, turned on her heel, and a moment later Martha heard the front door slam shut again, Hope's trainers fast on gravel, then quieter, then the silence of another morning far into the watery land.

Martha slowly tidied up, thinking of Laurie heading across the country for another keynote lecture, surrounded by people, being busy, wanted, fêted. She looked at her hands under the running water of the tap, clean, lonely. Maybe she was angry after all.

'That thing you said about anger . . . '

'Yes?'

He waited and Martha sighed, his way of making her fill in the blanks was infuriating, part of his role as her coach, she knew, but infuriating all the same. It wasn't as if she wanted him to say 'You do this, you'll get that'. Although, right now, she wouldn't have minded if he had. Sometimes, Martha thought, the hardest part about being an adult was having to make all your own bloody choices all the time.

'You said it was powerful.'

'No,' he said.

She looked up, 'You did, you said anger can be powerful.'

He shook his head, ever such a little, 'I said directed anger can be powerful.'

'Does it matter?'

He nodded, 'I wouldn't have corrected you if not. Directed anger has power. Misdirected, it can be dangerous to those around us. Sublimated, it becomes dangerous to us personally. So, we come back to it. What's your anger, Martha?'

'Nothing, really, not any one thing. I don't have any reason to be angry. I'm lucky, I know that, we have the kids and a nice home and, it's tough with my dad now, of course, it takes a lot of time, but I don't mind, I couldn't . . . '

'That's a lie, and you know it.'

Martha reared back in her chair, 'A lie?'

He laughed at her, 'All this noble "I'm not complaining, poor little me, I'd never complain", it's just not true.'

'I'm not complaining,' she was annoyed now.

'Sure you are, you're hiding it behind some bullshit veneer of politeness which is actually martyrdom, and even more unattractive—'

'I'm not trying to be attractive to you.'

'I didn't say you were,' he grinned then, a big broad smile with more than a hint of self-satisfaction and Martha found herself thinking that he probably would be very attractive if he wasn't also so smug.

'What you said about anger ...' she tried again.

He raised an eyebrow, waited.

'You said ...' she struggled, gave in, 'you really think I'm angry?'

He looked at her, waiting.

'What do you think?' he asked.

'Fuck. Yes, I am. I think. I think I'm angry that Laurie gets to go off and be with people and do all the fun things, even though I know she's tired and it's hard for her and she misses us.'

'I don't care about Laurie,' he said quietly.

'But it's hard because her getting all that attention, success, and she worked for it, and she deserves it, I know ...'

'I really don't care about Laurie. This is about you,' he spoke slowly and deliberately.

'Right. Sure. So I'm angry, I think ...'

'Think?'

'No,' she winced, 'I know. I know I'm angry because Laurie gets to be special, and I have to stay at home and be the ... the ... mother. I have to be the mother.'

'Thank you.'

'Thank you?'

'For being honest.'

'About being a horrible person?'

'Why horrible?'

'Because I'm not supposed to feel like this.'

'Like what?'

'Like ... angry. No, worse, it's worse than that.'

'Go on.'

'I am angry, that I get left behind, doing all the same old family stuff, but more than that, I'm ... I'm jealous.'

Martha screwed up her fists and brought them to either side of her face.

'And that embarrasses you?' he asked.

'Of course it does. I'm hugely embarrassed that I feel jealous of my wife. I think I'm probably jealous of my kids too, all that life ahead of them. My whole family are off having interesting lives and I'm stuck out in my office in our garden in the middle of the bloody countryside, this flat land and all this sky and ... it's not what I thought it would be like. I feel left out. And when you start off feeling outside, always outside ...'

'Because you're gay?'

'No, or maybe partly that, but I've always felt outside ... I just wanted ...'

'To be part of a whole? A community?'

'Part of something, yes.'

Martha didn't feel much better when she went home after that session, but there was some relief, a small scab picked, a small pain revealed. She chose to ignore the mess in the kitchen and went straight out to her office in the garden where she powered through an enormous amount of work. By the time the twins came home from swimming and Hope from her dance class, by the time Laurie drove in, exhausted from her long day, Martha was feeling much more cheerful. Maybe he was right, maybe she just wanted her own community, and maybe these people were it, her children, her wife. Maybe she wasn't that awful after all.

That night in bed, shoulders and hands touching, Martha easy and almost sleeping, Laurie said, 'I heard a thing when I was driving this morning, a parenting thing on the radio.'

'What have we done wrong now?' Martha groaned.

'Not sure,' Laurie said, turning on to her side, stretching her body against Martha, whose skin was always warmer than her own, 'it was about the difference between sporty kids and academic kids.'

'Ours are going to end up stacking shelves because we don't push them hard enough to study?'

'Obviously, but it's more to do with how only a certain number of people really succeed at the highest levels of sport.'

'Whereas anyone can be a mediocre architect or web designer?'

'Exactly,' Laurie smiled in the dark.

'Then you'll be pleased to know,' Martha yawned, 'that Hope has an entirely new approach.'

'Voodoo dolls of teachers to ensure she passes exams even though she's at dance class all the time?'

'Apparently she's going to work at her peak in every area possible.'

Laurie was suddenly very cold, 'She said that?'

Martha turned, curling away and into her own pillow, 'Something about everyone, individually, being responsible for the whole. He's good for her, this dance teacher. Now go to sleep, the kids are all right and I'm knackered.'

Martha slept and Laurie lay awake, looking out into their dark room. It had to be a coincidence, plenty of people talked about the individual needing to take care of the whole. It made perfect sense for a dance teacher to encourage his students to put the whole before themselves. Like that radio presenter had said, not every dancer became the prima ballerina, it made sense to train everyone for the corps and then target the few who danced into the spotlight.

Still, Laurie couldn't sleep. She finally gave in and got up at four. She covered Martha with the duvet, whispered that she had had an idea and needed to do some work – both women were used to the other waking in the middle of the night with a great idea, neither was fazed by the other getting up to work – and went upstairs to the attic.

Laurie pulled back the bookcase and let herself into the hidden room. She sat on the old strip of carpet that covered most of the narrow stretch of floorboards, reaching her arms out wide, fingertips almost touching the walls on either side of the small space. She stretched her toes towards the wisteria-covered window at the far end, then lay down flat. Secure in the knowledge that everyone in the house would be asleep for at least an hour, she reached her hands up and back to the door behind her, checking that it was definitely closed. Then she covered herself with a thin rug, and lay still, staring at the window, waiting for the dawn.

She knew Hope wouldn't want her to interfere, to meet the teacher. Hope had always liked to keep the different parts of her life separate, only ever invited her mothers in when she was ready, hated the enforced interactions of parents' evenings, open days. Regardless, Laurie would find a way, meet him and assure herself that there was no connection, could be no connection. All would be well, there was nothing to do now but wait for the light.

Fourteen

There were two types of dance in the community, both created in the night. The first was slow, rhythmic and repetitive, a dance of carefully choreographed steps, in which each person danced alone and, simultaneously, with the whole community. In good weather it was danced outside in one huge circle. In bad weather the circle moved inside, and circles danced inside each other, concentric, clockwise and counter-clockwise, from the big group outside, to the smallest inside. Each of the circles part of one bigger dance, forwards and backwards and forwards again, continuing until the community moved as one. Keeping going past the stumbling children, the ailing elderly, the heavily pregnant women or the exhaustion of dust-dirty workers just in from forcing growth out of the hard land beyond the home fields.

They were told that Ingrid had danced the first dance. She was in labour with Lukas, their second child, it was her birth pain that danced the dance out of her. Five steps forward, three steps back, five forward. Slowly walking round and round, her eyes down to the hot, holding earth, a slight, light rocking between each sequence, rocking backwards to death and forwards to life, rocking through the shock of her labour, Ingrid's body dancing as it wrenched their second son into life.

She was four months pregnant when they turned away from the world, almost six months when they found the shack and broke the ground that became the compound, Johan was born in their first cold winter in the desert. When Johan was just two months old, Abraham and Ingrid conceived the first child of the land. Abraham had dreamed that four would bring more, and so it was important to become four as soon as they could. The night of Ingrid's labour with the second baby, Abraham's fear showed in his nervous back and forth around his beloved as she walked through her pain. Eventually she demanded that he stop, that he follow, that she needed to lead them into parenthood and he must hold, be the ground from which she could move forward. Five steps forward, three back, five forward. Five forward into community, three back to the past, five steps again into the new, walking over the past to ensure it was well trampled down.

When the baby finally came they had been dancing the circular pattern for ten hours. All through the night and into the morning, they had created a new round path in the land outside the one-room shack that was their only shelter. Lukas was born forward into the light, Ingrid was the channel, stretched out between old and new, past and future, while Abraham held his wife and both of his sons, flesh and blood proof that the vision was right.

As soon as Ingrid could stand, they walked again. Ingrid obeying her husband's command, as every birthing woman on the land had done since, returning from a place of singular pain to the embrace of the community.

The second dance was revealed on the day of Abraham's first exhortation to the community, the first time he spoke to them for a full two-hour stretch. It came after he finally accepted that his second son Lukas was profoundly deaf.

Lukas had been such a happy baby, smiling, friendly, forever burbling his own words, own phrases, talking to himself in his baby babble, almost as if his was the welcome that brought the newcomers to the community. It seemed to Ingrid that it was easier to attract other acolytes once they had two sons. Before, when they were just a loving couple with their one baby, fervent in belief in the vision, it might have been easier to ignore their passion. Now there was not only land and a shack that had grown to a house of four rooms, a field growing the crops they'd sown the year before, there were also sons. Some visitors came for a short while, intending to try out the community, shift it across their shoulders, weigh it in their arms, and when they found it just right they stayed on, helped plough another field for the crops that would sustain them and others, helped build the big hall, create a dormitory for all to share the sleep of the hard-working just. Others arrived, certain of their dedication, but left days later, less sure once they had heard the extent of Abraham's vision, the dream he told at night by the pit fire in the yard, or crammed into the house once the year turned towards fall and then winter. There were still others who were keen to work and to stay, but Abraham did not want a community of just anyone, each and every member was chosen, by their own path and by the dream.

By Lukas's second birthday, there were twenty-one adult members of the community and seven children as well as Lukas, who had grown to be a sturdy little lad, with copper skin a little darker than Johan's, and his mother's black eyes, deep and steady. The community was growing, the little ones learning to take part in community life, and still Lukas chattered happily to himself in his own language. It was another summer, both dormitories were finished, the kitchen block nearly built and the community's land had increased twofold, before Abraham accepted his son's deafness, before he accepted what had been clear to so many others but not voiced.

Abraham spent a whole day fasting in the desert, it was just after dawn when he walked back to the house. Ingrid who had also not slept, had gone about her day with an eye, an ear for her husband, welcomed him home. She washed the grime and dust from his skin, held him as he trembled, helped him shave when his hands were finally still. She gave him a little water, then more, then a full cup. She cooked him eggs and toasted bread on the fire that she had kept deliberately low so that the coals would make good, crisp toast, just the way he liked it, just the way he missed, out here, so far from the electric toasters, just another extravagant luxury of their childhood, their adolescence, their utterly other lives.

Washed, fed, watered, Abraham was ready.

When the community were gathered, Abraham began telling his dream.

'The morning that I awoke into the dream, from the long sleep of a false life, I told Ingrid that we would find a promised land and create the new life, the real life. The new life that exists only in the whole. I cannot lead unless you follow, I cannot dream unless you dream with me. I woke into a new promise, a new covenant. And like my namesake, I have already sacrificed my son. Our boy will never hear lies from another's lips, will never be drawn away by the siren song of futile love. Back then, I promised Ingrid there would be a sign we were doing the right thing. This child is that sign, reminding us that we are all broken, failed and failing. And still we get up, still we keep on. The path is the promise, the journey itself is the promised land.'

Abraham went on like this for another hour, the first of his long speeches, channelling the community's own voice, speaking for them. All of it written into the book, in Ingrid's careful hand, so that afterwards they could look back and see how right he had been, how inspired. This was the first time that Abraham held them mesmerised, the first time he knew he really had them, not just because he had started the community and therefore he was in charge, not just because he set the rota for the field or the meal pattern for kitchens, but as the vessel of the community's spirit. When he told the community that he had always known his second child would be born broken, that it was a promise upheld, the child both sacrifice and gift, he said it holding Lukas high in the air for all to see. The tired toddler had had enough, and like any fractious child he made his presence known. It began, a frenetic, foot-stamping, tantrum of a dance. The community followed the child and the second dance was born. It was wild and far freer than the first, it was about frustration and fury and pent-up anger, and letting it all out in pure movement.

*

Two babies were conceived through that new dance, one of them Abraham and Ingrid's third son Samuel. This was the boy that they adopted Laurie for, raising her to be his help-meet, raising her for their son, in conscious readiness. Even as a little girl, Laurie took her duty to Samuel seriously, paying attention to him when he was across a room, at the other end of a line, even while listening to Abraham teach, some of her attention was always on Samuel, her covenanted – and his on her. The first time Laurie fully realised the extent of her responsibility to care for Samuel, she was seven years old, they were newly covenanted, and Samuel's world was pulled apart.

'There is no other, and yet there is. Each of us perceives ourselves to be one, to be other from others, we believe we think alone, dream alone. Yet there is also the whole that all of our work here on the land, in communion, aims towards. We are many, already. One day we will be many more. Here and now we number sixty-seven individuals, each one of us tasked with the same imperative, to serve the whole. And so we are both sixty-seven, and we are just one.'

He looked around at the group of people gathered before him. It was midday and the sunlight was strong, even on this winter land, it was bright enough that people were blinking, winking, wincing to watch him. Even so, no one raised a hand to shield their eyes, they were uniform in their atten-tion, arms to the side, feet slightly apart, heads raised, eyes raised, listening with the body as well as with the mind.

Sixty-six people, men, women and children, two of them babies, strapped to their mothers so that they too could stand to attention, stand attending. Each one stared up at Abraham, where he stood in his place on the porch that fronted the main house. Those below included his wife and his own three sons, Johan, Lukas and Samuel. Abraham made no exception for those who were his blood family, there was no leniency just because Ingrid had founded the community with him, his boys were not let off either. Some thought he worked his sons harder, expected more of them, that he pushed his lads too far on occasion, but there was no denying they were always ready and Ingrid, his helpmeet, his first chosen, was ever-attentive.

For weeks now there had been a rumour that Abraham was preparing to choose another wife. Even Laurie had heard the story, whispered by Samuel in anger and fear. Ingrid had given Abraham only sons, and Samuel had no younger siblings. Ingrid was in her mid-forties, Abraham was almost a decade older, but with many years left to grow his own line, Samuel was worried, his father would take a new wife, his mother would be hurt, he would no longer be the last of Abraham's children.

Abraham looked out beyond the group assembled before him, he looked to the big hall, to the sheltered corral where the babies played, to the kitchen gardens close by. He looked further out to the fields, marked by fences for which he had dug the holes himself, years ago. He had hammered in the posts, strung the wire all along their newly created boundary with only Ingrid to help him, the two of them and their belief in the vision, their faith that had drawn the rest. He looked out further still to the open desert, scorching in summer, brutal in winter. The harsh land that Ingrid had brought him back from more than once, when despair at the failures of his people kicked off an even deeper despair at his own failure of leadership. And yet, he would do what he must do now. Abraham was a servant of the vision as much as any of them, his own will bowed to the greatest good of the whole, out here in their hand-hewn home, beneath a wide blue sky that neither knew them nor cared. Only Abraham could lead them on.

He drew his gaze back to the group. It was time.

'There is no other. There is only the whole.'

He reached out his hand and beckoned Ingrid to join him on the porch. She moved immediately to his side, no uncertainty or hesitation.

'My helpmeet,' he said, genuine love and admiration in his voice, one arm around Ingrid's shoulders, measuring the shivering of her body. From her place alongside Samuel, Laurie could see the tremor that Ingrid was trying to control. Abraham held her tighter, his arm heavy, soothing. Ingrid looked at him, he at her, a focus for the community who looked up to them, the couple who had created their new life. The tall white man, his dirty blonde hair greying now, green eyes still bright in his tanned face, wrinkled from the years of hard work to build this land on which they stood. The beautiful black woman, dark-skinned, bright-eyed, her body strong and taut from her own years of physical work in service of the whole. Below them stood their three sons, the perfect American blend birthed for the community, for the future.

Ingrid returned his look. The trembling subsided. She nodded assent, Abraham squeezed her shoulders one last time, and then he stepped away from his wife. He left Ingrid standing on the porch alone and went down the five steps to the community itself. Laurie could feel Samuel beside her, feel his anger, his yearning to run to his mother. He did not move.

Abraham walked into the crowd and with each step a new space was made for him. As they had been trained, the community did not make way for Abraham, to do so would have been to suggest that he was not of them, and they were all one, of course they were. But they did move, a half step, a shoulder shifted back, just enough room for Abraham to take his next step and his next, so that he might be both leader and of the community at the same time.

He stopped, looked about, and then saw her, walked to the woman.

Janet started to speak and Abraham held a silencing finger to her lips.

Laurie glanced from one place to the other, from Abraham tracing his finger across Janet's lips, to Ingrid, watching from the porch, her mouth a tight line, her eyes dark. Her boys looked up to her, on the porch, and she nodded to the three of them, a nod barely there, seen only by the boys and by Laurie, the rest of the community transfixed by the sight of Abraham and Janet. Ingrid nodded again, a little more directly this time. Her eldest son Johan grabbed Lukas, pushed and prodded him into place. Lukas, her middle son, was no great intellect, never would be, but he would throw himself into the dance. It was her youngest boy that Ingrid worried for, the last baby that she tried not to love more than the others, the last baby that Abraham tried not to blame for ending his hope of more children with Ingrid. They both failed. Samuel was Ingrid's promise as much as he was an ending, and she watched him now as he stumbled into place in the dance, frightened and angered by his father's actions, Laurie standing alongside him, Laurie trying to help.

*

90

The dance began with Abraham leading Janet, each of the community members taking their place, finding a way into a line that was a circle and an unending whole. Ingrid joined in as the sung note began, linking into the long file of people, she took a place at the end of the dance. When the note died and the dance picked up, curled around, began to spiral, Ingrid was on Abraham's left side and Janet, his new wife, the plain wife, breeding-stock wife, was on his right. It was a dance that lasted three hours, on slowly freezing ground, the dance when Abraham took his second wife and the community celebrated their beginning. Samuel did not celebrate, but he danced, and he hid his anger well enough. Only Laurie could see his fury as she danced alongside him, playing helpmeet, calming the one to whom she was covenanted, soothing him into compliance, into safety. For now.

Fifteen

Laurie held off speaking to Hope about the dance teacher, she knew only too well how secretive and self-contained she had been at seventeen. Even after years of warmth and generosity from Dot and Henry, she still hoarded her secrets, holding to herself the possibility of breaking away from their comfortable shambles of a home. She chose to tread softly with their daughter, to enthuse about her dance practice when it went from three to four nights a week, and then extended to full days on Saturday, half Sundays as well. She was also away working fairly often, they had more money coming in and Laurie liked the safety it afforded, she liked being able to suggest they might plan a family holiday and not have to look for bargain breaks. She was careful and aware, trying not to alarm Hope, not to risk her becoming secretive, as all too many of their friends told them their own teenagers, especially their daughters, had recently become.

Martha meanwhile, was busier than usual with her father. After her mother's death he had reluctantly sold the farm, but kept the old farmhouse and two acres it sat in because he couldn't bear to leave the land. The house, though not big, was a lot for just one person, and already the garden was becoming too much as he approached his late seventies. He had always been robust, had passed on his strong, tall genes to his daughter, everyone had called him Big Jack as long as Martha could remember. They'd named their own Jack for him, and had called him Little Jack until he was eight, when he declared, seriously and determinedly, that he would no longer answer to the name, he was no longer little. By the time he was fourteen, that was definitely true, but his family could still get a rise out of him by prefixing his name with 'little'. Martha's father had done his best, but since his wife's death he seemed diminished, his passion, even for the land beyond the home fence was dwindling. Martha had taken to visiting twice a week, a four-hour round trip, a house to clean when she got there, and an increasingly fractious father to placate. Martha didn't want to placate him, she wanted to bundle up Big Jack and move him in with them, move him to a bungalow, move him to a rest home if she had to, anything to get him out of the old crooked house she had loved as a child, which now felt like a death trap of narrow stairs, sharp corners, and dangerously steep outside paths. Martha was busy caring for her father and for their children and she left it to Laurie to deal with the extra-curricular activities. Laurie waited too long.

'Fuck.'

Martha was pale, but for a vivid red dot in each cheek.

'What?' Laurie looked up from her desk, as ever a quick glance to the bookcase behind the door to make sure nothing was revealed, 'What's wrong?'

'Hope. Fuck.'

Now Laurie was alert, standing, 'What's happened?'

'When was the last time you saw her naked, in a swimming costume, in her underwear?'

'What's happened? Is she sick?'

'Tell me,' Martha said, 'when?'

'I don't know, weeks ago, months maybe, she's seventeen, she locks the bathroom door now – what's happened? Has she hurt herself?'

Martha shook her head, 'Has she been eating?'

Laurie shrugged, 'Sure, we make food, they eat, the twins never stop eating.'

'I'm not talking about Ana and Jack.'

'You've seen her eat, right? Why? What?'

Martha held up her hand, counting out the meals, 'She takes that cup to school with her breakfast in it, muesli or whatever, to eat on the way. She has lunch at school, she says, she comes home late after dance class with Ana and Jack, picks at whatever I've cooked for them.'

'They're always eating – you said yourself, last supermarket shop, that we needed to start getting three loaves of bread not two, and more eggs, cheese – I cooked two chickens last weekend for them to pick at after training and they were all gone by the time I got home on Tuesday night.'

'And the empty plate thoughtfully put back in the fridge,' Martha said, 'I know.'

'I think that was a hint.'

'Jack's hint, yes, not Hope's. Have you actually seen her eat, recently?'

'I haven't . . .'

Laurie didn't finish her sentence and neither of them

wanted to admit that Laurie hadn't been around enough recently to see anything.

'For god's sake, Martha,' Laurie said, 'just tell me what's happened.'

Martha explained that she had heard the front door slam, the twins had already left for training, she knew Hope had a class and, assuming all three of the children were gone for the morning, she had walked into Hope's bedroom without knocking, something she never did if they were home. She'd surprised Hope, half-dressed.

'She's horribly thin.'

'She's small,' Laurie said, 'she was always underweight compared to the charts when she was a baby. She grew just fine, though.'

'This is different. She's all bone, sinew.'

'Dancers are.'

'She's seventeen, and neither of us see her eat any more, ever. Do we?'

Laurie shook her head, realising Martha was right, she'd been away a lot, but it was also true that she couldn't remember the last time Hope had sat down to dinner with them all.

'Sorry,' Laurie said, 'I know I've been rubbish, too busy, too much time away. I'll talk to her teacher.'

Martha was suddenly uncomfortable. She had been meaning to tell Laurie about the coaching sessions, and had never found the time or the right words to do so. With four sessions done and two to go, it felt too late now to reveal it, especially as it was about to end anyway. Martha had not had a secret before, not from Laurie, it felt strange and also, she had admitted to herself, exciting to have one. And she also still felt a little odd about Laurie knowing she was seeing a counsellor, especially as the most recent sessions had been all about Laurie, Martha's fears that Laurie was growing away from her, her concern that she was not interesting enough for Laurie. He had been helpful, listened intently to her as she talked about her life, her family, her wife. It was very nice to talk to someone who was genuinely interested in how she felt, but she really didn't want him to mention the sessions to Laurie.

'I'll pick her up after class and while I'm there I'll check out the other girls, see what they look like,' Laurie said.

'Yeah, OK,' Martha agreed, 'though you might not get much time to talk to him, he's usually got another class coming in straight afterwards.'

'I won't make a fuss, promise, I'll just check it out. Do you think Hope saw you were worried?'

'No,' Martha made for the attic door, heading downstairs, a day's work to squeeze into the morning before she headed off to accompany her father to a doctor's visit, 'I did my best, "Here's your bra and your school shirts, where do you want them, I'm in a hurry." Made myself look all busy, guaranteed we'll get the "my mother didn't care she was all wrapped up in her own life" bollocks.'

'Well done.'

'Thank you.'

That evening Laurie sat in a long dark corridor, listening to three dance classes simultaneously. Hope had refused her offer of a drop-off to class, she was planning to meet up with friends from the village, they'd get the bus in together, but she agreed to the ride home, if Laurie was going to be in town anyway, then sure, come and pick her up.

'But please, Mom, don't do any ballet-mother shit.'

'One, what's "ballet-mother shit"? And two, I thought this was dance, not ballet?'

Hope smiled, 'One, it's what Kerry's mother does all the time, dropping her at class, and packing a banana in her bag for between classes, hanging around with extra hairgrips and crap like that. She used to be a dancer, so we think she's vampiring up all of Kerry's energy, trying to hang on to her youth through us.'

'You know I suck at that kind of mothering,' Laurie responded, quietly thinking Kerry's mother was smarter than she and Martha, and the extra banana was a great idea, 'How old do you think she is?'

'Kerry's mum? She had her young, and she's by herself, I don't know, thirty-three, thirty-four, something like that?'

'Right. Definitely needs to hang on to her youth, she'll soon be as old as me if she's not careful. And two? The ballet bit?'

'It is dance, you'd probably call it modern dance . . .'

'You don't?'

'No one calls it that any more, Mom.'

'Oh. OK.'

'And it has ballet elements,' Hope went on, 'but it's a practice as much as anything, like yoga or something, that's what Kerry's mum says. It's dance and . . . I don't know what to call it, other stuff, about rigour and discipline. But it's definitely not about hairgrips and perfect turnout. It's more real.'

More real, from where Laurie was sitting, had turned out to be more silent. Totally silent. From the furthest of the three studios she could hear the grunt, pump and sweat of a Zumba class, from the second the repetitive beats of a tap class, probably for small children given how few of them were hitting the beat at the same time. But from the third room, the one she sat directly outside, nothing at all. No music, no teacher counting time, calling instructions, no sounds of effort, no noise. As she waited, the Zumba class emptied, a dozen or more women and two grinning men left the room glowing and chattering, they were replaced by a perfect line-up of pre-adolescent ballet girls, ballet mothers in tow, hairgrips and bananas at the ready. Then the toddler tap dancers were replaced by Irish dancers, same sound, but these dancers were older and much more in time. Clearly those who'd built the town's proudly touted brand-new dance studios hadn't bothered a great deal with sound-proofing, and even so, there was nothing from inside the room where Hope was meant to be working.

Finally, when she was ready to try the door herself, no matter how much it might embarrass Hope, Laurie heard a noise from inside the room, an exhalation of breath, an inhalation, and then a single note, held far longer than most people might expect from untrained singers. Even after all this time, Laurie found herself wanting to join in, wanting to hold the note, to find her place in the chorus. And both hearing it, and realising that she wanted to join in, ached to join in, made her retch.

The door was opened by a girl Laurie didn't recognise, not Hope, not Kerry. The girl was younger than Hope, she was red-faced, her hair and the T-shirt covering her leotard were damp with sweat, her bare feet red from sustained effort. From where Laurie was sitting she could see inside through the open door. A man's back, his own T-shirt also sticking tight to him, effort clear in the beads of sweat on his shaved head, with a row of young women before him. Each one of them as ecstatically shining as the girl at the door. Each girl individually bowed low before the man, who bowed back in turn, then each one left the room, in silence, breathing hard, desperate not to show the effort she had just endured, a desperation Laurie knew only too well.

Finally there was just Hope left in the class, Laurie sat, waiting for her daughter to bow, to leave the room, waiting to grab her child and get the hell out of there, get further away than she could imagine possible, get away before he saw her at the door. And then he reached out, put his arm around her daughter, pulled Hope to him, they turned and came to the door together, teacher and pupil, mentor and disciple, priest and acolyte. He was smiling, as if he knew Laurie would be there, waiting. As if this was exactly the image he wanted to present.

He was standing in front of her, Laurie was still sitting, rooted to her seat with horror. Hope was glaring, a look that said get up Mom, stand up, be nice, be polite. A look that was full of shame because this man that she clearly revered was seeing her in another context, an ordinary girl with a mother like any other. Laurie nodded at Hope, then she stood up and looked him full in the face. His beautiful face.

He held out his hand, his accent unchanged after all these years, his long curly hair all gone and yet it suited him, the jawline stronger, skin as smooth as Ingrid's had always been, eyes as green as his father's – his father's eyes, it was all Laurie could do to stop herself vomiting – and his smile was enticing, as disturbing as she remembered. As she had tried to forget.

She put her hand in his and they touched for the first time in decades.

99

He took a step closer, too close, now she had to crick her neck to meet his eyes, and she knew that he had done it on purpose, wanted her to feel uncomfortable, wanted her to be physically out of her depth as well as emotionally.

'You must be Hope's mother, how alike the two of you are. I'm Samuel. I'm so very pleased to meet you. I'm sure you don't need me to tell you, but your daughter Hope is a special one.'

Sixteen

They were the special ones. The youths tasked with making a difference out in the world. Chosen because of their faith in the vision, their obedience to the discipline of community, and for their physical beauty. There were only three of them this year, in other years there had been five, maybe six, one sad year there were just two, and then they were not allowed to leave, the rule against couples very clear, understandable for any who knew the temptations of the flesh.

The world was not unknown to them, some of them had lived away, as Laurie had. Lived away and returned, welcomed back – through a process of reincorporation, a gradual return to the body of the assembly – and then integrated fully, a disciple again. Anyone was welcome to leave and to return, they had been told this many times, they believed it, had seen it happen. There were stories of those who had not left honestly, openly, the matter of runaways was something else, a Pandora's box of rumour and whispers, but those who came back of their own volition, as Laurie had, were proof of the redemptive love of community, proof that gossip about the punishment of runaways was nothing more than a story to scare the little ones in the corral.

Sometimes a special one went out into the world for a third or fourth time. They led the others, kept them on task. It was useful to have at least one who knew what might be coming, it maintained the discipline of the assembly. No master without a disciple, no disciples without discipline.

This year Laurie and Samuel were being sent to the world with Marshall. He was a serious young man, almost into his mid-twenties, old for a special one, but Abraham had made an exception for his uncommon beauty, his extraordinary skill in attracting sheep to the flock. In the past four years that he had been a special one, Marshall's abilities had brought thirteen new disciples into the community in just three journeys a year. Dangerous journeys where the whole community held them in their hearts for the length of their fortnight away. Two weeks into the world, a month back in the regime to remind themselves of the mission behind their foray, and then out again, and again. Marshall had been unsuccessful in just three of those engagements with the world, a fact he counted as failure and when the community knew he considered this a failure, when they understood how tough he was on himself, they had yet another reason to love him even more. This was to be his last venture away, after this summer Marshall would return to the community for ever, he would settle with the wife Abraham had chosen for him – chosen in consultation with both Marshall and the girl, but chosen all the same – and then Marshall would take his new seat on Abraham's council.

The girl who had patiently waited these five long years,

waited to become his bride, was not a special one. That would not have been right, no one couple should ever feel too valued, too important. Where one might be beautiful, the other should be plain, if one was especially smart, the other ought to be less clever. One who was fervently community-minded would be partnered with a known waverer – all the better to keep an eye out, an ear open, for any middle-night doubt, all the better for unity. Marshall's intended, Aysha, was plain, quiet, and good. She was pale pink white where Marshall was mixed-race brown, like all of those who were matched by Abraham, they were to be part of the melting-pot world, beyond division because division had been bred away. Aysha had not been covenanted young, as Laurie had, Abraham said it was in his vision that she should wait. When Marshall arrived in the community, Abraham smiled and told Aysha her beloved had arrived. While her childhood friends were already married and giving new life to the community, new babies playing in the corral, Aysha waited for Marshall's final return, his mission over. It was lucky she was patient as well as good, another girl might have grown tired of waiting. Abraham had chosen well, as always. When Marshall, Samuel and Laurie returned, hopefully with at least one new disciple each, then there would be the commitment, the wedding between the two, witnessed by community, held truly in the time and space that only this assembly of the committed could offer. It would be a day of celebration, bringing to fruition their covenant from years earlier, and Marshall would have earned his new place. He would never have to leave the safety of the promised land again.

*

The farewell was always a solemn occasion. Everyone gathered in the meeting space outside, waiting for Abraham, who would hold the hands of each of those special ones leaving, touch their heads in blessing, and then open himself to the voice of the vision, allow himself to be taken, as they all were in the dance, so that the words of advice he gave the special ones were true to the dream that had brought each of them here. This was a precious moment, where Abraham allowed himself to be revealed in community, to be fully overcome by the vision, so that he might speak the correct words for their path over the next fortnight. The words were not true because Abraham willed them to be, or because he chose them with care as any preacher might, but because he allowed the vision to flow through – yielding himself as a channel, humbling himself before the community, and in doing so giving an even better example of true service. Service to which they might all aspire.

Several of the women had helped Laurie prepare that morning, her hair pulled back, pinned just so, perfectly arranged so that it would come down with a single twist. Her dress, simple, white, pure and modest, but also shaped to show off her waist, her breasts, her collarbones. She stood between Marshall and Samuel, both of them dressed in light, white suits. All three looked simple, crisp, perfect. They would not arrive in the city dressed like this, they would travel in ordinary clothes, inconspicuous young people, travelling as any others might, but for the farewell they were decked out as the pure bride and her grooms, ready to give their all for community.

*

Abraham shook himself, his tired eyes wide in his weathered face, his hand heavy on Samuel's head, and he began, 'Samuel, you are mine, a son of my flesh as well as a son of our community. Your mother gave you life and she also gave her life to this community. Your mother gave her life for the vision, you know that, my son?'

Samuel looked into his father's eyes, green to green, he nodded. He hated it when Abraham spoke in public about Ingrid, her sacrifice, how much she had given to start the community, how quickly she succumbed to disease after he took Janet as his second wife, refusing medical treatment, giving herself up to free the man she loved. He hated Abraham for speaking so blithely of Ingrid's death and he could never say so in public. Samuel said nothing, waited, gave his father the space he demanded.

'My own son, and yet you have freely given yourself to service – as have all my children, those of my flesh and those of my heart.'

Abraham looked around at the gathering and his face broke into a broad smile. The rush of gratitude that came back at him for such a small gesture was always thrilling, but he would not allow himself to be derailed from his position as channel, the one route for the community's vision.

'You go now to the greatest service of all, to return with the newly hungry, the newly thirsty. When you bring back those from the world, those who have never known the love of community, the strength of assembly, you give them the greatest gift, you give them communion.'

And here those who had been silently standing to attention, standing to witness as they always must when Abraham spoke, lifted their eyes to the sky, their hands held up and open, in the community's preferred manner of applause. Those with their hands highest, eyes widest, had themselves been brought in by special ones, brought to the challenge and the safe harbour of community, of which Abraham now spoke.

'We here know true freedom, true hope, we know the full passion of the most honest engagement. Not for us the limited lives of those who bond with just one person, in the slavery, the constriction, of the private home. Pathetic private lives. Here, in our life on the land we know a full communion of souls, the passion and pleasure – and yes, the pain, we must be honest here, the intense struggle that is surrender to the whole, and the deepest reward that follows. For some of us, coming to community is easy, there is no difficulty in giving up the selfish self. For others it is much harder, we fight to break the ties of personality, but it is in losing the individual self, ceding to whole, that we truly become.'

He looked around the assembled group and smiled, 'You Joshua, you Elizabeth, Daniel, Mary, Sara,' he pointed to a group of teenagers, each one with arms raised in applause, each one thrilled to hear their name on Abraham's lips, 'you are the lucky ones, you and our smaller children in training, the toddlers and babies in the corral, our community babies, loved and raised by all of us. Not one of you has ever known the barbed chain of nuclear family. You will take us forward, blossoming into the fruits of our hard experiment on this unforgiving land. You have never known the pain of remaking yourself, a sacrifice I began for us and which I willingly continue.'

Abraham stopped, letting the mention of his own sacrifice resonate. In the absence of his words, the only sound was the ever-present high-pitched song of the eight great pylons that bestrode the expanse of the compound, reminding them always of the world beyond, their humming wires as much a part of the life of the community as Abraham's preaching or the hot dust that swirled around them.

Then Abraham walked slowly – he never walked fast, never ran, every movement was deliberate, considered – to Laurie.

'Our sister, our daughter Laurie knows this pain better than most. She came to us a baby, rescued from a family and a system that discarded her, brought to the care of our community. Saved. And then she was wrenched from our love by the same system that also fears us,' he nodded, 'and rightly so, for our joy, our passionate surrender to each other is the antithesis of all that tired society wants for its small citizens with their narrow, ordinary, personal lives.'

Now, even in his deliberation, Abraham was more animated, more fervent, he turned Laurie to face the community, standing alongside her, a good foot and a half taller, much broader, he led her through the gathering and up to his preaching place on the porch, so that everyone could look at her, love her in their looking.

'This child, who was given to us for safekeeping, was wrenched from our love by an authority that despises the community.'

He hugged Laurie close, so tight against him she could feel the muscles contouring his ribs, wondered if she could also feel the scars rumoured to be there from that part of his private self-sacrifice which was whispered, not witnessed. She wondered too, if others who were watching also had memories of Abraham holding them tight in the years immediately after covenanting, memories she had tried so hard to erase.

She forced herself to pay attention to where she was, to the land, to the faces staring up at them, forced herself to listen, to be here, to be now, not then.

'Our daughter, our sister, made her own way back to us. Travelled alone to come home, that we might help her again find the bliss of community. What dedication, what strength. We send her out now knowing that we are ever hers, and she will always belong to us.'

And ignoring the uncertainty she always felt when too close to Abraham, Laurie allowed herself to be lifted high on the approval of the community, and in doing so, she was confirmed once again in her hope, in her fear, that she had done the right thing in responding to Samuel's letters. The letters she had never mentioned to Dot or to Henry, the secret phone calls that none of her siblings knew about, not even when Samuel began to suggest that she return to the community, a place she remembered only in bad dreams, and certainly not when Samuel started to whisper that he loved her. The covenanting had become a faint recollection to Laurie, her choice to dismiss that time in her memories of life on the land, but Samuel believed in the promises they had made back then, believed they were destined for each other. In a wooing that lasted over a year, he had called her home.

Laurie had hidden away pocket money for months, she'd found second-hand clothes that would be more appropriate in the community, and she had lied to the family that had helped her find her voice, had taught her how to be loved as herself. She had done so because Samuel was right – whatever else he might do, Abraham spoke the truth – deep within, Laurie understood that there was no love outside community, that personal, individual love was selfish. The only true love was that which gave its all. She had come back to give her all. She had come back in order to be sent out, a special one.

The note began, deep in the breath, the chest, the back of the throat of someone in the assembled community. It was taken up by one voice after another, until everyone sang the note together, harmonic and full, breathing in to sing out, singing out to breathe in. As the note finally died, the dance began. Laurie's body danced the dance because it was all she knew.

Seventeen

At the door to the dance studio Laurie put a protective arm around Hope, pulling away from Samuel's hand, 'Yes, she's very special. Our Hope.'

Hope squirmed under her mother's arm, 'Mom, please.'

'Mom,' Samuel said, 'that's nice. So you haven't forgotten your roots?'

'Not at all,' Laurie said evenly, 'I've lived here a long time but I think it's really important to remember where we come from, don't you? I'll never forget the people I grew up with, they made me who I am today.'

'Good to hear,' Samuel's smile was as even as Laurie's, his look as steady and direct, 'I have another class in twenty minutes, and I need to prepare. The group I teach next aren't quite as special as Hope and one or two of the others in her group, but it takes all sorts to make an ensemble, some to lead, others to follow, all of them to train in strength and discipline – I imagine you know all about that, with your new-found success? It must have taken a great deal of training to bring you to this stage in your career – far more than most people ever imagine, I'm sure.'

Laurie forced herself to smile, wanting to bite back, to ask how he knew about her work, to demand he say what else he knew, but she swallowed back her horror and tried not to choke on it.

'So,' he continued, 'I need to prepare. If you ever want to get together and chat about the States, I'm your man. It can get lonely being in a strange land.'

'Mom, come on, Samuel needs time.'

Hope had pulled on her T-shirt and jeans, adding a big jumper that Laurie now realised was intended to cover her sharp and bony frame.

Laurie made her choice. She offered Hope her keys, 'Go wait in the car, I want a word with your teacher.'

Hope glared at Laurie, 'Seriously?'

Before Laurie could respond, Samuel interrupted, 'Discipline is part of the practice, Hope.'

Hope dropped the attitude immediately, 'Sorry. See you in the car, Mom.'

She bowed again to Samuel who returned her obeisance with a nod, and she also made sure that Laurie knew she wasn't off the hook with a quick glare as she grabbed the keys, and then she was gone.

They were silent. Laurie didn't know how to begin.

Samuel took his time, he slowly closed the door to the corridor, turned back to Laurie and smiled, 'Your daughter is quite lovely when she's obedient, don't you think?'

Laurie ignored his question, 'How did you find me?'

His smile broadened, 'It might be a coincidence.'

'All things are meant.'

He smiled even more now, 'Good to see you haven't forgotten everything. True, all things are meant . . .' He waited for

111

Laurie to continue and when she did not, he finished the phrase himself, 'every action possesses both a force and a consequence.'

'Which are you? Force or consequence?'

'I'm both Laurie, you know that. Haven't you been waiting for me to show up one day, to bring you back to life?'

'I have created my own life. It had no need of you. It has no need of you.'

'I've heard. There's the lovely wife and the lovely home and the three lovely children.'

'And what do you have Samuel, do you have anything of your own?'

Laurie did not want him to rile her, didn't want him to see she was angry, frightened, but it was too late to bite back her words. He closed his eyes and breathed in and she knew it was a breath of pleasure that she had snapped at him.

He opened his eyes and looked straight at her, 'We were covenanted.'

'It was a childish game.'

'It was witnessed.'

'By a bunch of crazy people, running away from the world.'

He shrugged, 'I understand you live way out in the fens? All that wide, flat land, it's not so different from the desert, is it? And the cosy little home you have created, your self-made "family" ...'

'It's real. My family and my life here are real,' Laurie half whispered, horrified at how much Samuel knew about her, and also not surprised. She remembered that Samuel had always had a knack of making people feel so treasured that they gave up their deepest hidden truths. Given the time Hope had spent with him, and the training both she and Samuel had had in listening and storing secrets, in building on half-told stories, he probably knew way more about them than she wanted.

'I need to go, Hope will be wondering where I am.'

He laughed aloud, then looked at the clock on the studio wall, 'Off you run. I have another group arriving, not acolytes in this session, just the ordinary people who help pay the bills. It takes a lot to cross the ocean, set up in a new town, persuade someone to leave their job.'

'You did that? You're why their other teacher left?'

'She was wasting her life. She realised it, with a little help.'

'What do you mean "help"?'

'Just that. I'm a life coach now.'

Laurie relaxed then, just for a moment, shook her head, 'Of course you are. Christ, everyone's a fucking life coach.'

'True, it's a crowded market, but I'm good.'

'Yeah,' Laurie's laugh left her, knowing he probably was, 'You always had a knack of persuading people to do things they didn't want to.'

'Or helping them work out what they really want. Your small-town dance teacher wanted to travel, always had done. Now she's off having the time of her life. She sends me postcards, the last one was from Peru.'

There was a knock on the door and Samuel opened it to let in half a dozen women, mostly in their thirties and forties, and a couple of men.

As Laurie reached the door, desperate to leave, Samuel leaned in, speaking quietly, 'See the effort these simple, small-town folk have put into how they look for a dance class? I'm winning already Laurie.'

'Hope will not be back, I'll make sure she never sees you again.'

He shook his head and took her hand, raising his voice, 'Loved meeting you Laurie, Hope really is one of the hardest-working girls I know, she's coming on incredibly well,' then lowering his voice and squeezing Laurie's hand hard and fast he added, 'You think you can stop her? She's enthralled with her own ability, she can't believe how skilful she is becoming – she knows I gave that to her.'

Laurie didn't answer, Samuel was telling the truth. Hope had never before shown the amount of discipline and enthusiasm she had been giving to these dance classes.

He went on, his voice even softer, 'You, of all people, know exactly how determined a young woman can be. If you stop Hope coming to class, she'll find a way regardless. Besides, I'm not here for her. Your talented, hard-working daughter is an added extra. I came for you, my helpmeet.'

Laurie pulled away, would have run if she could, 'Sorry to take up so much of your time.'

She was heading down the stairs as he called after her, 'I'll give you a call in the week. There's so much about Hope's future we need to discuss. Now then, my lovelies,' he clapped his hands and the next class clapped back, repeating his rhythm perfectly, 'what shall we do this evening?'

Laurie stood at the front door to the studio building, the reception area quiet now that the studios behind her were full again. The distant sound of rhythmic clapping, the closer beat of pointe shoes on the floor, a repeated piano tune, one and two and three and – and – and. Her heart racing, palms sweating, scared she would faint, vomit, scared her legs were about to give way, she leaned against the door that led out to the street. She took in a breath, held it, breathed out. Three more times until she was steady enough to face Hope, ready to deal with the fear forcing her past into her present. She shook her head as she walked out into the street, behaving as if life were going on as usual, even while it felt as if she was running as fast as she could from what she had left behind. One step towards the car, another, another. That training came in handy, Laurie could walk, she could breathe, she could keep going. She would work this out. Another breath, held, and onwards.

She and Hope drove to the pool to pick up the twins, the car was quickly full of the race stories, an adversary beaten by a whole half a second, a final sprint that didn't quite work, started too late or too soon. Then home via their favourite Indian takeaway, the over-priced one that Martha loved, spending the extra because Martha had been working all day and Laurie wanted to treat them all, generously, gently, treat them because they were her precious, fragile life. They ate in front of the TV, Jack's turn for the movie choice and then they all had an early night because the twins had a competition the next morning, Martha was working for a client all weekend, and Hope had class at ten. A class that Laurie couldn't bear her to go to and had no way of stopping without explaining why.

They were lying in bed before Martha had a chance to ask Laurie about the dance class, the teacher.

'Does he think there's a problem?'

'I don't know,' Laurie replied, grateful that she could answer honestly.

'But did you ask him about her weight loss?'

'I didn't get a chance, between Hope standing sentinel so I didn't embarrass her in front of him, and the next lot coming in, there wasn't enough time.'

Laurie wanted to say so much more, about who he was, why she was horrified that he knew their daughter, terrified that Hope already trusted him, but to say any of that she would have to explain things that Martha would never understand, about a Laurie she never wanted Martha to know.

'OK,' Martha mumbled, hoping that her tell-tale twist into Laurie's side would convince Laurie that she was already half asleep, 'I'll have a word when I take Hope in tomorrow.'

'No, it's fine,' Laurie spoke into the dark of their bedroom, very clearly, her stomach churning at the thought of Samuel meeting Martha, how he would charm her, enjoy getting to know her, having something else to hold over Laurie, 'She'll hate it if it looks like we're both having a go. I'll give him a call on Monday and arrange to talk to him properly.'

'Good, Hope trusts him, she'll listen to him.'

Martha yawned and snuggled in tighter, if Laurie thought she was sleeping she wouldn't have to tell her that she was seeing Samuel as a counsellor, she wouldn't have to tell something she wanted to keep for herself, and didn't even know why.

They lay still in their dark room, Laurie wide awake and fearful, Martha pretending to sleep and secretive, hiding from each other even as their bodies twisted together.

Eighteen

'I didn't tell her I'd met you.'

'She knows you've met me, picking Hope up, dropping her at class.'

'I mean, I didn't tell her about ... this.'

'This?' he asked.

'You know, this, what we're doing.'

'What are we doing?' he asked again, his gaze direct, a half-smile twisting the corners of his mouth.

'Nothing.'

'At all?' he asked. 'That's disappointing, I believed you when you said you felt you were making progress.'

'No, I am, I think. I'm glad of these talks, sessions, of this. It's just,' Martha stumbled, 'this is just ...'

'Something you haven't told your wife about.'

'Yes.'

Samuel didn't say anything, he looked at Martha, waiting for her to go on.

'I don't know why,' she added, faltering.

'Sure you do.'

There was silence, a yawning silence in which Martha squirmed, trying to work out why the hell she hadn't said anything on Saturday night, why she hadn't told Laurie she had been seeing Samuel for four sessions now, why she had chosen to take refuge in sleep, dodging the words that kept forming in her mouth, and then simply pushed the thought away the whole of their busy Sunday.

'I think . . .'

He waited.

'I think . . . I feel,' she twisted in her seat, uncomfortable at what she was about to admit, 'I like this time. With you, this, here.'

He nodded, 'Why?'

'Because it's . . . it's for me. Only me. It's not about being Laurie's wife or Hope and Jack and Ana's mum, it's not about my dad and needing to be a good daughter for him, it's not even about my work, it's about me. And I know that's selfish, and I know it's stupid, but . . .'

'Why is it selfish, stupid?'

'Because I'm a grown woman.'

'And?'

'And of course I could have stuff just for me, no one's stopping me, but that's not how it's worked out, not at the moment anyway, for whatever reason I've ended up being all about them . . .'

'I think you know the reason,' he said, looking straight at her.

She was confused, 'I do?'

'Of course you do.'

His tone was sharp, this was new, Martha was used to him being warmly encouraging, pushing her, yes, but not more,

118

not sharp. She shook her head, this was harder than she'd expected. When she'd come to their session today, she'd known Samuel would bring up Laurie's visit to the class, and that she'd have to admit not having told Laurie about seeing him for coaching.

She tried again, 'OK, so maybe it's . . .'

He interrupted, 'You can do better than that.'

Martha groaned, 'You're really pushing today, aren't you?'

'Isn't that why you're here? For you?'

Martha nodded.

'Then be honest about you.'

She paused, and then tried, 'I think I didn't tell Laurie – no, I know I didn't tell Laurie because I don't want her to know.'

'Good, go on.'

'I want something of my own. I gave up having a private life once we got together, anyone who goes from single to coupled does, and then we had the kids and it changed again, the kids mattered more. Everyone does it, to some extent, when they're in a relationship, when they have kids. They give up who they are, who they were.'

'Has Laurie?'

'Laurie's different. Where she grew up . . . she didn't have a normal childhood. I knew she needed me, and the kids, right from the start, I knew they all needed me to make it, to make us, an ordinary family. It was on me to help us be . . .'

'Ordinary?'

'Yes.'

'And are you?'

'Ordinary?' Martha shook her head. 'Is anyone? The thing is, Laurie didn't grow up in a family, not really.'

'What does that have to do with you not telling Laurie about seeing me?'

Martha frowned, 'I'm not complaining about her.'

'OK.'

'It's just ... I think I give a lot. And I want to. For us, to be a family, and looking after my dad, I don't mind it, really, I don't.'

'OK.'

'I just want something of my own. This time, being here ...'

'With me.'

'It's something of my own.'

'Something secret?'

Martha sighed, it felt like a relief to admit it, 'Yes. I want a secret.'

Samuel looked at the clock, their time was up, he smiled, 'Then we'll keep it between ourselves.'

'There's also ...'

'Yes?'

'Laurie's worried about Hope, she's been working so hard, and she – Hope, she's lost weight ...'

'I noticed that too.'

'Good. So we're not making it up.'

'Not at all.'

'Right,' Martha was calmer, easier, 'Laurie wants us to both come and speak to you about it. We want you to help, maybe you could speak to Hope?'

'I will.'

'And what about this?' she asked.

'This?'

'These sessions, you and me. Here.'

'This is your time Martha. It's your secret to tell, if you want.'

On Monday afternoon Laurie left a message for Samuel, on Tuesday she left two. She was leaving her third message on Wednesday when he picked up, 'Persistent, aren't you?'

Laurie heard his voice, light, amused, and then sharp, 'I said I would call you in the week. I said it, Laurie, I meant it.'

'We need to talk about Hope.'

'The hope of true unity? The hope of salvation through community?'

'My daughter Hope.'

'Ah, that Hope, as you will.'

Laurie could hear him smiling, laughing at her, 'When?'

'When I say so.'

There was no smile now.

'I'm concerned . . .' Laurie trailed off, worried about giving him the satisfaction of knowing her fears, and then started again, aware that he not only knew her fears, he had probably been part of creating them, 'She's too thin. She's working too hard. Martha and I are both worried.'

'Then why don't you both come and see me? I'd be delighted to spend some time with your lovely wife.'

'No.'

'Yes. Hope's my star pupil, my best girl. It makes perfect sense that I meet her parents. Come for a drink, or supper. Do you call it supper? Some of them do, the ones you'd call posh, I think. Do you say "posh"? How British are you now, Laurie?'

'We don't call it supper.'

'Shame, I like those ones, they're quaint.'

'And we can't both meet you. Martha can't, she's busy.'

'Too busy to worry about her little girl? Come to tea then, even if you don't do supper, you must do tea?'

She sighed, irritated with his games, 'For God's sake, Samuel, no one in England does tea. It's for tourists. We work, like everyone else, we don't have tea.'

'Then tomorrow, let's pretend you're a tourist, come at three, that gives us time before I have to prepare for my six o'clock class, Hope's class.'

'I don't . . .'

Laurie knew she sounded feeble.

'I insist.'

Samuel knew it too.

He gave Laurie his address and hung up, no goodbye. She was glad to have him off the line.

While Martha fussed about whether to wear jeans or a dress, what the hell she was supposed to wear to tea when no one ever had tea, Laurie snatched ten minutes in her hidden room, a lie about a last-minute edit to a paper she was giving next month. Ten minutes to armour herself, a preparation for the unknown. She found herself wondering, once her breath was a little calmer, her tight fists relaxed, briefly, if Samuel was also preparing. If they were, in fact, doing exactly the same thing at exactly the same time as they had done so often before, and that thought made her tense all over again.

Martha drove them into town and found herself almost admitting the truth several times, almost saying that she knew Samuel better than just a passing acquaintance at the studio door – or rather, that she didn't know him at all, but he knew a lot about her, about them. The problem was, she didn't know how to say it. Should it be, 'I've been seeing him, Samuel, as a coach' or perhaps, 'Listen, I've been seeing a coach – it's this guy, Samuel', either way it sounded as if she'd been keeping a secret from Laurie. Because she had been keeping a secret from Laurie. And so she swallowed the words back, said nothing.

Laurie was so engrossed in her own anxiety that she barely noticed Martha's silence and spent the time imagining Samuel's flat. Frugal, cold. An over-stuffed rental place, chintz and darkly pretty for tourists. A room in someone else's home, the best room, a place he had commandeered by finding a nook and burrowing in, a cuckoo biding his time.

She did not picture a light and airy apartment, 'Penthouse, come all the way up,' he had said, his voice scratchy at the other end of the intercom. Laurie had placed herself directly in front of the camera in the entrance way, she didn't want Samuel judging Martha without her there to watch him, to judge him in return.

The lift did not have a button for the penthouse, and both women looked around in confusion for a moment. When she heard Samuel's voice telling them, 'I'm bringing you up now, doors closing,' Laurie realised he was already watching them, not just at the door, but the half dozen steps across the lobby to the lift and from inside.

Martha raised an eyebrow, 'Very fancy,' Laurie nodded back, too unnerved to respond.

The lift opened out into a bright room, an entrance way, light falling from above through a wide, domed skylight. Directly opposite were double doors and as the lift doors closed behind them Laurie felt a moment of terror. No way to call the lift back, the only place to go was on, into Samuel's home. The pale wooden doors ahead of them opened and he stood there smiling.

Samuel looked good, Laurie had to admit, he looked good. The long limbs that had been slightly lanky in his late teens, now fitted his body well, a grown man's broad chest, broad shoulders. He had filled out, but there was not a spare ounce of flesh on his frame. With his long, curly hair gone, the shaved head gave him a gravitas he had lacked as a young man. As a boy he'd veered between wanting to be whiter like his father, blacker like his mother, never fitting, never comfortable. Now Laurie saw a man who presented himself at ease in his skin, the same sparkling green eyes, and that awful, charming smile.

He came forward and hugged Martha, 'So glad you could both come to visit.'

Taking his cue, she responded neutrally, 'We're both concerned about Hope.'

When he hugged Laurie he whispered, 'She's lovely!'

Once he had given them a drink – Martha accepted the cool sharp rosé he offered and Laurie declined, citing the drive home as her excuse – Samuel sat them both down on the blue velvet sofa and placed himself opposite in the way Laurie recognised only too well. It was how they had been trained as special ones, to command maximum attention. Martha recognised it too, it was how they sat in the counselling room.

'Laurie, Martha, you're worried, and you're right, Hope has been losing weight, I'd been intending to speak to her about it myself, but I'm so glad you brought it up first. In my role it can be very difficult if I find the parents haven't seen what is going on with their child. In many ways a part-time teacher such as myself, one who does not have the child with them day in, day out, is in a harder position than a school teacher. We're more likely to notice changes but less likely to have permission to address them. Now we have the opportunity for the three of us to deal with the problem,' he hesitated, 'if it really is a problem of course.'

Without giving them a chance to reply, he went on, 'You want to know about me, why your girl wants to spend so much time in my class, what I'm doing that's special – and it is special, I promise – and I'm happy to tell you.'

He said he'd come into a little money, that he had grown tired of American parents and their mollycoddling ways, he'd tried France but found the dance tradition there too traditional, the same in Italy, and again in Spain. And so, against his first instincts, he found himself in England and had chosen to move beyond the city, away from city children and city parents. He wanted to create a new kind of work and all he needed was the right adherents.

'You'll understand this,' Samuel said, speaking directly to Martha, 'your kind of work needed people to believe in it before it took over the world, the internet has become everything to all people, but it would have been nothing without those first believers.'

'I'm just a designer, I don't write a lot of code, I'm not the one who instigates stuff, I leave that to the devs.'

He smiled, 'And I didn't invent the jeté, the time step, jazz hands,' and here he reached out for Laurie and waved his hands right in her face.

Martha laughed as Laurie jumped, 'Babe, relax,' and Laurie hated the complicit wink Samuel gave Martha.

He went on, 'Neither of us invented the form, but we work with the form to create something new, all of our own. And that is the point of the work, to do what has not yet been imagined, to invent. For Hope, it's important to her to have something of her own. We all need that, in our own way, don't you think?'

He looked from one woman to the other and, not giving either a chance to respond, he went on to explain that it was the light which had brought him out here, to this nondescript town on the edge of the fens, given him a reason to settle.

'I've always looked for land and light, the right combination, dance is a visual as well as physical art. Out here, with the broad sky, the land wide and open, it's impossible to hide. Almost like our deserts back in the States, don't you think Laurie? Impossible to hide from oneself – when we face the self, then we can create.'

'He was so full of shit,' Laurie was driving, slower than her preference, but her hands on the wheel were tight, her entire body was tense, she knew she needed to drive carefully.

Martha was too busy looking out of the window to notice Laurie's hands, she was looking at the light, as she had been ever since they left Samuel's apartment when she had walked out into the street saying, 'He's right of course, the light here is special.'

All through the walk to the car and then the stop-start drive in early-evening traffic, Laurie had held her tongue, it was only when they were finally on the narrow road home, high hedgerows on either side that she spoke up, 'Seriously, so full of shit.'

Martha turned away from the huge sky outside, which even in her anger, Laurie noted was especially deep, the dark blue of early spring turning to night.

'You didn't like him?'

'I have no idea what's to like, he talked about himself the whole time.'

'He talked about making art, the spirit behind it. I know we don't know many people who talk about spirit . . .'

Laurie's hands were even more tense on the wheel now, 'We don't know anyone who does.'

'Not with such firm conviction, no, but . . .'

'What?' Laurie asked.

'He listened when we told him we were worried about Hope, I like that he'd noticed it too.'

Laurie didn't like that he'd noticed it, would have preferred his fulsome words about Hope to have been a lie to placate over-anxious parents, allowing him to keep their money and fob off their daughter with excessive praise.

'You think he'll speak to her?' Laurie asked, 'I'm not even sure that's the right thing to do. It might make her more self-aware.'

Martha had to concede this was possible, 'But she's already that, clearly. She takes him seriously. He was right, it'll be easier if she links eating properly to her dance training. She's too seventeen to listen to us.'

'I know,' Laurie said, turning into their hidden driveway, 'So what are we going to tell her?'

'About where we spent the afternoon? Work, I needed you to talk me through some kind of building specs, something

127

for the site I'm working on. They'll never question it, they don't care about our work.'

Worried as she was, Laurie had to smile, 'You're very devious.'

'And I'm right.'

Martha got out of the car relieved that Laurie hadn't asked how Samuel knew what she did for work, how he'd been able to speak to her about form with such knowing. She only had one more session booked with him, maybe she'd just say nothing, let it pass. She'd tell Laurie later, or not. It had felt strange keeping a secret, sitting in his apartment, and she'd enjoyed it. It was something extra, all of her own.

Nineteen

Three weeks later and Hope was thinner and more distant. Whatever Samuel had said to Hope, if anything, the problem was definitely getting worse. The time for careful handling was over.

With the twins out at a competition several hours' drive away – another parent had drawn the short straw and was driving – both Martha and Laurie were home, and had agreed that they would tackle Hope about the extra dance classes she had taken on. They'd read the books, they knew they should focus on the things that were more public, less likely to prompt shame and worry, so the dance classes were the obvious way in. Much as Laurie wanted Hope to cut any links to Samuel right away, they weren't going to ask her to stop classes, just to cut down. For the past month Hope had been going to two classes before school, two after school, all day Saturday and every Sunday morning. In terms of hours and commitment it was very similar to the twins' schedule so both mothers knew they couldn't try asking her to spend more time at home, nor were they going to suggest that she concentrate more on her schoolwork. Hope had never been a great student, but she had done better than expected in her last lot of mocks. Laurie knew this would be down to Samuel's insistence that everything was connected, that hard work in one area necessitated hard work in them all, and she certainly didn't want Martha to attribute Hope's schoolwork success to him. They had been biding their time for the right moment and, even though they knew there were no right moments to tell their daughter they thought she was too thin, working too hard, too driven, the moment was now.

They were sitting, waiting, in the kitchen when Hope came in from her Sunday morning class, and Laurie called her to come in for a chat.

Hope stood at the door, 'Chat? That sounds ominous.'

'Sit down, Hope,' Martha said, and Hope, slowly, deliberately, came into the room, pulled out the chair at the head of the table and sat down.

'Yes?'

Laurie had to stop herself smiling, it was genuinely laughable, their seventeen-year-old dictating the terms of their worry, deciding how concerned she would allow them to be. This new Hope, asserting a brutal independence over her own body, was uncharted territory, and it was unnerving because she wasn't shouting, she wasn't crying, she was very cool, very deliberate, and the person she most wanted to please was neither of her parents. They would not win Hope back now with mere love.

They tried to explain their concern, Laurie doing most of the talking, Martha backing her up. Hope waited, listened and then took a deep breath. Laurie watched her and wondered if Samuel had been teaching the same techniques that she practised herself.

Speaking carefully and calmly, Hope answered them, 'I will not leave my classes and I will not allow your jealousy to derail my plans. I've been warned about this.'

'Jealous?' Martha asked.

'Warned?' Laurie's tone was sharper than she'd intended and Martha glared at her.

'Samuel told us you would be jealous,' said Hope.

Now it was Martha's turn to bite back, 'What on earth are you talking about? Jealous of what?'

Laurie knew what Hope was about to say, could have said it with her, word for word.

'Samuel explained that you feel the need to control us – all of you – our families. That you have controlled our lives until now and so you find it hard to let us go, to let us live our lives. He said we should feel sorry for you ...'

'Compassion,' Laurie interrupted, unable to stop herself.

Hope was shocked out of her teenage arrogance for a moment by her mother's knowing, she quickly righted herself, 'Yes, actually, he did say compassion. He said we should have compassion for you because your lives were already set, and you no longer have the courage to break the patterns you've made for yourselves. He said that you'd see us doing it, opening our lives wide, and you'd be jealous.'

'Right,' Laurie said, trying to make herself speak of Samuel as if he were distant, different, trying to speak as if she did not know exactly the magic that he was working on her daughter, 'And he thinks that of all the parents, or just us?'

'All of you,' Hope answered, 'and also you especially.'

'Why us, especially?' Laurie asked.

'Because you are already outside, being gay, so you know what it feels like to be different. You want to be part of something . . . '

Martha frowned, repeating Hope, repeating her own words to Samuel, 'Part of something?'

'Yes. And you're conflicted.'

'Sure we are,' Laurie was furious now.

Hope smiled and continued, refusing to be put off, 'He thinks that you both – of all people – should understand what it is to be different and yet to also want to be part of the whole.'

'Everyone understands that,' Laurie said, 'it's normal, Hope. Everyone feels inside and outside, everyone feels like they belong and also that they don't.'

'Sure, but if everyone feels like that, why would you want me to do less, be less than I can be? Let me be amazing. Let me be different and amazing like you.'

Laurie shivered, the last thing she ever wanted for Hope was that she was different like herself. She tried another tack, 'We're worried about you, is that so wrong?'

'Not at all, but you don't need to be worried. I know what I'm doing.'

Laurie looked over at Martha and saw that her wife was sitting up very straight, her shoulders rigid, she knew what it meant, knew that Martha was going to speak up, say what they had agreed not to say, she looked at her, reached out her hand to take Martha's, willing her to stop, but it was too late, fear had taken over.

Martha pulled her hand back from Laurie and spoke carefully and very firmly to Hope, 'You're too thin, darling. We've both noticed it, and we're worried about your health.

We're happy for you to dance, we'll support you in training and your classes, just as we do with Ana and Jack, but not until you put on some weight. Until you're healthier, you are not going to any more than two classes on weekdays and one at the weekend.'

Hope reared back, her careful mask of calm dropped for the moment, 'You don't understand me at all, you can't – or you'd be more careful. You would be motherly.'

Hope glared at Martha and nodded, as if, having spoken the words aloud she had surprised herself, and now needed to confirm that what she had said was the truth. Both women heard their daughter acknowledge a gene line over her birth mother and it was horrible.

Martha nodded back, speaking slowly because that was all she was able to manage, 'You will always be my baby, and I will always be your mother, we both will, we both are. And as such, we say you need to limit the number of classes until we can trust that you're well. We need to take care of you, Hope, that's our job.'

Hope left the kitchen, the front door slammed, Martha and Laurie heard her running across the gravel outside, then distant, then gone.

Martha sat at the table and slowly allowed herself to breathe, 'Sorry. I fucked that up.'

'We fucked it up, not just you.'

'I don't know what else to do,' Martha was crying now, a few tears, her cheeks hot and red, her fists clenched.

'Me neither,' Laurie took her wife's hand, prising apart the tense fingers, nails digging into palms. She hated that Hope had pulled up a division between the two of them, birth and genetics, hated that their daughter had made clear a line they were always happy to blur, hated that Samuel was no doubt behind it.

Martha got up to put on the kettle, always her method of choice when confronted with a problem, 'This is different, isn't it? It's not just going to pass?'

'No, I don't think it will,' agreed Laurie.

Martha sat in front of her computer, opening and closing files. She spent an hour trying to figure out how to tell Laurie that she'd been seeing Samuel for coaching, how to speak to Samuel about the bad influence he was having on their daughter, and then she gave up because it all seemed too impossible and she started work. Another hour later and she deleted everything she had done, none of it worth saving.

Laurie decided not to bother with work at all, and so she cooked, a casserole for whenever the twins came home, and whether they had eaten on the way back or not. The four of them ate together and the mothers heard the stroke-by-stroke account of their wins – two apiece – and their losses, better than expected, good times swum regardless. Neither Ana nor Jack were concerned that Hope wasn't home, they were used to her being out late as they often were, and although Martha thought Ana might have been checking her phone more often than usual, sharing the texts with Jack, neither mentioned Hope being out so late. Martha whispered to Laurie that perhaps they'd over-reacted, perhaps it would all be fine after all. Laurie knew her wife was whispering a wish in the hope it might come true, and that neither of them believed it would be fine just yet.

Hope came in just as the twins were finishing up. She put barely three spoonfuls of food on her plate, and ate less than two of them, looking pointedly at Martha as she did so. She made a point of talking to her brother and sister about how hard they had worked, how exhausted they must be from their training and races, how incredible it was they both intended to be up at five thirty in the morning to get to training. She said it all with a genuine pride in her siblings who basked in their big sister's approval, and it would have been a genuinely touching family scene, but for the fact that both Laurie and Martha knew every word was a dig at them, another stake in Hope's claim to work hard, to push herself, to push her body.

Later, when Martha looked in to see if Hope was sleeping, she was met with a blank stare.

'Do you want me to wake you in the morning?'

'What for?'

'School, it's Monday tomorrow.'

'Not for class?'

'You have a Monday-morning class?'

'As of today, yes, we have an hour's class every day at 6.30 a.m.'

'You're not going to a class at six thirty in the morning, Hope.'

'But Jack and Ana are allowed to go to swimming training.'

'Jack and Ana are not—'

Martha stopped, she wanted to say not starving themselves. She tried again, 'Jack and Ana only go to training three mornings a week.'

'So I'll go three mornings a week.'

Martha smiled, 'Good try. Look, we screwed up this afternoon, Laurie and me, let's try to have a peaceful talk tomorrow, after school, yes? You get up at the normal time, have a good day at school, come home—'

'I have class after school. Am I allowed to go to that?'

'We said you could go to two classes after school – if tomorrow is one of the two this week, then yes. Come home after class and we'll talk about it, all right?'

'Do I have any choice?'

'No. We're worried about you, darling, that's all. It's worry. It's love.'

'It's stifling.'

'Yes, it probably is,' Martha said as she closed the door, 'but it's the best I've got.'

As usual, no matter what had gone on in the hours before, Martha fell asleep within five minutes of Laurie turning out the light. For years they had laughed about Martha's ability to turn off, whatever was going on, whatever was happening, sleep was her safe place – she slept when she was happy, she slept when she was unhappy. The twins were exactly the same, even when they were newborns, cuddled next to each other in the little crib that had dwarfed Hope, they slept like angels, right from the first day they came home. They slept like Martha, who now lay quiet beside Laurie.

Laurie tried to stay in bed, she tried to relax her legs, her arms, quiet the churning in her stomach, but there was no relaxation to be had, every time she felt her limbs begin to soften, begin that blissful soft easing away, her mind snapped back to an image of Hope defiant, Hope enjoying the challenge. After half an hour she gave up, five minutes later she was upstairs. The door that was no door was pulled closed behind her, a mat on the floor, bare walls with no distractions, a tiny leak of moonlight through the vine-covered window and Laurie took herself back to the time and place she had tried so hard to forget, to when she too had been defiant, running from the safety of Dot and Henry's home, running to the challenge of community.

Twenty

When Laurie returned to the community, she had to remember again that nothing was hers to do with as she chose. Not her time, her body, or her own will. She was drawn back by Samuel's careful insistence, by his letters and his phone calls, the sound of his voice in the night whispering her home, his helpmeet, his covenanted. Abraham welcomed her as a stolen daughter and promised that, after the necessary reckoning, the realignment, he would welcome her as part of the community.

As part of her realignment, Laurie was sent to work in the kitchen, under the strict supervision that was required of all new members. Every moment of the day and night was accounted for, days full of tasks and completion, with each completed action judged and found wanting or approved before moving on to the next. It was her last day of realignment, if all went well, if Suzie, her supervisor, reported that she had been successful, Laurie would be welcomed back as the full member she had been when she was taken away. She had not left of her own accord, that was known and understood, she had been lifted from the community's embrace, and still, she was required to realign to be worthy of their embrace.

She embraced realignment. In those many long phone calls with Samuel he had warned her it would be hard. The first week was all lectures and learning, hours attending talks along with the three others newly requesting entrance. One of the lectures was delivered live, the rest were recorded, they were from when Abraham was a younger man, his voice more forceful. After that week there was a questioning, from Abraham himself, in the presence of four long-term community members. Those who answered well enough, who understood the lectures well enough, went on to the second week. Those who did not went through the first week again, and again, and again. Many left who could not pass the first week, who could not retain the words they heard and repeat them, report back, some were too weak to keep trying until they could, some simply could not bear to sit in that dark room and listen one more time. There was one member of the community who now sat as an elder, Kathryn, who had repeated her first week seven times before graduating to the second week of realignment. Seven was a special number of course, and her dedication was obvious, her endurance strong. Later she spoke of it as a blessing, the gift of seven weeks listening to Abraham, seven full weeks in the dark, ceding to the truth, giving away all of her previous life – seven weeks to become her true self.

That first week was easier for Laurie, she had been raised on these stories, they were already part of her. Passing her first week was a great deal easier than the second, the week of duty. Up before dawn and bed after midnight, waiting at attention should any member of the community need her. Some members used those on duty more than others, some enjoyed using those on duty.

Laurie fetch my shoes.

Laurie make my bed.

Laurie take these babies.

Not that way, Laurie, this way.

Laurie feed the children.

Laurie water the garden – with this cup.

The whole home garden, with one cup. It took all night, she did not sleep, and the job was fully done.

Laurie kneel.

Laurie stretch.

Laurie stand on tiptoe. For an hour.

Laurie do this, do that, do not cry, control your tears, our control allows us to contribute, our control allows us to hold the whole. We are joined by our joint control, joined by our choice to hold – each one of us individually, each one of us together.

After the rambling, chaotic and warm home life with Dot and Henry, Laurie had thought her second week was the hardest. It was not. Her third and final week of realignment, the week under Suzie's command, was far tougher.

For the third day in a row, Suzie had Laurie peeling beets. Her hands stank of the vegetable and were stained dark red. This was the sixth day of her last week of realignment, if she got through this, Laurie would be back in community proper, she would be home. It was worth it, she told herself, to spend the first day in the kitchen under Suzie's command scrubbing every corner of the old dark room with a fine brush. Suzie was right, of course, to insist that cleanliness was vital in the kitchen, Suzie was right, of course, to give Laurie a second day of scrubbing, and a third. Cleaning would benefit the community, cleaning would benefit the other kitchen staff, cleaning meant being on the ground, literally humbling herself for the others.

'After all,' Suzie had said, 'you've spent all this time in a family unit, you need to remember what it is to be part of the whole, not important. You need to remember what it is to not matter individually. Oh look,' she said, pouring her coffee dregs on the floor, 'You've missed a bit.'

Laurie wanted to explain how it had been with Dot and Henry, how there had never been enough money to elevate any one of the kids above the others, that theirs was not the kind of moneyed home Suzie herself had left behind. Dot and Henry revelled in loving their kids into brilliance, that was all. Laurie wanted to explain this, but when she tried to speak the words caught in her throat, it was impossible to talk of her parents' generosity, their warmth, their welcome, without also remembering how much they had given her, the patience with which they had let her be, let her become a family member, instead of a hidden, silent child. It was impossible to consider sharing how life with Dot and Henry had been without also reminding herself of what she had left behind. Laurie didn't want to question why she had left, all she wanted to do was to concentrate on why she had come back, to the embrace of the compound, to be one of many, one with many. All she wanted to do was be part of, alongside Samuel whose words had called her here. So she accepted the tasks because she was trying to be good. Sucked it up and hated Suzie.

The third day of peeling, Laurie's hands red and raw, a kitchen knife in her hand, sharp and bright red with the blood of the beets, Suzie was berating her again.

'You're really slow, you know that?'

'I apologise, I'll try harder.'

'Trying is not doing, trying is not succeeding. You can't come back and pretend to have forgotten it all.'

'I haven't. I will succeed at working faster.'

'Great, I have a stopwatch, let's time you.'

Suzie took out an old watch and timed Laurie's beet peeling. It wasn't fast enough. Laurie did better on the next, and the next, on the fourth her shaking hand slipped and she cut a long line across her left palm.

'Oh no, have you injured yourself? Well, you'll have to recount that, won't you? Can't have any clumsy self-harmers in the community. Pity.'

Suzie turned to walk away and stopped, Samuel was standing at the door to the kitchen. He spoke to the rest of the kitchen staff, all of them trying to get on with their work, Suzie was the lead this week, and as such, her word was law. If anyone had spoken against her bullying they'd have had to recount it in the evening session, acknowledge their own lack of deference to the lead. Samuel wasn't kitchen staff and he wasn't cowed by Suzie. Unlike her, he was of the community by birth.

'You know, Suzie, the reason for appointed leaders is to practise leadership.'

'Yes, I do know that, thank you Samuel.'

'Then you know that you're leading badly?'

'You are not kitchen staff and you do not get to judge me.'

'True,' he smiled, 'but I called Laurie back, so I have some responsibility for her wellbeing, for her reintegration in community.'

Suzie picked up the huge tray of beets Laurie had been peeling, sprinkled them with salt and with oil, slowly and carefully placed them in one of the two huge ovens.

'She's integrating just fine. She'll get there, maybe not this week, but she'll get there.'

'The thing is,' Samuel said, advancing into the kitchen, 'she needs to get there this week, there are plans for Laurie, things that you could never understand, because you're simply not special enough, are you?'

Suzie was plain and she was ungainly and she knew exactly what Samuel meant when he called her not special, she blushed.

'Oh look, you've gone all red, like a beet. A great fat, red beet.'

He walked closer as Suzie turned away to the sinks, began to wash her hands, 'I'm busy,' she said, 'we have a meal to prepare.'

He stood right behind her, tall and lean and strong, close behind her, almost touching and Suzie pushed herself up against the sink, the water running on her hands. Others in the kitchen became very busy with their work, looking down at their own benches and tables. Laurie suddenly understood that Suzie wanted Samuel, that none of this had anything to do with her and everything to do with Suzie's crush on Samuel.

He was whispering to Suzie, 'Those hands are dirty, aren't they? Really nasty. You should wash them better, here, let me help.'

He reached both arms around her.

'This is a tight fit, isn't it? I'll have to squeeze right up.'

He pushed right into her from behind, Suzie's belly rammed into the side of the sink, and as he did so he turned off the cold tap, leaving on the hot. He held her wrists, pushing her hands under the now hot water, the hotter water, all the while pushing himself against her, pushing Suzie into the cold steel of the sink.

Laurie watched in fascinated horror, and then she spoke, carefully, 'That's enough, Samuel. Suzie's hands are clean. You should go. We have a meal to prepare.'

That night, finding each other in the dark, Samuel ran his tongue along the cut deep in Laurie's palm.

'I wanted to take that knife and stab her with it,' he said.

'I know,' she answered, 'but the burn will last longer.'

'The water never gets that hot, our generators are too slow.'

'Not that, the burn of shame, how much she wanted you, even while you were hurting her.'

'She wanted me because I was shaming her?'

'Yes,' she whispered, leaning into him, 'it's the shame that works us, every time.'

Twenty-One

In the morning Hope was gone. Her dance clothes, her gym bag, her schoolbag, all gone. Laurie stood at Hope's bedroom door, her stomach churning.

'Where's Hope?' she asked as she went into the kitchen, the twins already dressed and having breakfast, Martha on her first cup of coffee.

'What? Why?' Martha asked.

'She's not here,' Laurie said.

'She was leaving when I got up,' Jack spoke with his mouth full of toast and peanut butter, 'she was probably going to a class.'

Martha caught Ana's signal to Jack, one of their hand gestures. She and Laurie had never been able to properly decipher the little codes between their twins, and in a way it didn't matter because they both kind of enjoyed it, liked that the twins had a special bond. She did not like what she saw now, and rounded on Ana,

'Ana, what?' Martha asked.

'Nothing.'

'Ana,' Laurie's tone was cold, 'what do you know? How was she getting there? You two get the first bus.'

'I don't know, Mom, honest. Someone was picking her up, I think.'

'You think?' Martha asked.

'Mothers! She's gone to a class, it's not a big deal,' Jack said, pulling on his jacket and grabbing his trainers, 'Ana, come on, bus in five.'

Ana began following her twin, she looked back at her mothers apologetically, 'She said she had a lift, but I don't know who with.'

'You knew we'd said she couldn't go this morning, didn't you Ana?' Laurie asked.

'Yes, but . . .'

'Mom, she's not going to tell on Hope,' Jack said, 'and we're going to be late. Ana, come on.'

The twins left, goodbye kisses missed, grumpy Jack and worried Ana rushing for their bus.

'That went brilliantly,' Martha said.

Laurie turned at the accusatory tone, 'What?'

'You know our kids never tell on each other, never have done.'

'Right, and what would you like me to have done?'

'I don't know,' Martha answered, worried and upset and preferring to be angry with Laurie than think about how she still hadn't told her about seeing Samuel as a counsellor. Samuel who Laurie started to complain about now.

'I bet it was him, I bet he picked her up.'

'You don't know that.'

'I'm heading straight over to those studios and hauling her out of there.'

Laurie was making for the kitchen door, ready to go upstairs and get dressed.

'No, don't,' Martha said, shaking her head, 'You're making it too big a deal, you always do this.'

Laurie stopped, stared, 'Always?'

Martha shook her head, 'Sorry, that came out wrong. But . . . your own childhood, I think it means you over-react sometimes.'

'I'm not supposed to mind that she's openly disobeyed us?'

'Of course you are. We both are.'

'Well you can be nice Mummy if you want. I don't care, Martha, I want her to do as she is told.'

Martha groaned in exasperation, 'She's a teenager. That's exactly what she's not going to do. If you were around more you'd know . . . '

She stopped herself finishing the sentence, but it was too late.

The two women stared at each other, a bird screamed outside, a magpie, a car drove past at the top of their lane.

Laurie spoke carefully, 'I'm not going to argue with you, not about Hope, but that's not fair.'

'It's not, I know, but it is true.' Martha looked down at her coffee cup, the liquid tepid and dark, 'And I'm sorry, I shouldn't have said it.'

'I have to work . . . '

'Yes, I know. And we're both benefiting from it, and you need to keep on while they're interested in you. I know all of that. And I agree with you about it. But I'm the one who's been around more, dealing with how things are.'

'Fair enough. Except that how things are is our girl is starving herself, our twins are keeping secrets, and Hope is plainly defying us.'

'She's testing us, and if we make a fuss, all we do is play into her story about how we don't understand her, how we'll never realise how important dance is, or being thin, or . . . whatever. I'm as worried as you are. I just don't think that rushing after her now, embarrassing her in front of her friends, the whole class, will help. It especially won't help if you embarrass her in front of her teacher, she obviously adores him.'

Laurie sighed. Samuel. He was at the centre of this and the more she didn't tell Martha about her past with him, the more her fears grew. And still, she didn't know how to begin telling Martha everything that remained unsaid. She took off her jacket, hanging it on the hook by the front door, then came slowly back into the kitchen.

'So what do we do?'

'We could speak to her when she comes home tonight?'

Martha offered it as much as a question as a statement.

'So we let her go to the after-school class as well?'

'If she goes, yes. And when she comes home we sit her down and explain it's not on. We need to know where she is, we're worried, we think she's giving too much time to all of this dance stuff, especially this year when she needs to concentrate on mocks and exams and all of that.'

'We tell her we've suddenly decided she has to be academic when we've always known she's not and we long ago decided not to give her a hard time about that?'

'No, of course not,' Martha said, 'we just tell her it needs some balance. Just balance.'

'Balance. Good.'

They left the discussion there, unresolved.

*

Laurie went up to her office, Martha went out to the garden to her office. Neither woman did any work, both thought about Samuel, what they knew about Samuel. Martha about how it felt weird now that she had met him with Laurie, now that Hope was defying them to go to his classes. There was something uncomfortable in how he felt too close to her life, and yet she still didn't want to tell Laurie about the sessions with him, she still wanted something for herself, only herself. And all of it made her think how rubbish she was to have brought up Laurie's recent absences when she had her own reasons for not wanting to rush into Hope's dance class and drag her daughter out, and that was nothing to do with being a better mother than Laurie and everything to do with Samuel, with liking how he made her feel, and liking how he made her think. She knew that in all likelihood, she was as unwilling to be embarrassed in front of him as Hope was, and she was even more ashamed of suggesting that Laurie was in the wrong.

In her own office Laurie was also not working. Unlike Martha, she wasn't thinking about Hope, or about her parenting failures, she was thinking about Samuel, trying to work out what he was doing here, what he wanted from her. She was trying to work out how to get him out of their lives before he got in any deeper.

Twelve miles away, Hope was working herself hard in a private class, and Samuel was pushing her harder, repeat and repeat and repeat and perfect. They were both enjoying the synthesis of good teacher and willing disciple, the results that showed in Hope's exultant achievement and Samuel's approval – an approval muted, and withheld, and given finally, grudgingly, but given nonetheless. In a brief break to allow Hope to drink three mouthfuls of water, no more, Samuel checked the clock. Laurie and Martha would guess Hope was with him. He was interested in which one would make contact first.

Hope didn't come home that night. The bus arrived, the one she'd have got had she gone to her after-school class. Martha was waiting at the stop with Ana to keep her company, Ana feeling guilty that she had known Hope was going to a forbidden class in the morning, trying to get in her mothers' good books in the late afternoon. Hope didn't get off the bus.

The next bus came in, thirty minutes more of nerves and irritation with her twins, both of whom now stood alongside, both of whom were now worried, and Martha wanting to be alone in her worry, alone for when Hope got off the bus so she could yell at her firstborn, not have to be the good mother, the sane, sensible parent in front of the twins. Alone too, with the guilt she felt for having trusted Samuel, for not telling Laurie about Samuel. Three people got off the bus and walked out into the gentle evening, a man, a woman, a boy of ten or eleven, surely too late for him to be out alone, no matter that it was early summer almost, just light still and a wide sky above giving up stars one by one, the flat land stretching out ahead of the bus on the narrow road, and no Hope.

The rationalisations were falling flat. Hope must have been at school all day, or someone would have said something. Ana and Jack, in a different year with different classes, would have had one or other of Hope's friends asking where she was, how she was. She must have been at school all day. She must be missing since school.

Ana didn't admit that she had texted Hope during the day and heard nothing, and neither did Jack. Later they would tell each other, in even later night messages between their bedroom walls. For now they did their best, they divided Hope's friends between them, called around, and no, she was not with any of them. Friends told truths to the younger sister, younger brother. Yes, Hope had been at school, yes she had been in all of her classes – and an interest, an excitement, something happening in the slow flat pace of village life, small-town life. They would have called more, widened the circle to include classmates who weren't particularly mates, but that both Laurie and Martha said no, too much interest wouldn't help, too much gossip was the last thing they needed. All they needed was Hope. Texts were unanswered, calls left ringing.

One more bus, the last bus, by which time Laurie was sitting in the car, one foot on the accelerator, the other barely resting on the brakes, ready to drive off the minute Hope failed to step down. Furious with Martha for not letting her rush into town after Hope at six thirty in the morning, sixteen hours ago. Furious with Ana for knowing that Hope had planned to go to a class that morning and not saying. Furious with Jack for not knowing anything, for being surprised by the fuss, the furore. If the twins didn't know Hope's plans, know her secrets, what else had changed, what else had they not noticed? What else had she not noticed? Furious with herself.

Laurie drove to Samuel's apartment at the slowest speed she could bear, the slowest speed she could manage without an accident, without a flashing blue light. Fifteen miles over the speed limit and every mile too slow. Eventually she parked, more deliberately than usual. The rush to get to the apartment was one thing, now she needed to be careful, ready. She needed to remember who he was, what it was like to be around him, how quickly she could slip back to the person she had once been, in his presence. She needed armour against him, she needed to stay as far from him as possible. She got out of the car, walked to the lobby door, rang the buzzer for his apartment.

'She's not here.'

'Bollocks.'

'You have been in England a long time.'

'Fuck off Samuel,' Laurie pushed past him into the apartment, 'Hope? Come on! We're going home.'

Samuel stood at the door, and watched Laurie open doors and check beautifully furnished rooms, empty of Hope.

Eventually she stopped, in the middle of the elegant sitting room, balcony doors open to the night, she stood still and lost.

'I told you when you buzzed, I told you at the door, I've told you five times more, she's not here. She didn't come to class after school, and I had no word from her to say why, not like her at all.'

'You did see her in the morning?'

'Yes, we had a private class. She gave it everything.'

Samuel came closer and Laurie held out her hand to fend him off, he smiled, stopped, 'I was tempted to pop over to your charming home and see how she was when she didn't show after school. Then I thought perhaps I wouldn't be welcome. Unlike you, Laurie, you've made yourself very welcome going through every room. Still, now you're here, would you like a drink?'

'I need to know where my daughter is.'

'Yes,' Samuel agreed, 'you do. Would you like a drink?'

'I can't drink, I'm driving.'

Samuel smiled and walked past Laurie into the kitchen, she heard glasses, a fridge door open and close, the pop of a cork, and then Samuel's footsteps as he came back.

'I said I didn't want a drink,' she said, turning to him now, able to move, finally. The horror that Hope might be with Samuel and whatever that might mean had receded, to be replaced by an even worse fear that she wasn't here.

He was holding out a glass of water, a full and sparkling glass of champagne in his hand.

'And I believed you, now you need to believe me, I don't know where she is.'

'But . . .'

Laurie stopped. She knew Samuel, she knew there was no reason for him to lie about this. If Hope had been in his home, he would have behaved differently, he would likely have been gloating, pleased with himself. As it was, he seemed mildly concerned, which was much more worrying. Laurie didn't want him to be concerned about Hope, she didn't want him to have any feelings about Hope at all.

'Drink the water, Laurie.'

He held out the glass and she took it, drank it down.

He nodded, 'Good girl.'

'Fuck off.'

'Sit down.'

'I can't.'

'You need to, you're shaking.'

Laurie looked down, he was right. Her hand holding the glass was not only shaking, her grip was so tight she feared she might smash it. She handed it to him and sat down on the big blue sofa. She bunched her hands into fists at her sides, pushing them into the yielding fabric. She tried not to notice the comfort Samuel was living in, the ease. She wanted to focus on why she was there, wanted to focus on Hope and yet, as always with Samuel, she found herself drawn to notice him.

He sat opposite her in an elegant modernist chair, he saw her hands, the way she looked around her, taking in her surroundings.

'You didn't pay much attention to the place when you were here last. Nice, isn't it? I want simple, clean lines. I don't like mess.'

Something about the way he said the word 'mess' shook Laurie out of her stupor, 'You sound like your father.'

'No, Abraham would have said he despised mess, that mess was an offence against community. He always went that little bit further with every emotion, it was part of his method, going to the edge of too far. But I'm sure you remember?'

'I don't want to talk about him,' Laurie said, 'I'm here to find Hope.' She stood up, 'I should go, Martha will be worried.'

'Yes, she's quite the little worrier, your Martha.'

'How would you know?'

'An educated guess,' he smiled, 'but I thought you wanted my help?'

Samuel's voice was low, soft, and Laurie found it astonishing that she almost wanted to stay here, to talk to him, to find out who he was now. She bit her lip, hard, and asked, 'Do you know where she is?'

'No, but I'm sure she has her cell with her.'

'We've been calling for hours. The twins have too. She hasn't answered any of us. I should have gone to the police.'

'And yet you didn't,' he said mildly and she wanted to slap him, 'because she's seventeen,' he went on, 'because the police wouldn't have taken you seriously. Seventeen-year-old girls can be so impetuous, can't they, Laurie?'

She didn't answer and, because he was genuinely interested, Samuel put aside the teasing he was enjoying so much and relented, 'I'll call. If she has her cell on, she'll answer me.'

Laurie looked at him, he was utterly certain of himself, and she had a horrible feeling he was right to be.

He took his phone from his pocket and scrolled through some numbers, pushed a button and then held the phone to his ear, 'It's ringing,' he said.

Laurie felt sick. She so wanted to know that Hope was safe, wherever she was, she desperately wanted her to answer – and she hated the thought of Hope answering only to Samuel.

The one-sided conversation that followed made her feel even worse.

'Hope ... you didn't come to class after school and you didn't alert me to the fact that you would be away ... indeed, an apology will be needed ... I see ... yes. I appreciate that Hope ... Hope, listen to me now please ... are you listening? I will not speak unless you are calm. Breathe. Hope, as you have been trained. Good ... Good. Thank you. I have your mother here with me ... Your biological mother ...'

He looked directly at Laurie as he spoke and she tried hard not to show him how painful his words were, his knowledge of their story. Tried, and failed.

He went on, 'She and your birth mother are worried about you, as well they might be ... no, no excuses, we have discussed responsibility ... Thank you. I shall pass you over to her and you can tell her where you are so she can fetch you home ... No, I don't think that will be the case at all, I expect she and Martha will be delighted that I've been so helpful. You may speak to her now, and later your mothers and I will talk about their concerns for you ... yes. Good. I'll pass you over. And Hope? I will not have you miss class again, not without prior permission, do you hear me? ... Good girl. That's right.'

He handed the phone to Laurie, raising his glass of champagne as he did so and finally taking a sip. As Laurie took down the details of the friend's house where Hope was hiding, Samuel savoured his champagne, he was happy and relaxed and Laurie hated him.

When Hope had rung off, Laurie stood up, 'How could you be so sure?' she asked.

'Sure of what?'

'That Hope would want to dance? You couldn't have known that she'd turn up to a dance class, she's just one kid in many. How could you know she'd come to yours?'

Samuel smiled, 'Oh Laurie, the dance is in us, I'm a dance teacher. But I came here for you, you know that. I'd have found a way to get close to you, Hope was just one of many potential routes.'

'Where did you get the money?' She looked around at the room they were in, 'How can you afford any of this?'

He shrugged, 'Ingrid's parents were rich – and they were not stupid. They gave her some money for the community, at the beginning, but not the lot. I met them, got to know

156

them, and they liked me, wanted to help me. Especially when I had no one else to turn to, nowhere else to go.'

'You made them like you.'

He nodded, 'Same thing. Just like I've made your daughter like me.'

'But what for?'

'For you, Laurie. It's very simple. I'm here for you.'

'Then you've made a mistake, I want nothing to do with you.'

He smiled and showed her the phone in his hand, 'Don't you need to go and find your little girl?'

Laurie was glad that she had to go, glad that she needed to go and pick up Hope, it gave her a reason to walk away and not hit him, not rip that smile off his face and make him bleed until he explained properly why he was here, now, after all this time. She wanted to know and she couldn't bear to know, and she had to leave.

As she was waiting for the lift, Samuel called after her, 'Don't be too tough on her, you know how it is to be young. She's safe, that should be all that matters. You know that too, your daughter isn't a runaway, welcome her home.'

Twenty-Two

There had always been talk about what was done to runaways, the children of the community whispered the stories at night, out-doing each other in frightening possibilities. Runaways were always found, they were rounded up, carted off. Runaways were put in the back of the truck and taken to a workhouse in the city, never seen again. Runaways were taken to the old bunker, hog-tied and left without food or water until they died, even if they did get free, there was no way out but the big door, locked against them, nothing to do but roam empty passages underground until death came, death always waiting in the dark. There were stories of secret passages leading from the bunker, corridors that had been built when nuclear war was going to end all wars, corridors that wound down to chambers deeper still where the earth was nothing but cold, nothing but dark. Stories about corridors that had caved in over the years, were rubble-strewn, open to the earth, far from the sky. Stories about bones piled up, the dry old bones of runaways, caught and kept in the bunker, dead in the bunker, dried up and turning to dust.

As little children, safe in the corral, they had not wanted to run away, they wanted only to be held by the community, loved by Abraham – and they were. As older children, once they were covenanted, there were reasons to dream of running away, reasons to consider a dark, dangerous tunnel and the cold earth a safer place than a bed from which one might be called at any time, called into his presence. But even so, the stories they had told each other, back when Abraham's touch was purely a wanted dream, not a suffering to be flinched from, those stories lodged in fearful minds – no doubt as the adults who first whispered them to the children had intended. And so the little children did not run away, and even the covenanted ones did not run away, no matter how often they dreamed of escape, and there was no one to prove the truth, or otherwise, of the stories of those dark chambers in the bunker.

The truth was both less dramatic, and more. Laurie only ever saw it happen once. It was the week before she was due to head out as a special one, chosen to go into the world on behalf of the community. She had seen others being special, watched them go out praised and celebrated, fêted even more on their return with new community members, new brothers and sisters to grow the dream. The return of the runaway was not a celebration.

Ben was twelve years old, he had been covenanted just six months earlier, and in the two seasons that had passed he had gone from a sunny, cheery kid born into the community, a boy loved by all, to a surly brat who hated everyone and everything on the land, who vowed to get away as soon as he could. One morning they woke up, and Ben was missing. While he had been brought up to know the community were his family, the state law said his biological parents were his guardians, and the law of the community maintained that it was up to the blood parents to bring him back.

After all, as Abraham said to the man and the woman brought before him to account for their son's whereabouts, 'Who knows what he will say to the world about us, and what lies they might turn his words to? We cannot risk losing our children again as we did before. We cannot risk false testimony, there are too many out there who would break us.'

The biological parents went out and scoured the surrounding land for a day and a night, they went to the old bunker and saw that the solid metal door was locked as it had been for years, they circled the perimeter fence three times and they rode the bus into the closest town. Ben was found there, hanging out at the depot, nowhere to go and no money to get further than the one ride he had hitched into town, with a truck driver who thought that all of those people in that community were weirdos and hippies, but who realised, as they came into the town limits, that picking up an underage kid and driving him away from the only home he'd ever known was probably illegal. Ben was brought back tired, hungry and unhappy.

The ceremony for his return was not a community event as most of them were, nor was it the full reconciliation to community that Laurie had undergone when she chose to come back. Laurie, Samuel and Marshall, due to go out as special ones the following week, were called to the far pasture in the late evening. The event to reconcile the runaway was to take place away from the community buildings, and in the low light of late evening. New to being special, Laurie and Samuel understood that Abraham meant them to know how important their own return would be.

They stood alongside the boy's biological parents, and Ellie, an older woman who had been in the community from the very early days. Ellie had trained as a doctor and had been the community's resident medic for as long as Laurie could remember. She thought it was strange that Ellie was there, and then, when her eyes adjusted to the semi-darkness, and she saw that Abraham was lighting the brazier, that he was heating the branding iron they used to brand the community's small dairy herd, she began to understand, much as she didn't want to.

Laurie didn't hear the words that were whispered between Abraham and the kneeling boy, his parents holding him on either side, gripping his arms tight, keeping him down and steady, his back bared to the night. She couldn't see clearly what happened either, but she would never forget the boy's scream, or the smell of his burning skin, or the way Abraham held him after Ellie had dressed the scar, tenderly as a father might hold a new-born baby, a prodigal son come home.

The family left not long after that night. They did not return.

Twenty-Three

Laurie and Martha welcomed their prodigal home. Martha was relieved and over-solicitous, Laurie was sharper, cooler, but she was most angry with Samuel, she wanted him out of her life, and she wanted him to have nothing to do with Hope. Tired after the excitement of causing so much fuss, carefully judging her actions so as not to spur Laurie or Martha into a row, but mostly worried about how much trouble she was in with Samuel, Hope just wanted to hide. She ate a slice of toast and jam and drank a cup of hot chocolate, more to appease her mothers than because she really wanted to, she ignored the texts from her friends and the beseeching looks of her brother and sister who wanted the whole story, right now. She kept her head down and then, getting up from the kitchen table, she spoke up, sounding far calmer than she felt,

'Mum, Mom, you're not going to stop me going to class. I'm seventeen, I'll be eighteen soon. I'm going to go to whatever classes I want to, just like Ana and Jack do. I will eat more, I promise. I'm not anorexic, honestly not, I've just been trying—'

She stopped, confused, and Laurie asked, 'Trying what?'

Hope shrugged, 'Self-discipline. I've been trying self-discipline. Practising how much control I can have, over me.'

'So, a lot then?' Jack asked.

Ana kicked him, Martha glared, and Laurie bit her lip to stop herself snapping at Jack. He grinned, Jack could never stand one of his sisters being in trouble, he always tried to deflect attention, he'd rather be told off himself than sit quiet when the spotlight of parental anger was on one of the girls.

Hope smiled at him, grateful, 'Nice try. I went too far, OK? Just a bit too far. I promise I'll look after myself. But you don't get to decide what I do about dance, you really don't. I'm going to bed now, I have a class in the morning.'

Laurie was about to respond, her hackles raised with Hope's assertion of self-discipline, but Martha put a hand on her arm, 'We'll talk about it tomorrow, Hope. Sleep well.'

Both Martha and Laurie knew from the look Hope gave them as she left for her bed, that she had no intention of talking about it, and certainly no intention of being talked out of it.

The twins sloped off too, feeling vaguely guilty that they'd known something was up and not told their mothers as soon as they'd realised. Finally, the women went to bed themselves, looking in on each child as they always did. Martha knew Laurie was still fuming, but at least they'd managed to avoid disagreeing in front of Hope, at least there was time before morning when they'd need to present a unified front.

'She's not going back to class, we can't just let this go.'

'Don't be daft, Laurie, it's obvious that trying to punish

her isn't going to work, we have to find a way to work with what's going on for her.'

'Work with it? She's seventeen. She needs us to be sensible parents and stop her hurting herself, not let her do what the hell she wants just because we're worried she'll behave even worse.'

They were lying in bed, whispering furiously into the dark. They'd had these arguments before, but usually Laurie was the one pleading for leniency for their children while Martha insisted that they had to stick to their own rules. Neither of them was used to taking the other side, and neither of them was being fully honest about why they were taking a different position now.

'He's clearly a bad influence on her,' Laurie tried again.

'That's not true at all, you said yourself that she agreed to tell you where she was because he told her to, and it's obvious that she's scared he's going to tell her off when she gets to class.'

'I don't want him telling her off,' Laurie's voice was quiet.

'She missed his class, he's allowed to tell her off just like any other teacher.'

'Except that he's not any other teacher, is he?' Laurie asked. 'Hope's been totally different since she's been working with him.'

'Yeah, you're right. Her schoolwork's been better than it has in years, she's dedicated to her dance classes and taking it seriously, she's not screaming and sobbing about some stupid boy who's treating her like shit. It's just the eating thing . . .' Martha's voice petered out, no matter how much she wanted to acknowledge the good things that had happened since

164

Hope had been learning from Samuel, she knew the eating thing was huge.

'Exactly, and you've got nowhere to go with that,' Laurie responded.

They lay in silence for a few minutes and then Martha tried again, 'Of course it's a big deal, I know that, but we need to work with him on it, we need to get his support. Hope's listening to him and not to us, so we need to get him to use his influence with her.'

Martha was surprised at the vehemence of Laurie's response, 'I don't want him using any influence on her.'

'Bloody hell, Laurie, he's just a dance teacher, what's the big deal about him?'

Unable to answer honestly, Laurie turned the question back on Martha, 'I could say the same, why are you so fine with him? You've only met him once and you seem to think he's a genius.'

'I haven't only met him once.'

'Picking her up from class doesn't count, you don't know him.'

'I do.'

Laurie was very cold and very wide awake, 'How?'

'I . . . I've been seeing him,' Martha said.

'Seeing him?'

'Oh no, not like that, not like that darling.'

Martha reached out her hand but Laurie flinched away, unable to trust what she was hearing, 'Like what?'

'He's training to be a life coach. He offered me some free sessions, he needed someone to practise on.'

'He's been practising on you?'

'Yes, but it didn't feel like practice, it's been really helpful . . .'

165

'Helpful for what? Since when did you need a life coach? What the fuck's going on, Martha?'

Lying beside Laurie, speaking softly and fearfully into the dark room, Martha explained. Her fear of losing Laurie to Laurie's new life of work success, her fear of not achieving what she'd hoped for herself, the exhaustion of looking after her father and her sadness as she watched him grieve his wife of almost fifty years, how it had given her no space to do her own grieving for her mother, and Laurie was around so little and Martha didn't mind, honest she didn't, she was so proud of Laurie, happy for Laurie, but even so, there was the extra burden it created in time spent looking after the children and their home, often by herself. And behind it all, the years passing and Martha, at almost forty, surprised that she was having an age crisis, embarrassed that she was having an age crisis, having one anyway.

Martha was close to tears, whispering her fear, her shame, and Laurie had to force herself to turn and hold her wife. She had to make herself stay in bed in the dark, lying close to Martha. She wanted to run from the house and drive fast to Samuel's apartment, she wanted to smash down his door, smash him down. He knew exactly what he was doing, had been working all of this behind her back, and now both her wife and her daughter were enthralled by him. He was his father's son. She wanted to shake Martha and ask her how the fuck she could have been so stupid, so needy, why she hadn't said any of this before. She wanted to kick herself for not seeing this gap growing between them, she hated herself for having allowed her work to matter so much, for letting herself, even for a such a short while, be someone defined by the world, not her own path. She saw herself using the term 'the world' in her thoughts, and it made her even angrier. Samuel had brought the compound into her life, Samuel was bringing that hell into the life she had so painstakingly built for herself. She wanted to grab Martha and ask her why on earth she hadn't said something sooner, about her fears, about seeing Samuel. Except that she knew the answer to that question. Samuel had been trained to make people feel special, wanted, important. Trained to make them want to be with him, and only him. She knew, because she had trained alongside him.

And she wanted to tell Martha everything, explain why Samuel frightened her, why he was dangerous. Except that everything was too much to tell.

Laurie called him later that morning, when Martha, tired but relieved, unburdened, had gone out to her office to work.

'You bastard.'

'That's not very nice, you got your girl back, didn't you?'

Samuel sounded bright, chirpy, the smug smile in his voice was unmistakable.

'I'm talking about Martha.'

'Ah,' he paused, 'I wondered when she'd tell you.'

'Really? Didn't you hope to keep it a secret, worm your way into my life without me knowing?'

'Oh, I've always wanted you to know what I'm doing, Laurie. That's why I'm here, to remind you of your role as my helpmeet.'

'I am Martha's wife.'

'So you seem to believe. Which is how I knew she was always going to tell you. You're that kind of couple, aren't you? All safe and cosy and joined for ever, just the two of us.'

'There are five of us. And the reason you don't value the life I have now is because of your own inability to truly get close to people, your fucked-up family.'

'You are my family,' he interrupted.

'And your fucked-up life,' she continued, ignoring him, 'is not going to get in our way.'

Samuel answered her softly, lightly, 'I'm here to help, Laurie.'

'We don't need your help.'

'Martha was very grateful for it. You would be too, if you'd just let me remind you—'

She cut him off, 'I haven't forgotten a thing, not a single day goes by when I don't remember you and everyone else, everything else, from back then.'

'Did Martha say how useful I've been? Putting her fears about you to rest? Enabling her to see her own power? You want to keep an eye on that one, Laurie, she's way stronger than she gives out.'

'What I want, Samuel, is to get you out of my life, as fast as I can.'

'That's not possible, as we agreed, I will continue to be Hope's teacher, encouraging her to see a wider world than the limited nuclear family you have provided for her.'

'Hope's leaving home soon, she's nearly eighteen, she'll see you for the controlling—'

Samuel ignored her and continued, 'And I will be here when you come to your senses and remember the truths of your past. Our shared past, our promised future. I am in your life, Laurie, whether you acknowledge that or not. I always have been. You were given to me, remember? They adopted you for me. I am the reason for you.'

Laurie couldn't listen to any more, she ended the call, her hands shaking. She was stupid, she should never have called him, never let him see that he had worried her. She could feel the adrenalin pushing her heartbeat, forcing her breath. The only thing she could do now was wait, prepare herself for whatever Samuel would do next. Maybe he would screw up somehow, maybe this new life wouldn't all fall down around them.

And at the back of her mind she could hear Abraham's voice:

No matter how well we build our fortress, none of us is free from the actions of others. We must understand our culpability in the actions of others. We are all connected. It is our duty to save each other.

Twenty-Four

Laurie, Samuel and Marshall were heading into the world for the sake of the community. Laurie had been warned that their work would begin as soon as they got to the city, no rest after their full day of travelling, the five-thirty walk, the six-thirty bus, the second bus, third bus. Tired old buses carrying worn workers, people coming home from night shift, others heading out to factory jobs, menial manual labour. Laurie had spent just one year back in community and had forgotten how many discontented people it was possible to see in the world on a daily basis. She thought of the constant self-scrutiny on the compound, of the need to always give up one's own desire for the greater good, of the effort always to greet another, support another. Community life was hard and it was a great good. As special ones they would save these poor people from the world, save them from themselves.

There were three cities within a day's journey of the community, Laurie, Samuel and Marshall were heading to the northernmost of the three. An industrial town, it had grown over the past twenty years to become a computing hub, old men complained that the young men did no real work these days, old women didn't understand the work the young women did at all, young men and young women were friends and sometimes they were lovers, but mostly their passion was technical, back-end, elsewhere. Once it had been an ugly industrial town, now it was an ugly tech city. Marshall had chosen it for Laurie's first time as a special one because – he said – she was different, like him, like Samuel, she was not white.

'Why's that useful?' she asked.

'The young men are white with beards, the young women are blonde with yoga bodies. To these people, that makes us intriguing, interesting.'

Laurie frowned, 'I don't want to be their pet foreigner.'

Marshall nodded, explaining, 'Sure you do, these people are intrigued by the different, adore the exotic.'

'You mean they're racist?'

'Some of them, yeah. But what I mean is that they're rich kids. We're going to save them from themselves.'

Marshall put an arm around her, drawing her close, and Laurie liked him making a fuss of her. She also liked the way it made Samuel glare. Laurie knew Samuel believed that if anyone should be holding her it was him, they were covenanted, he had brought her back to the community, but Laurie had never had so much attention paid to her before, she was enjoying it.

It was Samuel's first time too, but Marshall didn't draw him close, confiding.

'Just because you're Abraham's son, doesn't mean I'm going to hold your hand out here.'

Samuel shrugged, disinclined to rise to Marshall's bait,

'And just because you're Abraham's chosen, doesn't mean that everything you do is right.'

'I'm part of the vision,' Marshall responded, smiling broadly.

'We're all part of the vision, some of us were born into it – some of you came along later,' Samuel answered, equally sure of himself, 'And I don't need you to take care of me.'

'We each have to take care of ourselves.'

'Then Laurie can probably take care of herself too, she's lived away, we haven't.'

'It's different for girls in the world, Samuel.'

Laurie walked into the bar with Marshall leading and Samuel following. It was nothing like the place she and her friends had gone to when she was at Dot and Henry's house, Dot and Henry asking no questions, told no lies. That shabby old bar had two pool tables, four regulars on a good night, a range of beers that Laurie could count on the fingers of one hand and a range of bourbon that she had never even attempted to count. When she was feeling generous, the owner Yolanda would ignore the fact that she'd known half these kids since they were in diapers, and Laurie and her friends would drink a weak beer or two, thinking themselves all the cooler for it. More often than not, Yolanda would sell the kids a Coke, give them an hour to play a game of pool, and then tell them to get the hell out of there.

The cavernous room they walked into now was loud, with pockets of glowing light from neon signs, alternating with deep dark corners where people shouted in each other's faces to be heard over the music. There was a steel-clad central bar, with space for dancing all around. There was a mezzanine above, where people stood watching, considering, choosing. The music thumped in Laurie's chest, pumped up from her feet, rocketed against the back of her head.

Marshall turned to the newbies, 'Don't accept a drink until I check out who's offered, don't leave the bar with anyone but me.'

Samuel frowned, 'So how do we—'

Marshall cut him off, 'Tonight is to get acclimatised. Tomorrow we make a plan. Laurie, you can have one drink, a vodka soda. Samuel, a beer. That's it. We meet at the exit in two hours.'

He handed over enough cash to buy their drinks and then left them, merging into the crowd with a practised swiftness. For someone so wedded to the community vision, Marshall certainly seemed at ease in the world.

Laurie watched him go and then grabbed Samuel, 'I'm all wrong.'

'What?'

'Look at me. Look at them.'

Laurie was wearing the clothes she had worn to travel back, from Dot and Henry's home to the compound, clothes to make her invisible on her runaway journey. Clothes that were nothing really, something she might wear to school, when she had gone to school. Jeans, Converse, a plain T-shirt, a thin string of iridescent beads around her neck, a fake silver bracelet from one of the women on the compound. She wore almost no make-up, her long hair was brushed and loose.

'You look great,' Samuel said, and he meant it.

Then he looked around. There were a few older men, late twenties, early thirties maybe, wearing suits, but very few. The guys his age were mostly in jeans, T-shirts, there were plenty of tattoos and almost as many beards, but he and Marshall weren't too out of place, they were nothing special, but not odd either. The women were a different matter, two different matters. One type of woman had dyed hair or a shaved head, pierced nose and belly button ring, dark-rimmed eyes, deep red lips. The other type wore a suit like the slightly older men, but fitted, elegant with extra-high heels and dark lipstick, eyes that were painted and flicked. Laurie was right, beside the wild women and the slick women, she stood out. She looked exactly what she was – scared, lost and different in all the wrong ways.

The evening wore on and Laurie watched Marshall working the room, standing at the bar, his good looks drawing glances from both types of women and some of the men. She watched him chat and smile, allow people to buy him drinks. He genuinely seemed to be having a good time. It hadn't occurred to her that this mission might be anything other than work, a struggle against the world. She watched Samuel too, giving it his best, he was charming and softly spoken, even in that loud space, and Laurie saw how women leaned in to him, eager to listen. She saw Samuel grow in stature, grow more sure of himself as the two hours passed, and she felt herself diminishing, pushing back into the darker space between the exit and the cloakroom. All three of them were different, exotic, special, in that bar, but only Laurie felt her difference as shame.

It was three in the morning before they came back to the tiny apartment they were sharing, Marshall in the one bedroom, Laurie on the sofa, Samuel on the floor.

Laurie lay awake, looking up at the ceiling, car lights bounced past, distant alarms rang out, the incessant noise of a city night was all new to her. She heard soft footsteps and then she felt a hand touch her cheek, wipe away the tears she hadn't admitted she was crying, tears a weakness in the community.

'You'll be fine, you just need to get used to it, it'll take time,' Marshall whispered.

'Samuel didn't need time.'

'Abraham's sons are part of the vision. Believing he's worthy of attention comes easily to him, you just need practice.'

'I dated before I came back, just like everyone else. This feels so different.'

'Because this is way more important, this is about the community. It's not dating at all, it's fishing, hunting, catching, keeping.'

'Oh.'

'Go to sleep Laurie, we'll work on it in the morning.'

He kissed her forehead and stepped quietly back to his room. Samuel lay on the floor, pretending to sleep, and hating Marshall for being the one with the sense to be kind to Laurie.

They worked on it. Marshall took Laurie shopping and used two days' worth of food money to buy her clothes that looked more like those the other young women were wearing. He rehearsed Laurie and Samuel in standing alone, making eye contact, looking away, looking back. He rehearsed them in flirting, Samuel standing directly in front of Laurie, Laurie looking up to him, eyes locked.

'Good,' Marshall nodded, 'now Laurie, move in, kiss him.'

The eye contact was broken as they both turned to Marshall.

'Kiss him, I'll tell you if it looks convincing, he can tell you if it feels good. Go for it.'

Laurie stumbled, 'I've kissed guys, Marshall.'

'Great,' he said, smiling lightly, 'then show me how well you do it.'

Laurie had kissed guys, fumbled a little, liked it well enough, though not enough to go any further, not even to feel part of the group, in the world. Her sister Alice assured her that not all of the girls who said they were sleeping with their boyfriends were actually doing it, that she had plenty of time. None of it had felt like this. Marshall was enjoying this. He waved an impatient hand and told them to get on with it. Laurie reached up, her face lifted to Samuel's, and kissed him.

'Get into it more,' Marshall said, 'Samuel, hold her tighter, feel her breasts against you. Laurie, push your groin against his.'

They pulled away again, both finding it too strange, too exposing, too interesting.

'Do as you're told,' Marshall said, his voice dangerously even, his tone remarkably similar to Abraham's when he was crossed.

They were trained to obey that voice, that command, and so they did.

'Hold her tighter, great. Push your breasts into him, your groin. Keep going, good, more. Good.'

Marshall coached them for a little longer and then he said, 'Enough of that,' he stepped between Laurie and Samuel, 'now who wants to practise with me?'

He was smiling and Laurie laughed, she thought it was a joke, Marshall looked at her sharply, his smile immediately gone.

Samuel frowned, 'I don't understand.'

'You and I both know that there were gay men in that bar, and in all the bars in this city, gay men who are as worthy of our mission as heterosexual men. Gay men we may also be able to entice, to bring home.'

Laurie stepped away and Marshall did nothing to bring her back to them. He pointed though, gesturing that she sit on the sofa in front of them, take up his vantage point.

'We cannot accuse ourselves of divisiveness, of couple-making, if there is a witness. Watch.'

Samuel did as he was told. He practised with Marshall, flirting, smiling, kissing, touching, hands inside clothes, hands down the front of just-opened jeans. They practised until Marshall had had enough.

'I need a break, you're wearing me out,' he grinned, but Samuel didn't grin back, 'Come on Sammy, this is our mission, we can't have a little fun too?' Marshall asked, turning to Laurie for confirmation.

Laurie didn't know what to think, kissing Samuel had been embarrassing, but it was also hard to watch Marshall enjoying Samuel's unhappiness, teasing him, calling him Sammy, which she knew he hated. All afternoon, their bodies had been too close, her mind too far away, out in the wide desert reaches of the compound, away in Dot and Henry's back yard at the edge of town, anywhere but this confined space where she was being asked to separate what her mind knew and what her body felt. And that took her further back, to when

177

she was younger, just covenanted, to the times she had long ago decided never to fully recall, and yet knew to be real. It took her back to those private times in Abraham's presence, in his office, after she had been promised to his youngest son, when she found it also meant being promised to the father.

'Whatever,' Marshall shrugged off her discomfort, Samuel's glowering embarrassment, 'being special isn't just about having everyone say how lovely you are, how comely. It's a commitment. It means giving it all for the community. Really, all. You're going to have to get used to it.'

Twenty-Five

Laurie was frightened by how used to it she got, how her training in the compound – training in giving herself over, in rising above her own feelings – made her capable of being so different from her usual, diffident self, and very quickly. Even in the easy and open welcome of Dot and Henry's family, Laurie had still been reserved, better at small groups than big ones, happier with a few friends at high school than rolling around in the big groups of a dozen or more like most of the kids. In making the choice to get used to it, the choice to be body and not mind, the choice to be bait, Laurie could be all those things she usually saw in others and couldn't reach, she was open and chatty and easy in any company, and she enjoyed it.

Abraham says: It is not our intention that matters, it is our action. We are as we do.

Laurie, Marshall and Samuel did being attractive, and so they attracted.

On their last night in the city they held the gathering. They would leave for the compound at six in the morning, if the gathering and the ensuing sharing, the dance, the hours that followed were successful, then they would be more than three by dawn. Samuel had invited two new friends, both women. Although Laurie had seen young men flirting with him, he had never returned their advances. Marshall had two friends coming, one man, one woman, and even Laurie had managed to convince one guy to come along, playing up to his assumption that she was part of a threesome with Marshall and Samuel, playing up to the assumption that she might be even wilder with him.

They began, Marshall leading, Samuel and Laurie assisting. A ceremony of personal revelation, a small group reckoning, each one starting with 'I acknowledge I have been at fault'.

Laurie thought their visitors were offering up their faults as gifts, badges of merit.

'I hate my parents and have been stealing from them for years.'

'I've been fucking my best friend's girlfriend for the past three months. I don't even like her, I just wanted to have a secret from him.'

'I can't remember the last night I went to bed sober, the last time I went out without a few lines of coke to get the evening started.'

'I love that my mother prefers me to my sister, I use it.'

'I have been screwing my father's best friend for years.'

And around again, and again, Marshall listening, probing, Laurie and Samuel as witnesses, recording each self-exposure, listing the iniquities.

*

Then the questions went further, Marshall was not interested in tales of drug and alcohol excess, he dismissed them simply as a reaction to living in the world. He told their guests, as Laurie had heard Abraham do so many times, that misdemeanours of behaviour were just the first layer, when removed they showed the deeper transgression, the misdemeanours of intent, insults of inhumanity.

'We don't care who you screwed or who you lied to, who you beat up or who you left behind. This stage of the process is no longer about your actions. You need to understand this. We care about you, not about what you did to others. This is about what you have done to you, what your lying to yourself has done to you.'

'I don't understand,' said one girl, Dara.

'You do,' Marshall insisted, 'but pretending you don't understand is one of your masks, your tricks. It lets the men around you think you need their help. And because some men get off on thinking they can fix confused little girls, some girls play up to that crap. The men here don't want to help you tell a story where you make yourself stupid.'

'But you ...' she was genuinely confused, this wasn't the gorgeous guy who had seen how lost and sad she was, who invited her here to understand her better, 'you said you wanted to help.'

'I said I could show you how you can be happy.'

'I can't, my life has been too hard, too difficult.'

'Again, that's bullshit,' Marshall leaned down right into her face, 'all lives are hard, all lives are difficult. If we're true to ourselves it is excruciating to survive even a day, skin on fire with shame, bellies burning at the recognition of how vile we are, how inept, so far from good, so far from true.'

She started crying and Marshall smiled.

'Yeah, you should cry. It is crap to look at your lies, and it should feel hard. But I don't want to help you, Dara. No one wants to help you, no one is going to wipe your tears and make it all better. It's time to grow up.'

Then he moved on to the next one, and the next, and when he had been around the five of them once, he did it again, and again.

Hours passed with Marshall questioning each one individually, each one standing just before him, each one revealing a little more each time, admitting their shame a little more each time. They told truths that were not about incidents or actions, but intent, the guts of themselves, offered up, picked over. As they went around the group, Samuel repeated their words back to them, their excuses for not owning up to their faults. Eventually, finally, they began to hear themselves as Marshall heard them, whiny, childish, petulant. They heard their poor-me stories as just stories, nothing more. All the props that had been holding them up for so long started to slip away. One by one they broke.

After the breaking came the dance, in that cramped apartment, the sofa pushed against the wall, chairs folded away, the smallest of dances, no room for more than the one tight circle, and they danced anyway. It was both a coming to their senses and a choice. Stay and join in, leave and ignore the revelation of your new-found self, go back to your failing life. Marshall had warned Laurie and Samuel that it could be heart-breaking to watch someone come so close to their truth and then back away for fear of what it meant to commit, really become whole, but even so, Laurie found it profoundly sad to see both of Samuel's women leave, one frightened, one plainly relieved, but both going anyway. Marshall's man was hanging on, as was the guy she had brought back, but it wasn't clear that either would stay. Only the woman who had come back with Marshall looked as if she might be ready to commit.

Laurie watched Dara as she danced, her gaze locked on Marshall. He was obviously the real attraction, not Dara's own true self. Laurie knew the girl would find compound life harsh, especially when she found herself kept away from Marshall at first, separated from the special ones, thrown into the rhythm of early waking, long hours of study, heavy days working in the garden, heavier nights of reckoning and reconciliation. She hoped Dara would make it. It would be nice to bring someone back, someone who stayed.

Eventually Marshall and Dara moved away, Abraham's prohibition against coupling in the dance lifted for those who were working at being special. The man that Marshall had invited left then, finally understanding that there would be no sex for him this long night. Samuel went out too, angry at his failure to catch someone new for the community, angry that Marshall was getting a fuck and he wasn't, angry about going back empty-handed, fearful of disappointing his father yet again.

Laurie and the man she had brought to the meeting, a man she had met only the night before, were left alone. It was one in the morning, they had been revealing, witnessing, dancing for seven hours, she was exhausted. He wasn't.

It all happened very quickly in real time, but in her mind and in her memory it was almost in slow motion, each move a deliberate invasion, his actions as planned as Marshall's questioning, as the hours before. This leads to this leads to this. After the past two weeks, after the preceding hours, after all that witnessing, it was hard to stop watching herself, hard to not just observe herself from above, from outside. Laurie chose to observe herself from outside.

It was only when he started pulling up her shirt, feeling, touching, pawing, pushing, ripping clothes aside, it was only then Laurie understood that the pain was her own, coming from her skin, her flesh. She pushed at him, straining against his physical strength, the strength of his intention.

Her words were dislocated, she reached for his name, struggled.

'Mark ...'

'Mick,' he laughed, he was having fun, he didn't know, or chose not to know, that she was not.

She tried again, 'It's late.'

He ignored her.

'This isn't what tonight is for.'

He ignored her.

'I don't want this.'

He almost stopped, puzzled, 'It's why I'm here.'

'No,' she said, 'you came for the witnessing, you said you wanted to know.'

He laughed and then he wasn't stopping. Her clothes were pulled now, wrenching against her skin, she found herself wondering if the marks would be visible, was it possible to get rope burn from a twisted cotton shirt, dragged across her shoulder? Abraham didn't approve of bruising, it showed a disregard for the self, which in turn showed a deeper disregard for the community, the one as part of the whole, the whole bruised by the one's lack of care, inattention to detail, clumsiness. Abraham could not abide clumsiness. It was hurting, the body, the body she was in, trying not to be in, hurting across her back where his weight pushed her shoulder blade into the arm of the sofa. Cheap sofa, cheap little room, damp stains on the ceiling. Laurie was looking up, up and out, beyond the room, beyond here. It hurt, the body hurt, but she had been in pain before, Laurie was trained in the community, she knew how to move beyond pain. She would choose not to hurt, not to feel it, choose to move beyond pain. It was only pain. That's what Abraham had said, those times after her covenanting, before the men in uniform with the bright torches and the fast cars and the loud, shouting voices had lifted her up and taken her away in the dark of night. Only pain.

Samuel was still seething when he let himself back into the apartment, a fast walk in the cold night, five blocks up, three down, round and round, had done nothing to calm his temper, ease his shame, to rid his body of the fury, his fists were still itching to smack Marshall's self-satisfied, arrogant, beautiful face. He was Abraham's son, part of the vision that had brought them to the land, Marshall was only in the second story, the later revelation. It was Samuel and his brothers, Ingrid's sons, who were the first community, the true founders. He ran up the stairs two at a time, sure that Marshall would be screwing the girl, that Laurie would be asleep, alone. That weird guy, her guest, had been ogling her tits all night, but Laurie was so detached from the effect of her beauty, he was sure the guy would have given up and long gone.

He wasn't gone. He was fucking Laurie. It was Laurie who was gone, eyes wide and staring up at the ceiling, one arm bent right back beneath her, that must have hurt, half her shirt pushed up and over her mouth, the guy had his hand over her mouth too, but Laurie wasn't screaming, she wasn't making any sound at all. Not even for the tears that rolled from her eyes. Just tears, rolling, one then another then another. No sound, no sob. The guy was grunting, moaning. Laurie looked across at Samuel, past the man's grunting groaning open mouth.

'Fucking hell, what the fuck? Jesus Christ, what the fuck?'

Samuel threw himself at the guy, now he remembered, his name was Mike or Mick, Nick, something simple, something nothing.

He grabbed the back of the man's shirt, shouting, screaming, spit and anger spewing out, so much anger, years of being the best son he could be, even as a constant disappointment, the best he could be.

The bedroom door opened and Marshall stood there, confused.

'What? What is this?'

Samuel had Mick down on the floor now, Laurie lay on the sofa, dishevelled, tears crying themselves, and then he understood. Laurie was ashamed for Marshall to see her cry. Dara was asleep in the room behind him. Marshall closed the door as quietly as he could, made Samuel see him as he held his finger to his lips. Mick thought it was a moment of complicity, and he smiled at the two men.

The two men of the community who proceeded, silently, complicitly, to beat the living daylights out of the man they had invited to be their guest.

Much later, whenever she thought of it – Laurie tried not to think of it – it all seemed to have taken such a long, slow time, though it can't have, not really. Her eyes were closed. She didn't see it, but she did hear it, and she smelled it too. Blood iron, piss acid, and underneath all of that, sweat. Hers from the effort of pushing him away, his from the effort of taking her, Samuel's and Marshall's from the effort of breaking him.

In the cheap apartment, Dara slept on while Laurie wiped the blood from the already stained and pitted veneer flooring. Dara slept on when Marshall and Samuel carried the man from the room, down the stairs, and took him somewhere else. Laurie did not ask where. Dara slept on as Laurie washed herself, surprised at the sting of the cold water, washing in freezing water to try to wake herself up, bring herself here, now, not then, on that sofa, not there. Laurie woke Dara with a cup of coffee at five, Dara went to her own apartment to get some things, she wouldn't need much, but cash would help. Cash was always welcome from those who had yet to give to the community, yet to contribute a starting share. Marshall and Samuel washed, Laurie packed their few clothes, they met Dara as planned at the bus station.

Laurie did not ask them what they had done with the man, she did not ask them if he was alive or dead.

The journey back to the compound seemed faster, heading away from the city, an easier journey than heading into it.

They left Dara at the gate of the compound, to begin the process of integration. She wept, she had obviously expected Marshall to take care of her. He told her that once she was part of the community she would understand why he needed to leave her now, then he walked away without looking back, a broad smile and a jaunty step, back to Aysha's welcome, Abraham's praise.

Two mornings later, when washing, Laurie saw a long, dark bruise running from her collarbone across her left breast and down to the ribs beneath her right breast. She would declare it to the community that night, her carelessness, clumsiness, her failure to keep herself good, a part of the whole, damaged. Her failure.

In that night's witnessing, they told some of what had happened, they had not talked about what they would reveal and what they would keep to themselves, but they all knew how witnessing worked, it was always safer to tell part of a story, rather than all, always wise to keep something in reserve. Marshall did not call what had happened to Laurie 'rape'. Nor did Samuel. None of them gave it that name, not even Laurie. Certainly not at the time and not years later either, when girls began to look back at what had happened when they were young and realised that they had neither said yes, nor meant yes. Laurie was not like those girls, there was no hook of time on which to hang the events of her past, no way to say, 'we were different back then, we didn't know back then, we thought it was normal'. Laurie had never thought she was normal, none of the community were. Later she realised that was part of Abraham's brilliance. He kept them all thinking they were different and better, that they had so much further to go to attain his hopes for them, and also that they were, already, soaring higher than so many ordinary people, those sleeping fools, unable to wake to the dream. So much of Laurie's history was re-made into a story that would make sense to others, that others could bear to hear. She had learned quickly, when she was taken to Dot and Henry, when she ran away back to the compound, when they returned from the city, that there was only so much other people wanted to hear. After a while, it was easier to behave as if the part of the story she had told everyone was the whole story, the only story. But Laurie had known and – even with her eyes closed – she had witnessed, understood her connection to the actions of others.

When she ran away from it all and came to England she had the bruise tattooed across her front, a complex pattern of lines running from her left collarbone to her ribcage below her right breast, it looked like a sash, a badge of honour. She wore it to remind herself of where she had come from, what she had chosen to leave behind.

I grew up in two homes.

My adopted family were wonderful, are wonderful, they are my family.

I was in a cult when I was a small child.

They took me away when I was nine years old.

I didn't stay in touch with anyone from there.

I never went back.

I would never go back.

Nothing remains from that time in my life.

Liar.

Twenty-Six

There followed a quiet time, after the fear and the raging.
Martha had finished her sessions with Samuel, Hope was
home more, she was concentrating on her schoolwork and
her friends as much as her dance, Laurie still felt sick whenever she thought of what Samuel must know about her from
Martha's work with him, she knew only too well how good
he was at uncovering secrets, exposing hidden shame, but at
the same time she couldn't bring herself to tell Martha why
she was so worried about Samuel, and so she held her tongue,
bided her time, hoped he might yet leave them alone. She
did not believe he would, but telling her whole truth was
impossible, so she said none of it.

Once the holidays started there was more time for the
teenagers to be teenagers, sleeping into the day, staying up
late through the light nights. They had a fortnight in Spain
taking Martha's father with them, celebrating her fortieth in a
villa with a long pool and hot sun. It was more expensive than
usual and they were all glad of Laurie's new work success.
Laurie was glad to be away from England, away from the

possibility of bumping into Samuel. One night towards the end of the two weeks, in a café, the kids all on their phones, grateful for the Wi-Fi, Martha and her father in animated conversation about a remembered holiday from years ago, Laurie found herself looking across the village square where they sat in the warm night, looking towards the shadows in the recesses of an old church on the other side of the square. Her heart thudded as she saw a figure standing in the dark, looking back towards her. A tall man, long-limbed, shaven head. He smiled and was gone, further back into an alley running alongside the church. She couldn't be sure it was Samuel, but she couldn't be sure it wasn't, she barely slept for the last two nights they were away.

The week before school started brought a cool twist to the night air, and then the pace picked up again, the family gathered themselves in the comfort of new pencils, new timetables and plans after the chaos of summer. A garden, just past its full-blown glory, ready to cut back in a month or so, ready for the turn to the dark.

Saturdays took on a quickly predictable round of training and competition for the twins, dance class for Hope, work for Laurie and trips to her father for Martha. Sometimes all three of the children would go out later to the same party, on other evenings the twins would hang out with their swimming team and Hope would head to her bedroom to work. She was readying herself to step out into the world, and her preparation made her mothers both proud and sad. Although for very different reasons, they too had found the rest of the world a siren call, they too had left and learned that there was no place like home because home was a time as much as a place, and Hope could no more come back to the time when home was all her world than Laurie or Martha could do the same.

Left to themselves, Laurie and Martha would watch a film and share a bottle of wine, one drinking two thirds and the other going out later to pick up the twins. They sat together knowing that this time was also a preparation for them, a readying for when they were just two, the couple they had once been. Single, couple, family, couple – and an aware- ness, rarely mentioned, but all the more clear since Martha's mother had died – that they too would return to single. One of them would.

On Sundays the driver of the night before was given the grace of a lie-in, while the other mother got up and took the kids to dance class and swim training, or class and a swimming competition in an even further town. After the racing and the echoing shouts, Martha or Laurie would drive home with Ana and Jack, damp, chlorine-scented, for whatever meal had been cooked in the meantime. Hope stayed in town for a longer afternoon class, and now the mothers did not worry about her dance obsession, because Samuel had been true to his promise to address her eating, and Hope had responded to his concern. Her dancing was a distraction from the pressures of her final year at school and, because she came home happy and ravenous, her mothers hoped the problems of spring had evened themselves out. Laurie still hated how much time Hope spent with Samuel, and she still did not explain why to her wife, she said noth- ing, held her breath, and hoped for a best she did not believe she deserved.

*

192

'We should have a party,' Ana said, lightly.

'Should we?' asked Laurie, her eyes on the road, the twins all swum out and victorious beside and behind her.

'Yes,' Jack said from behind, where his knees banged the back of Laurie's seat at every bump, 'Good idea, Ana. My idea, Ana.'

'Yeah Jack, the good idea that stays in your head is just an idea. The idea I present to the parents is an actual thing, it is a party. The party.'

'If the parents say yes,' Laurie said mildly, changing gears to slow down for the slow city driver ahead, definitely not a local, judging from the care with which they were taking the bends, 'Why and when?'

'Hope's birthday,' said Ana.

'Halloween,' said Jack, with a vampire snarl and narrowed eyes.

'Yes, I know when her birthday is,' said Laurie. 'Aren't you all too old for a dressing-up party?'

There was a moment's pause and Laurie caught a glimpse of Jack in the rear-view mirror, rolling his eyes as he mouthed 'wrong mother' to Ana.

He was right. They should have asked Martha first. Martha loved parties. When the children were little she had master-minded dozens of increasingly extravagant parties, so much so that it became a school-gate joke with the other parents, the impossibility of their own children ever having an event as intricately planned or as well executed. Martha's parties weren't lavish, they were often cheaper than the parties of many of their children's friends, but they were thorough. If there was a game, it was played with every rule attended and all the gear necessary. When the party was in the evening there were lights, not just inside or in front of the house, but all around it, up the drive and right into the winding road above.

'It's her eighteenth,' Ana said, trying another tack, 'it's a big deal.'

'Huge deal,' Jack chimed in.

'Does she want a party?' Laurie asked. 'She hasn't said anything.'

'That's why it's a good idea,' Jack smiled, proud of his thinking, 'she still thinks you guys are angry with her, she doesn't want to push it.'

Laurie looked at Jack in the rear-view mirror, then across to Ana, 'Is that true?'

'Why are you asking her?' Jack asked.

'Because I'm a girl and I know these things,' Ana smiled, smug.

'No,' Laurie said, 'we were never angry with her, I'd hate to think Hope believes that, we were worried.'

Jack shrugged, 'Angry, worried, it comes out the same.'

'Yeah, but not from the same place, idiot,' said Ana, 'and Mom, she knows you were worried. We all do, even him,' she gestured to her brother in the back, who jolted her front seat on purpose this time, 'but you know, it means she's being a bit . . . '

'Too good?' asked Laurie.

'Yeah,' the twins said at the same time, and Jack added, 'way too good. All that homework.'

Laurie nodded, grateful for this insight into her eldest daughter, 'OK, so if we have a party, who's going to help set up? You know Martha will want to make a big deal about it, I've got to go away for that conference, you both have—'

'No competitions that weekend,' Jack pre-empted her question. 'We can help. And Mum will love it.'

'Love it,' Ana echoed, mimicking Martha's soft voice because she knew it always made Laurie smile.

'She will,' agreed Laurie, 'I'm surprised you asked me first.'

Ana grinned, 'But if we win you over, then Mum's easy.'

'So you have me twisted around four little fingers. Even though I don't like parties,' said Laurie, turning into their driveway, 'and I really don't like dressing up.'

'Yeah, but Mum does, and Hope wants it,' Jack said as he untangled his legs from the back of the car, 'you can tell them both it was your idea, we don't mind.'

Jack was out of the car before Laurie had pulled the hand-brake, his door slammed behind him and his long, lean body heading on towards the house, the party sorted. His hunger was next on the agenda.

'Well?' Ana asked, turning to her mother, her big blue eyes wide and hopeful, 'Come on Mom, she's eating, she's not being crazy about dance, she's barely mentioned Jon-the-bastard for ages.'

'You really think she'd like it?'

Her eyes narrowed as she looked pityingly at her mother, 'We only said it because we know Hope wants a party. She didn't ask you herself because she knows you hate parties.'

'I don't hate them, I just don't . . . love them.'

'Yeah, but you hate all that spooky Halloween stuff. Hope wants a party. Mum will love a party. Jack and I want a party. Let's just have a party, Mom. OK?'

Laurie stretched the rake through another swathe of red and gold leaves and counted her blessings. She did not believe in a god that might grant blessings, but she was grateful anyway. That Dot and Henry were getting older but well and happy. That Martha's mother's slow decline had been foreseen, even though it was so painful and that there had been time for them to say goodbye. That Martha's father was healthy even as he missed his wife dreadfully. Gratitude that she and Martha had found each other so early, and stayed together through their tougher first years. Her brother Karl had died three years ago, only forty-two with three children and a sudden heart defect that showed too late and too fast to fix. An old friend had lost her wife to cancer, only this January. So much that was ordinary to be thankful for, a partner, a home, work, children. So much that she had been trained to despise, which was now everything she valued.

Laurie shivered, it was a fine bright day, the sun still had a touch of warmth, one of those days the fens did so well, so much sky and all that water to reflect it, filling the air with liquid light and possibility. No reason to feel fear, but she felt a shiver of uncertainty anyway. They were lucky. Did that make a difference? Laurie understood that a day where things are everyday, normal, was the luckiest of all. And noticing that she had noticed it, that life was ordinary, thankfully ordinary, she shivered again.

She looked over to the big kitchen window, across the green space she was tidying in preparation for Hope's party at the weekend, and realised why she had shivered. They were watching her. The four people she loved more than her own life, had been watching and waiting for her to see their tableau. Martha with carving knife raised high, Jack wearing an Uncle Fester mask with his hands to his own throat, Hope with her foot raised to her mouth, taking a bloody bite out of her instep, Ana somehow twisted so that her head was under Hope's free arm.

They fell about laughing at her horror, her half-shriek, half-laugh when she realised what she was seeing in the moment of seeing it, when her fear and relief came in the same instant, and then they came running outside, all four whooping in pleasure at Laurie's shock, the successful completion of twenty minutes' planning and execution, another five minutes waiting for her to see them, to jump and scream and laugh. Five people giving in to the bliss of kicking through and rolling in a massive pile of freshly raked leaves.

Later, Laurie caught herself wondering if it was her fault, maybe acknowledging how happy she was had brought back the dark. Abraham would have been sure to correct her for thinking herself so powerful, for thinking she had any control of fate, but he was long out of her life. Unlike Samuel.

Twenty-Seven

Laurie had been cooking for two days. No matter that Hope insisted her friends were just going to get drunk and not taste the food anyway, or that they wouldn't be capable of telling the difference between a pumpkin pie and a sweet squash, or that she was dreading the party that had grown larger by the week, Laurie insisted that if they were going to play American tradition and decorate the house inside and out, then they would do the same with the food, American standards, American sizes. It turned out that Hope was only half right, the kids did, of course, get drunk – they were teenagers in their last year at school – but they also ate. Homemade hamburgers with fresh ketchup, both prepared to Dot's old recipe, devoured by boys who were almost men, while girls who usually refrained from eating in public, and certainly not in front of the boy or girl they were trying to lure, set about the sweet pies, cream piled, spice scented, gobbling them down like children in a fairy tale, risking the witch's wrath as they ate from her magicked table, risking hating their bodies the next day. Strategically placed around the three rooms in use for the party – kitchen, the old sitting room, garage cleaned up for the night – were bowls of marshmallows and cinder toffee, white chocolate-coated strawberries and dark chocolate pretzels. While Jack and Hope and Martha had draped walls in ribbons of black and blood-red crepe paper, hidden luminous skulls and zombie faces in dark corners that would be darker come evening, Ana, who was closest to Dot and Henry of all the children, helped cook and stir and dip in a kitchen that smelled progressively less like England and more like the parties of Laurie's early teens.

At six the house and garden were deemed ready and all five rushed off separately to dress up. Dressing up was Martha's passion, the more extravagant the better. She also decreed that the family's choice of costume should be secret from each other, to add to the excitement of the evening. Both Laurie and Martha had expected some reticence from Hope about the dressing up. She had loved it as a child, but enforcing fancy dress on an eighteenth birthday, even one that coincided with Halloween, had the potential to prompt a row and, now that things were calm, Laurie wasn't sure it was worth the risk. They talked about it before suggesting it to Hope.

'It's not like we haven't dressed up dozens of times for her birthdays before,' Martha said, 'and she wants a party, we didn't expect that.'

'True, but eighteen-year-olds aren't known for their will-ingness to make idiots of themselves. Ours even less so.'

'Sadly, given what it's taken her to get there, I think you'll find that our almost-eighteen-year-old is feeling especially proud of her body right now.'

'How is that relevant?' asked Laurie.

'She's a perfectly adequate student and a far more dedicated dancer, and now she's eating as well, all that work is showing in tone. If it was an ordinary party, she'd have to wear jeans like all the rest of them, this is a chance to show off, I expect she will.'

Both women were right. Hope at first frowned, not sure her friends would enjoy dressing up, not sure she would. But after talking to a few of the girls at school, she pronounced herself happy to invite people to a Halloween eighteenth.

'I didn't think you'd agree,' Laurie said when she and Hope were in the car, the week before the party, on their way after class to pick up the twins.

'Neither did I,' Hope agreed, 'and then I remembered how much Mum loves dressing up and now we're older she doesn't get much chance for stuff like that.'

Laurie turned her eyes from the road for a moment, to look at her eldest daughter, 'You're very lovely sometimes, you know that Hope?'

Hope nodded, 'I do. And I also know exactly what I'm wearing. I'll need money.'

If it was a bribe, Laurie chose not to hear it as one. A sum was set for each of the children to spend – or to keep and spend elsewhere if they could find, beg, borrow or recycle a costume instead – shopping trips were made singly or with friends, bags hidden inside other bags when they came into the house, and clothes tried on in bedrooms with doors firmly closed, all five conspiring to make their first appearance a surprise for the others, a joy, a joke, a gift.

Jack was downstairs first, their gorgeous boy, tall, strong, vibrant and glorious in his Marilyn Monroe outfit, his twin arrived a few minutes later and they both burst out laughing. An entire childhood of refusing to dress alike, their fraternity had been identical only in their profound disdain of matching twins. Now, here they were, wearing the same nipped and tucked dresses, wigs and wiggles. Their swimming teammates, who had secretly encouraged them to pick matching costumes, were the ones playing the joke.

'Damn,' said Ana, 'you look hot.'

'You do too.'

'That is so unfair, guys in frocks always look hotter than girls. And guys in drag get thought of as cool, girls in drag never do.'

'Tell people you're reclaiming the feminine, then you get to be cool too.'

'You know a lot of big words for a swimmer, Jack.'

'I have no idea what you mean, Ana,' Jack said, swaying and sashaying his way from the room.

Laurie's choice of witch costume was no surprise. Not keen on dressing up, she had long ago decided that dressing as a witch every time would make it all far easier. One year it was the Wicked Witch of the West, another she'd been Morgan le Fay, once she had terrified the children who'd come from Jack and Ana's Year Two class when she welcomed them at the front door as Hansel and Gretel's witch, offering a tray of gingerbread biscuits. This year she was her favourite, Glinda. Partly her favourite because of the absurd frock that came with Glinda, and partly because Martha couldn't stand Glinda's voice and Laurie's impersonation was painfully skilled.

Compared to her wife's glitter and the twins' glamour, Martha's costume was almost tame, a simple black shift that fell to just above her knees, showing off her toned arms and legs, a plain pair of black sandals, a slightly raised heel. She looked elegant and understated, dressed for a cocktail party in 1965, and quite beautiful.

'I thought this was fancy dress?' said Jack.

'You look amazing, Mum,' from Ana.

'You really do,' said Laurie, 'what's the twist?'

Martha smiled and turned off the lights, and there, patterned on her arms and legs, her toes, across her collarbone, and spiralling up from her neck, stretching over the fine bones of her face were webs, silvery strands of luminosity. When she reached up her arms she revealed delicate filaments stretching from the side seams of the dress to her hands, crosshatched to form wings of webbing. When she unpinned and shook out her thick dark hair, there were dozens of silver threads trailing down her back.

Martha turned the light on again and she was returned, elegant, understated.

Jack and Ana applauded and then grimaced as Laurie kissed and praised her clever, beautiful wife.

'Stop it, mothers,' Ana said, 'you're only setting us up to fail in our flawed heterosexual relationships.'

'Nah,' said Laurie, 'you lot'll be fine. Especially Jack. Jack's going to do very well for himself, straight girls love a guy in a frock.'

'See?' Ana nudged Jack in the ribs.

Then, as one, they all yelled up the stairs for Hope.

Hope came downstairs carefully, slowly. She turned the corner at the dogleg of the stairs and took a breath. She had been coached in this moment, she lifted her chin a little,

relaxed her neck and shoulder with a light shift, an undu-
lation of skin and bone, sinew and muscle she was learning
to love more with each of Samuel's classes. Another breath,
another yell from Jack below. Her bare feet and bare arms felt
cool, almost cold. Her hair was pinned up tight at the back,
stretching the skin from her eyes, her forehead, her chin,
helping her to hold her head up high, just so. Her dress was
tight across the front, tighter at the waist, falling loose to just
below her knees. She had seen the picture, faded now, that her
dress was based on. This was the best replica she could make,
in quiet, secret, late in her room. She hoped it was right. She
took another step and heard the crunch of a car, two cars on
the gravel outside. Jack's voice was even more insistent, come
on, they're nearly here, get a move on. Two, three, four, five
more steps. She turned the corner.

Laurie saw Hope's white dress, thin cotton, light, sharply
pressed. She saw how her hair was pulled back, twisted just
so, pinned into place – a knot Laurie knew would undo
with just one flick of the wrist. She saw her daughter's face
devoid of make-up – almost devoid, there was a fine layer
of lipstick, a tiny touch of blusher, hint of mascara – and for
those touches Laurie was enormously grateful, because they
meant she was here, and now, and so was Hope. For now.
She saw Hope's feet, bare, her wrists and fingers missing their
customary bangles and rings, she wasn't even wearing the
silver ring she'd worn continually since Dot gave it to her on
a visit for her thirteenth birthday, Laurie stared at the band
of ridged skin where it was missing. She saw that the sleeves
of the cotton dress were regulation three-quarter length, so
that Hope's fine wrists seemed even finer, extending from the

buttoned cuff. She saw the tight waist and knew that she and Martha had been somehow fooled. Their daughter's ankles and wrists were too bony, her waist too small, the rounded neck of the dress – hand stitched of course – showed sharp collarbones, too sharp. All of the dress, all of the image, all of her Hope, in the wrong place, wrong time, and that time and place brought into the centre of their home.

The others were exclaiming about the dress, the look, making guesses at the costume, where it came from, who Hope was meant to be. Laurie was trying to remember where she was, that this was her home, her life, that she was safe. Breathe in, breathe out. Now. Not then. Safe.

'So who are you?' asked Jack.

'It's *Witness*, isn't it?' asked Ana, 'That old film Mum likes?'

Martha asked, 'Is it?'

Jack said, 'Only cos she fancies the woman in it. And I don't blame her.'

Neither Hope nor Laurie spoke yet, both waiting.

'Eeeuw,' Ana pushed him away, 'You can't fancy the same woman as your mother, that's just weird.'

'I never said I fancied her,' Martha protested, joining in, trying to get Laurie to join in, 'or if I did, it was ages ago.'

'I can so,' Jack said to Ana, 'straight mothers and daughters fancy the same men all the time, they do in the movies anyway.'

'Straight dads and sons do too, apparently,' Martha said, and then turned her attention back to their birthday girl, stepping forward and kissing her daughter, 'Baby, you look beautiful. Absolutely gorgeous. Is it *Witness*?'

Hope shook her head, 'It's a . . . a dance thing. You'll see. When the others get here.'

Jack grinned again, 'Crazy Christian flash mob. Can't wait.'

Hope turned to Laurie, 'Mom?'

Laurie looked at her daughter, wanting to speak and not sure what she could trust herself to say. She wondered if Hope had known there would be a reaction, expected one, planned one. She wondered if Hope prompting her now was part of it, whatever the game was, whatever Samuel had created to cause her pain.

'Mom?' Hope asked again, smiling softly, looking like her own Hope, uncertain, needing reassurance, 'Don't you like my frock? My look?'

Laurie held her daughter very tightly, held her and tried not to recoil when she smelled rose oil on her girl's skin, her baby's skin.

'I love you my darling, anything you choose to wear makes me happy.'

Then the doorbell rang and the twins rushed to answer it, Martha hurried to the kitchen to make sure the hot food was ready.

Laurie and Hope were left alone, there could only be a few moments before everyone came through to the hallway and it all began.

Hope was still smiling at Laurie, 'You know where I got the idea for the dress? What I copied the pattern from?' Laurie shook her head, Hope went on, 'Sure you do, I've seen the picture.'

'There isn't a picture,' Laurie's voice was dull, she knew what was coming next, 'I don't have any pictures of that. Then.'

'Oh Mom, you're so beautiful in the photo. All of you are, you and Samuel and the other guy. Marshall?'

'Is this to punish me?' Laurie asked.

'For not telling me you already knew Samuel? For still not telling Mum?' Hope shrugged, 'I worked out you knew him the first time I saw you talk to him. I wish one of you would tell me what happened though, why you're so weird about him. He says I have to wait until you're ready to tell me.'

Laurie wondered if Hope was telling the truth, the doorbell rang again, she wanted to shake her daughter and demand how much she knew, she wanted to run to the door and bar it, stand at the gate and refuse entry. Too late. She'd opened this door herself. The people coming in were calling Hope's name.

'It's my party Mom, I have to go be nice.'

'Hope, wait,' Laurie held out her hand and grabbed Hope's fragile wrist, 'Look at you, look how thin you are. You promised us that was over, I thought we could trust you.'

'And I thought you and Mum were totally honest with us, that's what you always said. Guess we were both wrong. Anyway, haven't you always said it's my body, to do with as I choose? What you've been drumming into us kids for years? Well here I go, turning eighteen and using my own body, just as I like.'

The doorbell rang again, another car pulled up on the gravel outside, the hallway and kitchen were full of friends, of squealing and delighted teenagers and with others far too cool to show their joy but pleased to be there nonetheless. Hope walked away, leaving Laurie alone and scared.

Twenty-Eight

It was a month after their return from being special that Samuel told Laurie about his idea to depose Abraham, explaining that it had come to him in the dance.

'But how?' she asked. 'The dance leads the dancers. You give yourself more to the dance than anyone, how can you have an idea while dancing?'

'It isn't my idea, Laurie, that's my point, that's how I know it's real, it's of the vision. The dance allowed me to think the community's desire.'

Abraham had often said that Johan was conceived before the community, Lukas was a pointer to the truth, Samuel was the first child truly born to the fully self-determining community. Samuel was the chosen son, smarter, beautiful, more aware and more knowing than anyone but his father. Or he had been while Ingrid was alive, but not long after her death, Marshall had arrived, aged just sixteen, and suddenly Abraham had a new favourite.

Samuel went on, 'Abraham always said I was born into the living community, true?'

'Yes,' Laurie nodded, wanting him to approve of her responses. She had come back for him, she had to understand him to make sense of her choice to be here, even now, even after what had happened in the city.

'So doesn't it make sense that I might understand the community's future through the dance?'

'It makes sense, I just – I don't know. You really believe the community wants this?'

Samuel stood tall, the sun was behind him, soft curls haloing his beautifully shaped head, arm muscles defined from the physical work they had been allocated since their return from being special. Field labour to remind them that no one was above working the land. He was strong and shining.

He nodded, 'I felt it, before the words even formed in my head. The dance wants this. It is us, all of us.'

'It is the embodiment of the community, yes,' she replied, parroting the words they had learned as toddlers, the words that came with the steps, the understanding of those words coming far later, coming from experience of what it was to be danced by the whole. 'What about Marshall?'

'This has nothing to do with Marshall. He was supposed to take care of us, of you, in the city. He didn't. We can't risk him failing the community in the same way.'

Samuel made it sound so simple, so right. And the force of being back in community, the patterns and rituals, made it easier to choose to follow him, allow him to persuade her of the next step, and the next. All she had to do was agree to walk alongside him.

Even while she was away, Laurie had thought of him. If it had not been right that Samuel brought her back, he would never have found her, a lost needle in a haystack of red tape and closed files. Of course it was right that she returned to the community. After what had happened in the city she craved the enclosed compound. She was theirs and always had been, destined to return, and not just to the community, but to Samuel for whom she had been brought to the community in the first place.

Samuel was persuasive and he was beautiful and the rhythm that was their secret, stolen fucking was another kind of dance, a meditation of forgetting.

He stood in front of her, 'Yes?'

Laurie accepted his offered hand, 'Yes.'

She didn't know if she meant yes to the new-found joy of her body revelling in his, or to his plan to free the community from Abraham.

Perhaps she was saying yes to both.

And then it all happened very quickly. Samuel caught her eye at the evening gathering, gave her the agreed signal, and what she had been wanting and fearing began. She was in Abraham's office for the first time in years, the same room, the same feeling, the same fear. The walls lined with books, dozens of languages of biblical translations. Abraham always said he understood every one, perhaps he did, perhaps he did not need language. Their community was mostly of the book, but there were hundreds of other books, piled in corners, propped up behind doors, each ready to be pulled from the shelf at a moment's notice, substance for Abraham's occasional change of rule, reversion of rule, reinstatement of rule. Abraham never did anything without textual backing and his books were filled with markers, highlighted a dozen times in different colours, broken nails left between pages, ripped from nail beds and left as a bloody marker in the books of Abraham.

When Samuel finally came to the office, so much later than she'd hoped he would, she was staring at the books, at the walls, anywhere rather than look at Abraham. Her shirt was on the floor, her bra askew, her skirt already undone, Abraham's shirt was awry, and his jeans unzipped, all exactly as she had agreed with Samuel.

She stood there, the sacrifice between father and son, and Abraham spat at her, his disgust, his fury, and worse, his disappointment, 'Viper.'

'You wanted to fuck her, old man,' Samuel had said, a knife at his father's liver, 'You let her in.'

Abraham laughed, 'You think I haven't fucked them all already? You think she is any different? You think *she* didn't want to fuck *me*?' he leaned in and whispered something and Laurie tried not to listen, tried not to hear what he said that caused Samuel to make his father's blood flow, Abraham whispering about the nights after their covenanting, the times she had been delivered to this room in the dark.

Abraham was hissing, 'They all want me, I fathered their dream, and they always all want that.'

Laurie stepped back in horror, what if Abraham was right? Maybe this wasn't all just part of Samuel's plan, maybe she and all the others he had taken after covenanting were just as he said, part of the dream. And maybe she had wanted him, she remembered so wanting his attention as a child, so wanting him to notice her. The insinuation confused Laurie and angered Samuel, and it was in their anger and confusion that they made the leap. From will we, can we, how could we, to the point where they were suddenly walking away from the old house, past the community hall, the gardens, the home fields, way out past the old testing station, then the fences, one-two-three, each one barbed and brutal, each one cut and re-twisted, hoping to keep community trackers distant for a while, for long enough. Laurie and Samuel were not runaways.

The walk was not as she had imagined. After all of Samuel's promises and whispers, all that had brought her back, she had expected more, but once they were on the trail of Samuel's new dream, he was different, cold, sharp with her.

Laurie was adult enough, woman enough – at all of seventeen – to know that Samuel was now all about the new vision. She was certainly adult enough after their time in the city to know it was only a very little, if at all, about her. And yet, she had hoped for more. Walking on into the desert beside the son and his stolen father, berating herself for stupid childish rebellion, her own desire all too obvious. It had been so frightening to do what they had talked about for so long, to come back, give herself again to the community, be special. So terrifying to do it all, as planned and then to take that next step. The one they were now walking.

As a child, a long walk around the far fence had been a thrill, rarely available, given how much of the community's time was regulated and ordered. A very few times, when she had finished her chores, if she managed to slip away before being given another task, Laurie had made her way to the lesser-used of two paths approaching the old house, one from either direction. When Abraham and Ingrid first saw the empty shack that was now the core of the house, it stood a little way back from an old road. Ingrid didn't have the heart to suggest it looked like any shack, or that most men would not have seen it as the beginning of a mission. In the months following they raised the first fence, leaving a wide gateway at the western end, to welcome other pilgrims. Two acres beyond the shack they fenced off the other end of the old road right across the tired and broken tarmac, closing the circle.

Sometimes people asked, 'Didn't the authorities mind? Didn't they make a fuss when you cut off the road?'

Abraham would laugh at the interruption to his tale, a good-natured, genial laugh, instilling a sense of ease in no one but his interlocutor, and answer quite plainly, 'They recognised a higher authority, they recognised the strength of the vision.'

He would go on with his story and later that day, late that night, the questioner would find themselves hustled out of the compound, back into the world along the one road, the gate locked behind them. It was a useful example, and those who had not questioned learned never to question.

Over the years dirt and sand swept across the broken tarmac that led in the other direction, away from the shack, and eventually it became less obvious, less of an exit. The compound grew exactly as Abraham had dreamed, so that there was only one way in and out. After a time the compound perimeter was extended north, east and south, wider and deeper. One year the main gate itself was shifted, reinforced, rebuilt a good two miles further west than it had been originally. By then, what was left of the old road was nothing but a sandy path, heading off in a straight line towards the dawn, outbuildings raised over it, newly irrigated gardens growing alongside, inner-compound fences erected above. If you followed the original line far enough though, if you kept going, eventually the old road resurfaced, cracked and crumbling, heading to a distant fence, beyond which there was no community.

In their planning, imagining this day, this moment, Samuel had refused to tell Laurie how far they would have to walk, now she wondered if it was because he hadn't trusted her to agree if she'd known how far he was planning to go. She would have agreed regardless, surely he knew that? They had passed the outer compound perimeter an hour ago, an hour and a half maybe, walking into the dawn. At first there had been a last wave of cool air, the moment where the land sighed out a gentle, soft breath, giving up moist earth, freeing secrets that were hidden rivers and untapped wells, before the hot day began.

Laurie was six and only just out of the children's corral when she'd first asked why they had to work in the hottest hours of the afternoon, 'Valeria says that in Mexico they sleep in the afternoon, that her mama and papa both slept every afternoon before they came here. Can't we sleep?'

Her question was dismissed, she was told to get on with her work. Later she was taken aside, informed she had displeased Abraham, that she must attend the reckoning and admit her fault. She had done so, sweaty little fists, hot, tear-stained face, and Abraham's cool hand on her cheek, a slap that was a caress because it was the only touch he had ever given her, and her skin smelling of his rose oil as it smarted.

She asked again, three years later, not long before the dark night when the men arrived in helicopters and tore through

213

the compound, checking papers, right to stay, right to go. Along with five other adopted children, she was taken away, for her own good, they said. Ripped out of the only world she had ever known.

'But why can't we sleep in the afternoon? We should work in the morning, when the ground is cool.'

She was told, of course, that it was not for the community to decide the hours they worked, it was Abraham's vision that gave them these rules, even Abraham bowed to the greater knowledge of the dream. Rebuked, she repented her insolence in asking not once in her young life, but twice – again the caressing slap, again the strange joy in receiving Abraham's attention, even if only for his displeasure.

Now, as they walked into the east, the sun rising higher with each step, the land around them becoming drier and rockier, she wanted to demand answers from Samuel, insist he show her the map she knew he had in his backpack. Instead, awed by the fact that Abraham walked, bound, between them, amazed and not a little fearful at what they had done, she said nothing.

Abraham had been quiet, oddly acquiescent. Laurie recognised a new tone in his voice, placatory, less the leader and more fellow journeyman. It was disarming because he sounded so unlike his usual self, and also because he was walking alongside, not in front – and she was surprised at how much she enjoyed this reversal.

The land beneath them was hard rock, sand and dust left behind, rock with narrow crevices an inch or less across, dozens of them in every sheet of stone. Every now and then a lizard looked up from a shaded crevice, a trail of ants led each other beneath into the dark. The sun climbed on. They stopped for water in the shade of a long-dead tree, its trunk wide, its branches reaching up fruitlessly. It had not had leaves for many years but still it stretched to the light.

'Don't lean against it,' cautioned Samuel, 'sit in the shade, but don't touch it. It's desiccated, it might go at any time, and it will be full of ants.'

Laurie stepped a little away from the danger of the tree, standing dead.

They drank water from the pouches she and Samuel carried. Abraham did not carry water, he had – he said – long ago given his needs over to the land, if there was water he would drink, if not he would go thirsty. Laurie had heard this since she was a small child, heard it as his constant refrain – *the land will give* – and when she watched Abraham drink from Samuel's flask, she noted that he drank slowly, not sucking as she had, showing no thirst. He seemed to believe his own story. Perhaps he was right, perhaps the land would give to him.

The sun high in the sky, land that had faded in the sun's light from yellow-brown sand and yellow-green plants to grey-green rocks and grey-brown stones and still they walked, Samuel leading them in a colourless landscape, everything dried to a shadow of itself. Laurie walked because she had been walking for hours, because it was too far to go back, because she had no idea where forward was, she walked on and as she did she raised her hand in front of her face and even her own skin, her usually light brown skin, seemed grey, monotone. The sun above and nothing around them but rock and sand and the deep grey of each step she took into the heat. Another and another. Always into the heat.

Eventually Abraham spoke, 'I made you special ones, what more could you ask?'

Samuel grunted and Laurie shook her head, wanting to explain but not wanting to defy Samuel's edict that they weren't to speak to Abraham in the long walk.

Abraham went on, 'You are gifted, beloved, made special, but there is a pre-ordained path, a covenant I made with this earth, you cannot unmake it. I must live out the vision. There is time yet.'

'Shut up, old man, this is the time. It is time, now.'

Samuel pushed him on. Laurie had imagined this moment so often. In none of her imaginings had she ever begged Samuel to stop, to turn back. She wanted to ask him to stop.

She agreed with Samuel that it was time to let the next generation take their place. What Abraham had begun, they needed to continue, to lead forward, further. They were young and vibrant and able, there was much for them to do yet, to achieve. She was seventeen, Samuel was nineteen, Abraham was sixty-five. He was old, too old. No matter that he was still fathering children, as had his original namesake, that he had taken two wives since Ingrid died. Now was the time for the new-born, the generation who were truly of the land. Abraham could be made to understand, Samuel had assured her. It was time for Samuel to take his rightful place, third-born, land-born, the son.

In those long late-night telephone calls to Dot and Henry's house, when he had whispered his hopes and dreams of a new-born community, Samuel had persuaded Laurie of the future they would create together. They were covenanted, they would be the new Abraham and Ingrid. Her return was the revelation that Abraham needed to understand that the new must begin now.

That was not how it had turned out. She had returned and Abraham had sent them off as special ones but with Marshall to lead, Marshall set between Samuel and Laurie. They came back and Marshall was named as Abraham's heir. This wasn't what Samuel had dreamed and so now he would make the dream come true.

They walked on, Laurie guided by Samuel, Abraham guided by Samuel's knife digging into his ribs.

They were still walking out across the desert in the late afternoon heat, the land shimmering all around them, the community way back and none the wiser.

Laurie hating the walk and hating herself when what came from her mouth was a whine, 'How much further? It's going to be harder later if we don't rest soon.'

Neither of the men looked at her. Samuel knew where they were headed, and perhaps Abraham knew too, his head was down to the hot wind, his neck bowed against the sun. Samuel was intent only on walking, one foot in front of the other, walking into a new time.

Laurie tried again, tried to hide the whine, but feared it only came out tighter now, shorter of breath, shorter of patience. She knew a woman of the community must never exhibit impatience, yet still the words flew from her mouth, 'I said, how far is it? It's not a difficult question. It's not as if he doesn't know.'

Laurie gestured to Abraham and as she did the old man

looked to her, his head lifting from the sagging neck, twisting ever such a little towards her, a sly look and a small smile.

'Don't smile at me.'

Laurie wanted to slap him, to stop the old man, finally they were away from Abraham's place of power and Laurie had hoped she would feel free. Instead all she felt was that Samuel was in charge, Samuel was forcing her to keep walking, heading to a destination that she didn't even know. Abraham and Samuel both knew where they were going, father and son, leading her on. Leading her too far.

'I said don't smile at me.'

Samuel sighed, 'Don't encourage him. Just keep on.'

'I thought we were in charge now?'

'No one is in charge Laurie, it's not about that. We're trying to do the right thing by the dream, that's all.'

Then Abraham smiled again, his head high, 'Haven't I always taught that we're each responsible for ourselves? There is no saviour but you, Laurie. Step into the dance, whatever your dance, step into it.'

Twenty-Nine

'Step into it.'

'No.'

Laurie's answer was firm, clear.

Samuel stood behind her, she could feel his height and strength too close, 'Step into it, you know you want to.'

'I don't dance, Samuel. My family know I don't dance. They don't need me to, they dance plenty, look at them.'

That great surprise gift of English weather, an unseasonably warm evening, had given their guests the best possible excuse to party outside, and the garden that Laurie had cleared just in case the party overflowed, expecting it to be the place of secret smokers, less secret stoners, had become a garden of dancers. She had blocked off the still-unfinished foundations for the new office and the pile of old rubble with screens that Ana and Jack had covered in pictures of Hope from all ages and seventeen other birthdays. The edges of the garden were littered with tea-lights lit in jars, old glasses, bottles, as many breeze-proof vessels as Ana and Jack could find, and the party was dancing on the grass, music coming from a clever combination of speakers that Ana had worked out, everyone dancing around the centre of Laurie's life, her family.

Martha was dancing with Hope, her strands of silver sparkling, Hope was a quiet white line in a space full of energy and growing abandon. Ana and Jack darted in and out of Laurie's view, now Ana was off in a group of high-kicking girls, Jack with a bunch of lounging lads, now the girls and boys were bouncing together in a mosh-pit imitation they'd picked up from old videos. Each time she thought she'd lost them they seemed to return to the centre, her wife, the twins, coming back to Hope, joining in with her calmer pace and energy. It was as if they fed from it, then rushed out again to the edges of the dark to work off the excess of energy.

Laurie stood at the side of the garden, in the shadow with Samuel and admitted to herself that she missed being part of the dance. She felt as revealed as ever she had in those awful, intoxicating reckonings, witnessed by the community, the exquisite pain-pleasure of shame, surrendering to being fully seen. Samuel's hand was on her back now and she remembered how it felt to have his hand on her skin, and she thought she might cry, it was such a relief and a searing pain to be close to him again, the only person who knew her true past.

Laurie watched as the dance shifted, calmer now, centred around Hope. She watched as her daughter began to lead the dance. Five steps forward, three steps back, five forward. Again and again. When Laurie realised what she was watching her hand went to her mouth, she thought she might throw up.

'Don't,' Samuel said.

'Don't what?'

'Don't make a fuss. Your baby is eighteen, she can do whatever she wants. She is doing what she wants.'

Laurie didn't move her eyes from the space in the garden where the dance was forming, people copying Hope, following Hope, 'This is what you want.'

'Yes, it is, but it's also what she wants. She's very strongwilled, your girl.'

The dance was more rhythmic and Laurie felt an old familiar ache, her desire to be both in and out at the same time, wanting to both lead and follow, and the impossibility of being part of the community without being swallowed up, losing herself. She watched as the dance scooped up Martha and Ana, the two of them opposite Hope in the circle. At first Martha was looking out for their children, checking that Jack was OK, that he'd found a place too, helping Ana with the steps, knowing that their younger girl was a mermaid, not a dancer. It didn't take long for Martha to join Hope's rhythm, Laurie could see her laughing.

'Look at it Laurie, tell me it's not glorious to see the community form around your girl?'

The boys from Hope's class had begun to join in, pulled by the gravity of movement and their friends. Most of them were a little stoned or a lot drunk or both, and still the steps caught them, an intoxicated stagger that made sense to their tumbling feet, swaying bodies.

Samuel was close enough to her now that she could feel the warmth of his skin, 'Look at Martha, she's loving it. Don't you want to join her? It's just a dance.'

'You know it's not.'

'I know that the last time you danced it was too long ago.'

Laurie shook her head, 'No. I dance, alone, to remind

myself of what it was like, of a place I intend never to return to, a person I don't mean to be.'

He took a deep breath, maybe she had surprised him, the dance ahead was stronger now, the beat more insistent.

'I don't want to go back,' she repeated.

'Neither do I. But if you haven't let go of the dance, fully, then it's still part of you. It wants you to dance it, Laurie.'

And then, as if she knew what Samuel was whispering, as if she knew exactly the moment to look – she couldn't have, it was impossible, but it was also the purest of choreography – Hope turned her head as she continued to step forward, step around, step away, she turned and looked straight at Laurie and held out her hand, 'Mom, come and dance with me.'

Laurie went to her daughter and Samuel watched as Hope took the next step, and the next, and Laurie danced with her.

Abraham says:

'When we give up the individual, there is hope and freedom. The idea that we are separate is a psychosis accelerated by the emphasis on the self, the individual's happiness at the cost of all else. But it didn't make us happy, did it? It's time to give it up, give in. Let us be together, let us be one.'

Laurie was dancing because the steps were so easy and she had wanted for so long to dance this way with others. She was also crying because she knew Samuel was laughing with joy, laughing at a completion, and she had no idea where the next step was taking her, had taken her, she was already in.

They went to bed happy and late, the garden and the house cleared of teenagers, the dishes piled up in the kitchen to wash with safe sober hands in the morning. Martha and Laurie turned off the lights in the garden, blew out the last few candles, looked in on their children who were no longer children. Ana's Marilyn dress was hanging on her wardrobe, her make-up removed, her wig carefully placed on her dressing table. Jack's room was as messy as his twin's was ordered, his clothes discarded on the floor, the wig long gone to one of the girls from his class. Martha thought Jack had been especially keen to lend it, a reason to spend more time with the girl, and both mothers felt the sad thrill of their boy growing up and away from them.

Hope wasn't quite asleep when they looked in.

'Thank you, mothers, great party,' she said, her voice croaky with singing and laughter and sleep, 'Go to bed.'

'We're going,' Martha said, 'happy birthday baby.'

'Happy birthday to me,' Hope answered, curling into her pillow, into what was left of the night.

'We did good,' Martha said.

'We did,' Laurie replied.

'And wasn't that dance great? Everyone got it, the steps, I love that Hope was leading it, that she wasn't too shy to be in the centre.'

'It was good to see her being proud to be the birthday girl.'

'I love dancing,' Martha said, twisting around so that Laurie would hold her as she fell asleep.

'I know you do, babe, good night.'

Despite her unease at Samuel having been in their home, despite her feeling that she had betrayed herself in some way by joining in the dance, Laurie was sleepier than usual, she wondered if it might be OK after all, if Samuel might be happy with just keeping Hope as an acolyte. If this was all it was, an occasional feeling of discomfort, past stories too close to new life, then perhaps it might yet be fine.

Laurie sank back, a long breath, the doors were locked, the children were in bed, their home was safe, and just as her limbs became loose, there was a jolt, a moment where she was falling, off-kilter until she righted herself, terrified, until she realised where she was, home, beside Martha, safe – and then she slept.

Thirty

The plan needed Laurie to fall. She would go to Abraham's office, get him to drop his guard, Samuel would force him to leave the compound with them, all three walking out and beyond the boundary. Then, when they were close to the bunker, Laurie would fake a fall. Abraham would berate her for clumsiness, they could both rely on his predictable insistence that an accident was her own fault, her own choice. Laurie would cry and, as usual, tears would irritate Abraham even more, he would become angry, agitated, she would act frightened, angering him further. Laurie didn't understand why it was necessary to manufacture an altercation, but Samuel assured her it was.

'Getting him to go down into the bunker will be the hardest part. He needs to think we're just stupid kids. I want him to believe it's all just an accident of my anger with him, my jealousy about Marshall, your desire to please me.'

'I don't desire to please you, Samuel.'

He grinned, 'You do. Anyway, the point is, we need him to relax into thinking that he's still in charge, smarter than us. We can say you hurt yourself when you fell, you need to rest in the shade, so we go into the bunker.'

'Can't we just force him into it? If we can get him off the compound, we'll already be in charge.'

'None of it's certain, we have to use what we know about him. Abraham won't believe we've outwitted him, he'll assume we've fucked up somehow. If we get him to believe that what we're doing is his idea, finding somewhere for you to rest, then at least we'll be one step ahead. I'm not stupid enough to think a knife is the only power over him.'

'You really think that me pretending to be hurt is going to do all that?'

'It will wrong-foot him, yes. Once we get him into the bunker and he's tied up down there, it'll be fine, but I don't trust him not to outwit us somehow, so let's have him thinking he knows better, it's safer that way. And I can teach you to fake a fall.'

Samuel taught her tripping and tumbling so that it looked real, stumbling to a halt and then over-balancing, seeming to over-balance, but in reality falling only because she chose to fall. The way he said it, it made sense, as if he'd worked it out long ago.

She asked him about it, 'How did you learn this? Who taught you?'

But he just shook his head, 'It's always better to choose to fall, that way there is some control.'

And they did have some control, until Laurie actually hurt herself when she fell. Rehearsing in the compound was one thing, tripping and falling when they had been walking for hours, when she hadn't had any water for ages, when Samuel was glaring at her as they got closer and closer to the bunker and she still hadn't fallen, hadn't followed the plan, was quite another.

She took a breath, shook her head to quiet all the confusion, the questioning about what they were doing, and she lurched to her left side. As she went over Abraham reached out his arm to help her. It seemed as if he knew what she was doing as she did it, and he was ready to stop her, to right her, but his reaction was just too late, and the speed of his grab meant that when Laurie fell, Abraham fell on top of her, knocking her further on to her front, her left arm twisted beneath. She put her hand out to break her fall and stone and bone met in a ripping of wrist, her thumb bent back and away.

She cried out and Abraham, far from reprimanding her, righted himself and held out his hand, 'Are you hurt?'

Laurie pulled herself up as best she could, the ankle that was twisted beneath her took her breath away, and there was another, even more intense pain at the base of her left hand, she fell back on to her side, looking at her hand. Her thumb was all wrong, a right angle turned back on itself.

'That's got to hurt,' Abraham said.

'Yes.'

'Give me your hand.'

Samuel stood over them, furious that his plan was slipping awry.

'Leave her alone, Abraham.'

Abraham ignored his son and spoke softly to Laurie as she allowed him to take her damaged hand in both of his. He saw she was trying hard not to cry.

227

'There is nothing wrong in admitting pain. Your fault does not preclude the possibility of pain, none of us is spared that.'

Samuel reached out and Abraham gently chided him, 'Really boy, even now? You always wanted the attention, didn't you? Even when it was your mother who was hurt, you always wanted the attention.'

Samuel was still, his voice cold, 'What?'

'You know what I'm referring to, when your mother was corrected.'

'When you beat her,' Samuel answered.

Abraham's touch was light on Laurie's arm, 'She was one of the community, we had a different rule back then, more ... physical. Do you think I should have treated her differently because she was my wife, or because she was your mother?'

'Both. Neither. No one should ever have been beaten. Your regime was barbaric.'

'We changed.'

'Too late. The way you treated your own wife ... ' Samuel couldn't finish.

'And a knife at your father's throat? In the small of his back? How is that different, Samuel?'

Abraham's hand was tighter on her wrist now, and Laurie was scared, ankle throbbing, thumb joint burning, pulling away in case he hurt her more.

Abraham went on, all the while closing his hand tightly around Laurie's dislocated thumb, 'It's a shame you didn't teach this young lady to fall as well as your mother taught you, all those times, falling and rolling yourself away to safety.'

Samuel understood that his father knew more than they had hoped, 'It was foolish of me not to think you'd recognise it. Ingrid trained all of us boys, when we were little, even Lukas. She taught us to fall and roll so we were out of your way.'

'Your mother never chose to fall, she had the strength to stand and be accountable.'

'She gave herself up for us, put herself in our place.'

The sun was beating down, the pain in two sharp points of Laurie's body, thumb and ankle, she thought she might throw up and still the two men continued, arguing back and forth, old anger, old hurts.

'You're an idiot, boy. She gave herself up to me. Ingrid was a good mother, but she was a better wife, she was held in my vision and she took that hardship upon herself. I like stoicism in a woman, it's a much underrated attribute. Now then Laurie,' Abraham's grip was tighter on Laurie's hand and thumb, she couldn't help herself whimpering a little in fear and in pain, and she hated Abraham when he smiled and said, 'Let's see how stoic you are.'

'I told you, leave her alone,' Samuel loomed over them both.

In response, Abraham looked up to his son, the young man standing with the sun directly above him, the light behind him shading his face to a mask, his fury clear in the ready tension of his fists.

Just before he wrenched Laurie's thumb back into place, Abraham said to Samuel, 'You're in my light boy, you should try to enjoy it. This little excursion is also part of the vision, always has been, I knew I would be led away by the weak son and the prodigal daughter. Everything is as it should be. Enjoy the brief moment that I'm in your shadow. It won't last.'

Laurie screamed in nauseating pain and an almost worse

229

immediate relief, then she screamed again as Samuel heard and understood Abraham's words, his theft of Samuel's dream, making it his own. Samuel roared and Laurie lurched out of their way, hearing the thud of Samuel's boot and the crunch of the old man's nose.

She was head down in the rough grit and dirty sand of the desert, scrabbling away from the violence between father and son behind her, crawling on her hands and knees because she couldn't put pressure on her foot, the hot earth beneath her reeling with their rage. But she couldn't get far enough away to miss the sounds, to escape the crunch, thud, stomp of Samuel's boots against his father's face, his ribs, his back. Not far enough away to avoid hearing Abraham curse his son, his weakest boy, the one he had always expected least from, finally fighting back. Abraham tried to fight too, but he was so much older, and weaker, and surprised, truly surprised for once, at the violence his son unleashed, coughing and laughing his own disbelief that the pretty boy was a man after all. Coughing, crying out, retching. Groaning, a strangled laugh, last laugh, and then thud, thud, thud. Samuel panting, sobbing, and then both men were silent, and then the only sound was Samuel's heaving breath and the high wind in the pylons, screaming out across the land.

Thirty-One

Martha and Laurie both woke late, the twins later still. Rare for their children to have a weekend morning off training, Laurie and Martha went downstairs quietly, careful not to disturb them. Martha got on with scouring the house and garden for glasses and plates missed in the night's unsober clear-up, while Laurie prepared pancake batter as Dot had taught her, ready for when her family woke up. Half an hour later, Ana and Jack were luxuriating in pyjamas at the kitchen table, laughing at the photos their friends had been sharing since the night before.

'Well Jack, if ever we needed proof that you're the real beauty of this family, here it is,' Ana said, offering her phone to Jack to read her friends' comments on his photos, leaving him delighted and blushing.

Martha came into the kitchen with half a dozen plates and a few glasses clinking in one hand, 'I have no idea how this lot ended up in your bedroom, Jack. Wine glasses I might point out.'

'That was Hope's mates,' Ana said, 'she wouldn't let them

in her room, and I didn't want her messy friends in mine, so they took over Jack's room.'

'They didn't care that it was a pit?'

'Sexy pit,' Jack smiled, yawning.

'No,' Ana said, 'just easy to ignore the stink while getting pissed on rubbish wine.'

Martha gave a fake shudder, 'Gah, teenage wine nights, we've had a few of those, haven't we?' she asked Laurie.

'Hell no, we were in America. Didn't touch a drop until we were twenty-one.'

It was the story she'd told Martha and her children all of their lives together, and for a long time it had been an easy lie. Now, with Samuel back in her life, Laurie felt odd telling only some of the truth.

'Yeah, sure,' Jack jeered, 'all those perfect American kids and their law-abiding American parents and not a gun-toting madman among them.'

Laurie was glad to change the subject, 'Pancakes are ready, did you wake Hope?' she asked Martha.

'She's not here.'

'What?' Laurie stopped, and already she knew something was wrong.

'I was surprised she got up in time after last night, but her bed's made and her dance bag is gone, so she must be at class.'

Laurie looked at Ana who was suddenly extra-interested in her phone screen, 'Ana, what's going on?'

'Why?'

'Does Hope have a class this morning?'

'I suppose so, if she's not here.'

'Does she have a class?' Laurie's voice was calm and very clear.

232

'I . . . don't think so. Only . . . I don't think any of the other kids in her dance class had anything this morning.'

'They weren't drinking like they were going to class this morning,' Jack said grinning.

'Jesus, Jack,' Ana said, kicking him.

'What? I'm telling the truth. They're all old enough, or nearly, like Hope, they can get pissed if they want to.'

Martha put down the plates she was still holding, 'Listen, both of you, if you know where she is, please just say.'

Ana sighed, 'I honestly don't know, but she said something, last week, about private tuition. She thinks that Samuel is so amazing, if he offered her a free lesson, she'd get up, even with no sleep, for sure.'

'Yuck,' Jack said, and Ana agreed with him, adding in a gagging noise for good measure.

Laurie tried to speak lightly, 'You don't like him?'

'Mom,' Ana rolled her eyes, 'all of the dance girls fancied him at first, but after a while they said he was just creepy, all these rules about what to do and how to be. It's only Hope who can't see it, and that's because he thinks she's so perfect. The other girls in her class only put up with him because he's a bloody good teacher and there's not exactly an excess of great teachers way the hell out here.'

Martha and Laurie exchanged a glance, Laurie placed the last of the pancakes on the pile, carefully picked up the platter and put it in the centre of the kitchen table. She took off her apron, kissed Martha and left the room.

The same autumn that had given them a glorious night just twelve hours ago, had woken with the full force of the season, and Laurie drove through horizontal rain, wind buffeting the car whenever she came to an open stretch. She parked just down from Samuel's block and ran to the lobby door, she pressed on the buzzer for his apartment and left her finger there until there was an answer. It wasn't Samuel.

'Sorry, who do you want?'

Laurie leaned towards the speaker, 'Samuel, this is his flat, the penthouse.'

'No,' said the distinctly local accent, 'this is my flat, the penthouse, has been for five years.'

'But ... but he was here. I've visited here before. I have been up in the lift to your entrance hall and I want to know where the fuck Samuel is, and where the hell my daughter is.'

There was a moment of silence, when Laurie thought perhaps her anger had done the trick, perhaps the woman had gone to get Samuel.

Then she heard the door in front of her click open, 'You'd better come up love.'

Fifteen minutes later Laurie was standing in the street, in the rain and the wind, her hand shaking too much to click the button on her car keys to open the door, let alone to get in and drive away. The very nice woman had explained about her six months in Japan, how she'd sublet the apartment through a lovely company, she was sure they'd have the fellow's references, his details.

'It won't take long to find him dear, though, if I were you I'd think myself lucky. If he's gone off with no goodbye, you're well off out of it.'

Samuel was gone, Hope was gone, and Laurie had no idea where they were. Eventually she calmed herself enough to get in the car. When she looked at her phone there were several missed calls from Martha and a dozen texts, each more worried than the last. All but a few pieces of Hope's dance clothes were still in their drawer, but three pairs of jeans, two pairs of trainers, and several jumpers were gone. Some toiletries were missing, not much, her make-up and jewellery were scattered all over her dressing table as usual, so it was impossible to tell if anything was missing or not. And the dress she had been wearing to the party was gone as well. When Laurie read this she started to cry, the image of Hope dressed to be special was too much. She gave herself a minute longer to howl in the closed cell of the car and then she calmed herself. She was here, in England. She had a wife and three children. She was not lost in the desert, she was not abandoned in a dark bunker, she had resources, and this would get sorted. All she had to do was find Samuel and get her daughter back. And work out how much of the truth she was going to tell Martha.

After calling home to tell Martha that Samuel was no longer in the apartment and she was on her way back, she took a photo of herself, eyes swollen and red, and texted it to Samuel.

I imagine you'll want to see this. Now tell me what to do next.

Laurie was glad Martha hadn't told her she was going to call the police. The nice young woman sat in their kitchen and explained how there really was nothing they could do, she'd only driven out as a courtesy, their daughter was eighteen, she hadn't been gone twenty-four hours yet, no one had committed a crime as far as they were aware, it really wasn't anyone's business – yet. If Martha had mentioned the police, Laurie would have had to find a way to ask her not to contact them, to ask her not to make it worse before she could speak to Samuel and try to make it better.

The policewoman drove away and Martha watched her car turn out of the driveway, 'She's a child.'

'She's eighteen, that's why they won't do anything.'

'Not Hope. That police girl, she's a child.'

'Yes.'

'Which is why she doesn't think it's a big deal. She thinks our daughter is screwing some older bloke and we're fucked-up lesbians who can't cope with it.'

'Yes, she probably does.'

'Maybe she's right?' Martha asked, imploring, 'Maybe it's not a big deal?'

Laurie shook her head, her heart heavy, 'It is a big deal.'

'Do you feel it, does it feel like a bad thing has happened?' Martha asked, terrified.

'No,' Laurie shook her head, answering honestly, 'I don't think a bad thing has happened, not to Hope. But you need to know why I'm worried. I need you to know about Samuel and me.'

Laurie didn't tell Martha the whole truth, she didn't even tell her most of the truth. She had never before told Martha about going back to the compound at seventeen, being special, what happened in the city, nor what happened later in the desert. She had never told anyone what happened in the desert, she barely allowed herself to think about what happened out there, with Abraham and Samuel. Even with Hope missing, she couldn't tell Martha that story. Besides, as she convinced herself, what good would it do? Samuel and Hope were somewhere together, so she told Martha that she and Samuel had been children in the compound, they had been promised to each other by Abraham, and Samuel had a weird belief that they were still meant to be together. Laurie told Martha half-truths and long-rehearsed stories, wishing she believed them herself, but there were words at the back of her mouth, the true story, the whole truths that caught in her throat, threatening to spill out in a scream.

'You knew him all along?' Martha's fury was quiet.

'Yes.'

'I don't understand . . . '

'I didn't know how to tell you I'd gone back to the compound. I've never told you about it, how it was when I went back. I didn't know how to explain—'

'Why you did that? Went back to those fucking awful people?'

'I did it because I was seventeen, because I was young, sure that I knew best.' Laurie wanted to add that she didn't know if they were all awful, not all of them, that it was so much more complicated than she'd ever said. So complicated that even Dot and Henry never talked about her going back either, never brought it up, knew that Laurie couldn't bear to think about it.

'Hope is eighteen, Laurie.'

'I know.'

'She's young, she's sure she knows best.'

'I know.'

'You could have told her about him, you could have told her where he was from. What he was like. You could have told me – you knew I thought he was helping me, had helped me.'

Martha looked at Laurie and Laurie wanted to run, hide, Martha looked straight at her and it was all Laurie could do to keep her mouth shut, not to speak what she had never spoken, the real story of her tattoo, inked into her skin to remind her of being special and all it had led to.

'You think he didn't just turn up here?' Martha was asking, 'It's obvious he targeted me, he targeted Hope, to get to you?'

Laurie nodded, 'Yes.'

'So what now? What do we do? Do we call that police girl back and persuade them we're not just pissed off that our daughter has discovered shagging with a middle-aged bloke? That we're not that fucking stupid? What do we do? How do we keep Hope safe?'

Laurie reached out and Martha would not take her hand, 'I think we wait,' she said, 'I think we don't provoke him. The police won't do anything until it's been twenty-four hours anyway, they think Hope is her own woman. He'll be in touch, he'll know we're scared and so will Hope, one of them will be in touch.'

'Are you sure?' Martha asked.

'No,' Laurie answered, telling the truth.

Martha started to leave the kitchen, to go through to the sitting room where the twins were still texting their friends, sending messages, asking Hope to contact them.

She stopped at the door and asked, without turning back, 'Did you fuck him?'

'No,' Laurie lied.

Thirty-Two

In the heat, in the dust, Laurie found herself focusing on small moments at a time. The sweat, dripping from her back, her front, her face, drying on her clothes and then almost immediately damp again, dripping again. The flies, a constant buzzing around her head, looking for moisture, attaching themselves to her eyelids, to Abraham's drying blood. Their feet on the ground, the earth absorbing sound as it soaked in the heat, not actual footsteps but a constant scuffle as if they were tiny ants, going about their mindless business, heading towards something unclear, unknown, heading there anyway.

For much of the mile or more to the shelter, Samuel took the bulk of Abraham's weight, Laurie stumbling alongside, trying not to cry out at the pain in her ankle. She didn't think the ankle was broken, surely she wouldn't be able to move at all if it was, but it was viciously painful, each step more exhausting.

Samuel had no sympathy, 'I need your help.'

'I'm trying,' Laurie answered, reaching out a hand to lift up Abraham's arm that had been bouncing on the ground for

Samuel's last few steps, the hand now scratched and bleeding lightly from rasping along the rocks they had crossed.

'Not hard enough.'

'I'm in pain.'

'You fell incorrectly, I trained you, you got it wrong.'

And on, for another horribly slow five minutes, then a break to catch her breath, again, and again. Whenever she thought of that last part of the walk, Laurie's main memory was of the heat, sweat burning as salt drops bled from her forehead into her eyes, stumbling and struggling to be useful, knowing herself useless.

Samuel finally announced that he could see the bunker, 'There. Not far now.'

Laurie peered ahead, she could see nothing in the landscape that was different from the rocks and dirt that were ground to sand, the occasional dead tree, and the odd hump in the distance that inevitably resolved itself into another rock formation as they drew closer.

'How can you tell?'

'He used to bring us here when we were boys, Johan, Lukas and me. He'd take us right up to the door of the bunker and then tell us to find our way back to the compound. He'd run away, fast, and Johan and I were left to bring Lukas back. The first time it happened Johan threatened to run off by himself, chasing after Abraham, crying in the dark. I had to beg him to stay with us both.'

'In the dark?'

'He couldn't bring us here in the day, it would have shown the community that he treated his own family differently.'

'Making you find your way back alone wasn't preferential treatment.'

'It was in his mind. He said that one day he would decide which of us would lead and it would be judged on how well we had worked together for the community. That's why Johan didn't run off after all, he knew if he got back ahead of us, he'd be found wanting, putting himself above the whole. Johan didn't give a fuck about Lukas, he never has, but he wanted to be chosen.'

'And now?'

'What do you mean?'

'We're out here, Johan is back at the compound, he doesn't seem to mind that Marshall has been chosen instead of either of you. Or, if he does, it's not obvious. He's not doing . . . this.'

Samuel stopped, Abraham's feet were already on the ground, he carefully laid down the dead weight of his father, groans of breath scraping from the older man's throat.

Laurie was surprised at the care, but when Samuel saw her frown he said, 'I want him to wake up in the bunker and know where he is. Where I've taken him. I don't want him to wake up out here.'

'Oh.'

Samuel stood back from Abraham's body, 'Laurie, do you really not know about Marshall?'

'What about him?'

'He's Abraham's son. When he came to the community, it was to find his father, the man who'd had an affair with his mother. The affair was one of the things Abraham was leaving behind when he and Ingrid came out to the desert. He promised Ingrid he would leave it all behind if she stayed with him.' Samuel shook his head, 'She loved him.'

Laurie was stunned, 'He's your brother?'

'Half-brother.'

'But all that stuff, when he made you . . . in the city.'

Samuel nodded, 'Yes, Marshall loved all of that.'

'I thought—'

'He was charming, beautiful? He is. Everyone loves him.'

'You don't.'

'I did, very much. Until I realised that Abraham saw Marshall as his firstborn, the true son, and Marshall saw that Abraham didn't love me, not really, he's always thought I was a threat, and Marshall started to use it, the constant comparison.'

'You're both Abraham's sons.'

'Yes, but Marshall doesn't remind Abraham of Ingrid. When Abraham looks at me, all he can think of is Ingrid, what he did to her.'

Laurie started to contradict, to offer the compound's ingrained belief that Abraham loved them all equally, but it wasn't true and she knew it wasn't. It had been obvious for a long time that Abraham favoured Johan over Samuel, that he favoured Marshall over them all.

'I don't want Abraham to anoint him as his successor,' Samuel was saying, 'and I think it's a really bad idea if the community is led by that arrogant bastard.'

'So we are here?'

'Yes.'

'But what if Abraham doesn't change his mind? What if you can't persuade him to agree that you should lead instead of Marshall?'

Samuel shrugged and picked up his burden again, 'Then he'll die in the bunker. As he told us when he deserted us out here as little boys, each of us knows the way home if we look inside. We just need to choose to take it.'

*

Laurie watched Samuel prise the rusted padlock from the old entrance. Immediately behind the six-inch-thick door was a passage that headed forward a few feet and then, from where Laurie sat with Abraham's slumped body, it disappeared into blackness.

Samuel took a few steps forward then turned back to Laurie, 'I'm going down.'

She watched him turn on the torch, saw that the beam seemed dim and useless compared to the brilliance of the sun they had been struggling through all day, saw that Samuel seemed to disappear into the dark, his light was there for a moment, then gone.

He came back up ten minutes later, calmly reached down to the bag he had left by the door, pulled out a rope which he slung over one shoulder and a roll of duct tape he pushed over his fist, 'The sun is going to set soon, we need to get him down there before he wakes.'

As children they had heard about the bunker, stories told by the adults who sometimes had to go way out into the desert to bring home roaming cattle. Built just after the war, when everyone was afraid of nuclear annihilation, it was said to have several rooms, each one deeper than the last, and, since a rock fall, only one way in and the same way out. Most of the rooms and passages were blocked off by broken-down walls, cracked ceilings, the desert pouring in. The children had their own version of the story. Runaways, escaping from the compound after one reckoning too many, made their way to the bunker hoping to find shelter from the open desert, wild creatures and the bitter cold of night, what they found instead was an impossible, impassable warren and, deep inside, a hidden room from which there was no exit, piled high with the broken bones of runaways, no way out other than the way in, lost far behind.

Thirty-Three

Hope knew this room, she had told Samuel about this room, that it was secluded, empty, unused except by the kids at school for secret parties. He must have come out here and cleaned it up, the floor had been scrubbed, her feet weren't sticking to it, she was flying, higher, harder, more.

Samuel had blindfolded her when she got into the car. He took away her small bag of clothes and toiletries and blindfolded her. She'd thought it was sexy at the time, hoped it was, but when she started to speak into the silent car, he told her to be quiet. Politely, but firmly.

'Silence please, Hope. I need to concentrate on where we're going.'

And now there wasn't much that she knew for sure, other than she was here, and so was he. She was hanging on to that, breathing into that, dancing her whole self into it.

A passing thought, were her feet bleeding, like in *The Red Shoes*? Bleeding feet might please him. Something must please him, surely. She would work it out, find the way to make him smile. Was he never going to smile at her again? Why was he watching her but paying no attention? She had tried to stop, twenty minutes, maybe thirty minutes in, but there was no stopping.

'No Hope, you said you wanted this, you wanted to be special, you wanted to make the effort. So make the fucking effort.'

There wasn't even any music, she was dancing to his time, Samuel's hand smacking against his thigh, his foot stamping on the floor, his body dictating the time of hers. This wasn't what she'd thought it would be like. None of it was what she'd thought it would be like, and Hope had been dreaming this for weeks, scheming, planning. For so long this moment had filled her waking thoughts, how it would be when it was just her and Samuel, when he was free to be with her and she with him. Yes, he was older, but that was part of the attraction, of course it was. What was the use of pining after the boys at school? Guys who knew nothing and were destined for less, country boys with no intention of leaving this flat, sodden land, or the smart boys hungry to get away, but only so they could party more, drink more, get stoned more easily, more often. She had nothing in common with the boys at her school, and she had nothing in common with the girls either. It wasn't that Hope thought herself so special, so different – although she secretly hoped she was special, more, better – it was about him, about him thinking she was special, more, better. And surely he wouldn't have gone to all this effort, helping her plot and plan, helping her arrange all of this if he didn't think she was worth it? She wanted to matter, and so she had to dance better, work harder, keep a more perfect time, syncing herself with his hand beating his thigh.

*

246

She had left with him, very early the morning after her party, waiting until her family were sleeping, knowing that his car was parked beyond the big hedge up on the road, knowing he had been waiting, biding their time until the twins and her mothers were asleep. Everyone unaware that the party itself was the real costume, her true disguise, to make sure no one would notice the bag she was packing, the things she was hiding, to ensure none of them would notice the anticipation and excitement that raged through her in the days leading up to the party.

She had thought it was odd when Samuel asked her to make the dress, to hand-sew it according to an old pattern he gave her, and weirder still when he asked her to wear it to the party. But she'd worn it as requested, she was ready to do whatever he asked. She had never before felt this desire to please, to acquiesce, and part of the reason it was so thrilling was how transgressive it felt to give her choices over to him. It was obvious there had been something way back between Samuel and Laurie, confirmed when he showed her the old photo, it was weird that Martha hadn't picked up on it, even weirder given how strange her mom behaved when she was around Samuel. Her mom was being stupid, it wasn't as if she wanted him now, if she ever had, really. Mom was gay, there was no reason for her to be worried about Samuel and Hope getting together. This was a new time, a different time. He was a good man, a gorgeous sexy man, and Hope was eighteen years old. Old enough to have her own life. Old enough to pack a bag and leave her home and the debris of the party and climb into his waiting car and drive blindfold into the dark with him, with no idea where she was going, other than that she was going there with him, because he wanted her to.

Because he wanted her. She hoped he wanted her. She wanted to make him want her, let the rhythm flood her body, tried again and again to give herself over to the time that Samuel was beating.

Now they had arrived and it turned out that the destination was just that closed-down old school hall, miles from anywhere but not far enough from home, not different enough from home. They were not in London, not even one of the nearer cities, they were further into the low flat land, and all Samuel asked was that she dance, demanded that she dance.

She tried to dance to please him. Nothing pleased him. She kept trying. And more, again, more, again. Hope was so tired. She'd had such expectations for tonight, those expectations were not this.

It must be the middle of the day, later even, but she couldn't tell for sure because the windows were covered, old newspapers and thick card over the light, if there was light. She asked for a break, a glass of water, she asked to stop. In response Samuel stamped his foot, clapped his hands, he changed the tempo again, changed her rhythm.

When she broke down, as she was always going to, eventually, she thought he would come to her, hold her, assure her it would be all right. He was a hard teacher, yes, but he cared. She trusted that he cared. Hope collapsed to the floor, crying, waiting.

He was still clapping as he came towards her, maintaining a rhythm she could no longer keep. She genuinely thought he was coming to comfort her, which made it all the more surprising when he slapped her, and that too was in rhythm. As was the next slap, and the next.

'Stop crying, Hope.'

'You hit me.'

Hope's tears were shock and they were the beginning of a new feeling.

'Stop crying.'

He slapped her again, in rhythm, again, and with each hit something new arrived, some twist growing deep in her gut, beyond where she was hungry and thirsty, beyond where the touch of his hand, so long wanted, had become fearful, painful. Anger was rising.

'Stop crying.'

Slap.

'Stop crying, Hope.'

Slap.

'You wanted this, Hope.'

Slap.

'Isn't this what you wanted? Isn't this it?'

Slap. Slap.

And finally, at last, she turned.

'Fuck off, fuck off Samuel, fuck right off.'

He laughed, and perhaps because he laughed, she rose up, strong and furious, she pushed Samuel back and he went sprawling, knocked off balance, surprised. He fell on his back and she ran for the door, her feet were bleeding, the toes bleeding, she could feel the pain now, she could feel everything now, every stinging slap of his hand branded into her arms and back, and she ran anyway, grappling with the sticky door handle, through the old entrance, broken chairs and desks still waiting for a rubbish truck that never came, would never come, she ran out of the building, down cracked concrete steps, and into the rain and the cold grey light.

She headed towards the river that had once been used by this school, a waterway for rowing and playing, for swimming on hot days, a waterway that was fed by the little stream that crossed their garden at home. She knew the river was overgrown, muddy, boggy, dense with vegetation, tall reeds and swamp grasses waiting to cut into her skin. Hope knew this area better than Samuel, knew the secrets of the flat land, where fields suddenly became marsh, where paths that felt solid and firm took another dozen steps and sank into land that was tidal, where the river had banks that faded into land and back again and nothing was as it seemed.

Nothing was as it seemed. Samuel did not want her, Samuel did not care about her. And, even so, he was running after her, shouting for her, calling her back. He was not saying sorry, he was roaring, damning her back to him, ungrateful bitch, stupid girl, cursing her back to him.

Hope did not turn to see how close he was, she knew the air out here was strange, something to do with low winds and high flat sky, it played tricks with sound, people might be much further away than they sounded, they might be far behind. Or they might not. She did not look back, she kept on, grateful for all the exercise, for the training, grateful that she knew how to ignore the pain and keep moving. She veered off the main path towards the river and on to a narrower walkway, even more overgrown. The light was diffuse, strange grey, cold from the sea and becoming misty too, always more water in the air at this time of day, tidal water, tidal land. Her shoes were all wrong to run in, even without the pain in her feet, her toes, they were wrong, she took deep breaths, as Samuel had taught her, deep breaths to calm her mind and think clearly. She had to hold back the terror that was forcing her to go faster, the upset that urged her on and away. She knew this land, this river, better than he did, she'd never get up to the narrow road and then on to the main road without him seeing her, but she could hide, bide her time. She could let him hurry by, still racing by after her, and then she could creep back to the old hall, follow the river the long way round, get into the building, lock the door behind her and get to her phone where he had left it on the table when he took it from her. She could call home. She could be safe, home. She just needed to hold her breath and wait. There would be a hiding place soon, the vegetation here was much thicker, brambles ripping at her legs and arms, she moved on even more slowly, bleeding toes stinging with each step to the ground beneath, boggy mud heavy, claggy, pulling her down. Her legs were tired, she had been awake too long, tired too long, the earth pulling her down to the water.

And then Samuel's ranting ceased, his panting breath, his running feet halted. Somewhere out there he too had stopped. Somewhere out there he was waiting.

Thirty-Four

Laurie followed Samuel down into the bunker. It was cold, even before they got all the way down to the main room beneath the ground, way colder than she had been expecting. And it smelled bad, not just decades of dust and decay, and no doubt the rodents or small creatures that had somehow burrowed their way down and not made it out again, but something else as well. Something darker that made Laurie heave.

'It stinks down here.'

Samuel didn't answer, he was struggling to lay down Abraham's body. Beyond the beam of the torch he laid on the ground there was just darkness, nothing but pitch dark.

She and Samuel worked on tying Abraham securely, and as they did it began to sink in to Laurie what they were going to do. What they were threatening to do.

'Samuel . . . ' she began, and heard him sigh almost before she had started to speak.

'It's too late now, we're not going to back out.'

'But if he says no, what then?'

'Then he stays down here. That's the plan. We're sticking to the plan.'

'But the community – we can't just leave him here and pretend we had nothing to do with it. We'll have been missed. They'll know he's gone, and we're gone, they'll know it was us.'

Samuel picked up the torch and shone it around the room. She saw a metal shelf, a few folding chairs, a folding table, all stacked against the wall. There were several dusty glass jars labelled 'Sterile Water', one labelled 'Alcohol'. Opposite the entrance they had come through, where the last of the evening sun sent a dim light echoing down the stairwell, there was a passageway partly filled with rubble.

'Where does that lead?' Laurie asked.

'No idea,' Samuel said, 'you know what they said when we were kids, you could get lost in here. For all I know it's been closed off by the rock falls.'

'Yeah, or the runaway bodies are piled up back there, maybe that's where the stink comes from.'

Laurie was trying to make Samuel smile and it wasn't working. He was distracted, shaking his head at the uncertain path illuminated by his torch.

'Samuel, what are we going to do now, next? What do we do?'

Samuel shook his head and frowned, looking forward into the dark, rubble-strewn tunnel, 'I don't know.'

Laurie stared at him, 'What?'

'I don't know. I don't . . . '

His voice petered out and Laurie's exhaustion and pain couldn't stand any more.

'You don't know? You've dragged us out of the compound

and beaten him up and now we're way the hell out here, and you don't know what to do next? Christ Samuel, I thought you had a plan, you said you knew what you were doing.'

'I knew we needed to come out here. I knew that much.'

'And now what?'

Out of the dark came a laugh, a hoarse, coarse, pained laugh, 'That kid has never known what to do. He knew how to fuck up, how to get his mother to make excuses for him, but he has never seen a plan through, never had a plan to see through. He's all fire and passion and the minute you call him on it, he crumbles, pissing out the fire with his own fear.'

Samuel roared, lunging for Abraham, and Laurie threw herself in front of him to stop the son attacking the father again, wrenching her ankle even more in the process, sinking to the ground in a rush of nausea and the vertigo of pain.

'Wait,' she hissed at Samuel when she could get her breath, 'let's at least try to talk to him.'

'Go ahead,' Abraham said, his breath catching, wheezing, 'I'd like to hear your thinking. Tell me, I'm not going anywhere.'

So they did. For almost thirty minutes they laid out the case. Abraham was sixty-five. When he had founded the community he'd been clear that older men must give way to younger men, to younger women too. He had said – and it was in the recorded lectures that they had memorised as children, lectures Laurie had relearned during her reintegration – that there would come a time when the community was led by another, and then another. He had always said it should not become a theocracy. Lukas could not lead, Johan didn't want to, Marshall should not, he was not born into the community as Samuel had been, so it was time for Samuel to step up. He would readily take Abraham's advice, he was happy to be counselled, but now he should help the community to the next level.

'And you think you're the right person to do that?' Abraham asked, 'Really?'

Abraham smiled as he spoke, and for the first time in her life, Laurie heard him as perhaps Ingrid had heard him, as maybe he had sounded to the first community members. He spoke softly, his tone serious, almost as if he was questioning the words that came from his mouth, she heard hesitancy in his speech, a grappling for clarity.

'When we came out here I had only Ingrid's faith in me and in the vision. I chose to believe in it, I had to, it was that or know myself mad. The country was still in Cold War insanity, we were brave, long before the crazies, before Jonestown and Waco. We were the good guys, Samuel, your mother and I, we were.'

Samuel said nothing, his torch trained on Abraham's face, and Abraham spoke from the cold ground, hurt, bleeding, his voice rasping where Samuel had punched him in the throat.

He went on, 'Even so, I thought I might be insane, worried I was, but Ingrid allowed me the freedom of finding out.'

'You beat her.'

'Yes. I have no excuse. Men did that, they hit their wives. I think they still do.'

'And their children?'

'Of course, spare the rod . . . '

Abraham said it simply. Whereas he'd sounded sorry about hitting Ingrid, hurting Ingrid, there was no sorrow in hurting his sons. He had moved on, was talking about himself again.

255

'Your mother was my rock.'

'You discarded her.'

Samuel's tone was still low but the vehemence was loud.

'No, she gave way. You boys never understood. Well, Lukas couldn't, and Johan – Johan is no threat to you, Samuel, or to me, he's soft. He'd move back to the city tomorrow for all those easy lies, mortgage, job, kids, simple worries about how to pay the bills and how his kids are doing at soccer. The falsehood that is family. If I was as brutal as you think I am, I'd have forced him to break from her, given him another wife.'

'But if he's happy?' Laurie asked.

'He's deluded,' Samuel answered for his father.

'Utterly,' Abraham continued, 'he will ask, soon enough, can't they live together, can't they be apart from the community, have their own place? So yes, Samuel, you are right to think someone needs to step up, someone tougher than I am these days. But it isn't you.'

And now Abraham started talking about Marshall, why Marshall was better for the community, right to lead and nothing Samuel could do would change that.

Abraham was not, as he often did, declaiming with great passion, he spoke as if he really wanted Samuel to understand, 'The community needs someone who will combine your passion, your self-belief, with careful strategy and solid planning. Forethought, it needs thoughtfulness, it needs . . .'

'Manipulation?' Samuel asked.

'Perhaps,' Abraham allowed, 'however you name it, you do not have it in you. You are all about the rush to do, to act. The next steps must be thought before they are taken.'

'You didn't work like that, not at first.'

'I had the vision.'

'I have a vision,' Samuel's voice was strangled with fury.

'No son,' Abraham said resignedly, 'you have ambition, they're really not the same.'

The sounds were stronger here, in the bunker, outside they had been whipped away by the wind, swerved sideways by the beating heat. Down here, in the dark, the torch dropped and lighting one corner, the noise was deadened, thick, flat. Kick and crunch and smack and the cries of both men were horrible. And then there was only one man crying.

When Laurie opened her eyes it was to see Samuel shine the torch on his own body, mark the blood on his hands. He shone the light in her face, and she didn't look up, she didn't want to see him.

'You should have stopped me,' he said.

'You should have stopped yourself,' her voice was flat, defeated.

'Yes,' Samuel agreed, 'but I didn't want to.'

And then he shone the torchlight forward and headed up the stairs and out into the desert night.

Laurie called after him, begging him to help her up, to help her out.

The heavy door thudded shut and the darkness was solid.

Thirty-Five

'Fucking hell, Mom ... just, fucking hell.'

Jack jumped off the sofa, his tall, strong body tense and angry, fists held tight, he raced out of the room, out of the house.

Martha called after him, it was raining and cold outside, but the front door was already slammed.

Ana looked at her mothers, angry, confused, hurt, 'I don't know why ...' she started, and then didn't know how to finish.

'It's not rational,' Laurie said, 'there's no good reason why I didn't say something sooner. Fear, shame, a whole pile of crap from my past. I'm sorry. I'm really sorry.'

Ana stared at Laurie for a second, and Laurie knew that Ana was seeing her fully, just another fallible human, more fallible for being a failing mother.

Ana left the room in the opposite direction from her twin. A few minutes later Martha and Laurie heard loud music coming from directly above, a challenge daring them to complain.

'That went well,' Martha said.

'I had to tell them.'

'I agree,' Martha was giving Laurie no leeway for hope, 'they're old enough to know you've been lying to all of us.'

'Not lying, not really.'

Martha sighed, rubbed her eyes, checked her phone again, and answered slowly, 'Not telling all of the truth. All of the relevant truth. I have no idea how it must have been growing up there. Of course it's affected you, but fuck it, Laurie, Hope's our baby. And you knew what that man was like and you didn't stop her. You didn't stop me. You didn't tell me.'

'I tried.'

'Not hard enough.'

Martha walked out of the room and left Laurie sitting alone, shamed and silent.

Fifteen miles away Hope shifted from her hiding place, she had given it ten, maybe twenty minutes. She had been counting time in her head as Samuel taught her. He hadn't made a sound in all of that time, no more shouting, no thump of running feet, no angry words, no breath. Just her own heart pounding, her own blood rushing in her ears, the sound of her fear. She carefully stretched up from her crouching position, ready to run, ready to go. The patch of ground where she had stopped provided fine cover, dense with marsh grasses and reeds, the dead heads of long-gone flag irises, ferns that whipped back where she moved away, slowly, so carefully, moved away from the safety of her hiding place.

She stuck to the edge of the river, she thought perhaps this joined up with the stream at the back of their place, for a moment she even considered getting into the river, just following it back, against the current, if the tide was coming in maybe it would take her home. A long stretch of fern whipped around her legs, ripping at her calf and nearly pulling her off balance, it was all she could do to stay upright, not fall, cry out, draw attention to herself. Hope kept moving, very quietly, very slowly.

Laurie wanted to follow Martha, there was so much more she wanted to say, words she was choking on it was so hard to keep them back. She wanted to explain how Samuel's very presence closed her down, made it impossible for her to think clearly, to trust her own judgement. Even if she had been able to explain to Martha how being around him both provoked old feelings and new ones, brutal feelings, the truth was that she didn't want Martha to know that side of her. Martha was kind and smart and she was fun, she was easy to be with and she was honourable. Laurie didn't know if she could ever say all of those things, the full stories, what had led up to them going to the desert, what happened there, she worried that giving voice to them might loosen the hold she had on the here and now. The tattoo was a reminder she wore on her body as a warning to herself, to never cede her own power again. But in thinking about it at all, there were memories, small, specific moments, physical feelings, she could not shake from her skin. It was too much for Laurie to deal with and it was too much for Martha to hear, so Laurie had never said it before and she didn't speak all of it now, and Ana slammed around upstairs and Jack ran off, and Laurie sat, still, in the centre of their home, knowing herself to have brought their family to this point. Sitting in shame suffused with dread.

*

Hope was alongside the old school's fence now, she had made her way round to the side of the building. The edge of the river had long given way to a proper water meadow, the ground was wetter, thicker, it had stolen her dance shoes and now the effort of pulling her blistered and bleeding feet from the deep mud that held them was exhausting. But she could see Samuel. He was sitting on the front step of the building, the steps she had run down, the steps she had had to come back to, to get away. He was holding a phone. She hoped it was his and not hers. She hoped he couldn't see the texts she had sent her friends, the messages about the amazing thing she was going to do, the intimations of sex and happiness that she was so excited about, the stupid wishes she was going to make on her birthday candles. Eighteen stupid wishes, and each one about him.

And then he stood up and turned and started to walk towards her. Through the old fence that should have hidden her from view, directly towards where she was crouching in the mud and the slime and the cold, wet earth. He walked slowly towards her taking photos the whole time, she could hear the camera button on the phone, click, click, click.

She stumbled backwards, tried to get up to run, stumbled again, fell on her back and dragged herself up, but the earth here was wetter, more river than land, pulling her in, pulling her deeper, and then he was standing above her, he was on dry land and she was low into the mud and the wet and she was lost. Had lost.

'Nice to see some spirit, Hope, I was worried back there, thought I'd made a mistake with you, that you didn't have your mother's strength. It's always good to see a girl fight back.'

'I'll fight you,' she said, 'if you come anywhere near me, I'll fight you.'

He smiled down at her, 'Hope, you're in watery, boggy mud. Your feet are sinking deeper even as you talk to me. You are shivering with cold and you are getting colder. You don't want to fight me, you really want to reach out and ask me to hold your hand. You want to ask me to save you.'

He waited, and she waited, and eventually, because she had no choice, because she was freezing cold and hurting and sinking, she did just that. She reached out her hand and he waited until she said the words, made her say the words. She was proud of herself for not crying.

Laurie's mobile beeped, it was a message from Samuel. She was terrified to open it and terrified not to. When she saw the photo of Hope, in bedraggled dance clothes, hair scraped back from her face, Laurie was more scared, and she also dared to feel a touch of relief. Even in this picture, Hope was dancing, that was something.

There was a text with the image.

> *Hope is working so hard on her dance, you must be very proud.*

Martha took one look at the picture and reached for her own phone to call the police.

'Don't, Martha, please,' Laurie said, 'wait until I find out where they are.'

'They can find out from the message.'

'Only on TV.'

'She looks exhausted, her feet are filthy, what the hell's happened?'

'I don't know, but please, let me try first. He's impulsive and I don't want—' she stopped herself from saying she didn't want to provoke him, 'I mean ...'

Martha shook her head, she didn't want to hear what Laurie meant, but she put down her phone anyway, 'Five minutes. Then I'm calling the cops.'

Laurie texted, *Where are you?*

She waited a minute, and when there was no response, she tried again, *What do you want?*

This time he texted back, *Warmer.*

Then she knew what to say, *What do you want me to do?*

See? That wasn't so hard. I'll let you know.

Thank you, Laurie texted back, then she added, *Please can Hope text Martha? Tell us that she is all right?*

If she's a good girl. Stay where you are. I'll call you back. Let's take this one step at a time. You know how things go wrong when there's no plan.

Laurie showed the texts to Martha, 'If we show this to the police, they'll believe something is wrong.'

Martha nodded, staring at the screen, at the photo of Hope. When she eventually looked up from the phone screen, Laurie saw the pain carved into her wife's face.

'I'm so sorry,' Laurie said, 'this is all my fault.'

Martha frowned, 'No. It's not. You totally fucked up and I hate you for it – you didn't tell me about him when you could

263

have, and when you knew she was infatuated with him you should have told Hope about him, about your past with him, and maybe that would have helped . . . '

'So how is it not all my fault?'

Martha's voice was resolute, her words clear, 'He came here, he brought this to us. He searched you out, he groomed Hope and he took her away. Whatever this is, he made it happen. This is all on him.'

Thirty-Six

It was a darkness more intrusive than any Laurie had known before. Out here in the desert, even on a night with no moon, there was always starlight, a fluorescent shimmer, tricking the eye that there was real light where there wasn't, persuading the brain to see, and so it did. Now though, her eyes were open and there was nothing. She closed them and there was nothing.

Then she heard Abraham laugh, cough, groan. The sound could have been all three, perhaps it was. It was impossible to tell where he was lying, to know where the noise of him came from. She felt as if Abraham was closer than he could have been, and also as if his laughter was happening inside, in her head, in her skin, in her gut, those too many times that Abraham had been inside her self.

Abraham wasn't known for laughter, knowing smiles were his stock in trade. There was the smile that said you'll understand soon enough, I'm coaxing you to your own revelation. There was the smile that revelled in a community member's confusion, when they discovered that sharing their transgressions, far from freeing them from the burden of guilt, was a step towards deeper awareness, the path Abraham wanted them all on, where there was no salvation but to lose the self entirely. And there was the sad smile, almost a sigh, for this poor person sinking back into a frail individuality that comforted the sleeping mass of humanity. Occasionally he gave a great grin of welcome when he saw true understanding dawn in another person, watched them take on the responsibility for themselves all alone, ridding him of the burden of dragging them, wrenching them, to awareness – a smile of relief and his muscles ached to make it.

The laugh again, and now it made sense, it came from where Laurie thought Abraham should be, opposite her, tied up, safe. Making Laurie safe.

'What's funny?'

'You are.'

She waited, tried not to ask, tried not to want to know, and even as she said, 'Why?' he laughed again.

'See? Very funny.'

'I don't see,' she said, irritated, tired, in pain, 'and neither do you, it's black as hell in here and neither of us can see anything.'

'I've known you since you were a baby Laurie, since we chose you for the community, for Samuel. I could tell you how you're sitting now, if you want?'

'Stop it, Abraham.'

'Our little secretive girl, always trying to carve out a moment of privacy for yourself, always thinking she was more special than everyone else.'

'That's not it at all.'

'Oh, it's not what you tell yourself, when you think you can't survive without time alone, but in removing yourself from community you are suggesting that you're better than the rest, that they don't need the private time you've deemed you cannot live without.'

'It's not like that.'

'Don't sulk,' he said and Laurie lifted her chin, straightened her back, looked directly ahead. Her movements were involuntary and even so they earned a 'that's better' from Abraham. And Laurie despised herself for the moment's pleasure she felt in receiving his approval.

'So,' he went on, sounding strangely strong, when only a moment ago he had been groaning in pain, 'How are you sitting now? You are leaning against the wall dug out of rock, one leg is tucked under the other. Until a moment ago you were chewing on the ends of your string of hair. You'd hoped I didn't see, because even though you have transgressed in every way possible, you're still scared of me seeing you break a rule that you learned before you could speak.'

Slowly, carefully, forcing herself to take her time, Laurie moved her right leg from beneath her left, straightened up, pushed back her long twist of hair so it was out of reach of her nervous hands.

'You're no different from the rest of them,' he was saying, 'you attack your body, bite nails, fall over, bruise yourself, cut yourself. You do it to get away from being with you and your truth. You are terrified of sitting down with you, only you.'

'I'm here.'

'Not really. You drag up memories, analyse your feelings,

pick at your life like a chicken carcass, dissected and devoured. Your life isn't that interesting, Laurie, no life is. Whatever you've done, thought, seen, heard, they're just experiences.'

'I'm not here to be lectured by you, Abraham.'

He laughed again, this time a short, sharp burst of laughter, and now she could hear the pain beneath it. He took a breath, his voice slower, more careful, she recognised it as the tone he shifted into when he was teaching. She didn't want to hear what he had to say and yet there wasn't a person on the compound who didn't crave Abraham's full attention, hunger for and dread his scrutiny. She could feel herself readying for it, both the fear of revelation and her desperation to be seen.

It was getting colder, it must be late, that transition when the desert floor shifts from burning to a sudden, deep chill, heat leached from the ground by a wide sky that goes so far up, sucking away the warmth. She leaned back to try to get comfortable, her mind skipping across the long walk here, the way she had thought it would never stop, one foot then another, one step then another. Further back, a time when they were deep in the dance, before she was taken away by the authorities—

'You want to be known,' he said, out of the dark, and she was startled into wakefulness, she could hear a smile in his voice, he knew he had frightened her, she had to be more careful, stop giving him power, stop making him matter.

'You want to be known,' Abraham repeated, 'yet you do not have the courage to reveal yourself. You want me to do the work for you. You want to have your truths coaxed from you, waiting on me to carve you into yourself. You don't even care that it hurts to have your lies cut away. Do you realise how tedious it is for me? That none of you have the courage simply to state the truth? That I have always had to be the leader? It has bored me for years.'

'Then let Samuel take over.'

'Samuel doesn't have the strength, and you know it. We had hoped that planning a strong helpmeet for him would help, but he has simply led you into temptation, into his own folly. Samuel is dangerous, Laurie, you should beware his ambition.'

'I think it's you who need to beware of his dreams.'

'We'll see. He will never have the strength to lead the community as I have, his dreams are all of himself. I have had to be the father-therapist to you all, as you cry out your sins and your jealousies and your disappointments. I have had to teach you and force you to comply to the most petty of rules—'

'You invented the petty rules!'

Again, a sigh that was maybe a groan, a pause, longer so that she thought he might be asleep or dead, that she might be alone, and then he spoke quietly, 'I thought you'd all step up eventually, but even you, who left us . . . '

'I was taken away.'

'Even you came back and sank into the rules and the rituals like a nun running from the man who wants to fuck her – running fastest because he is a man she really wants to fuck. Is it possible, Laurie, do you think,' his voice was very soft now, very calm, 'for you to be here, in the dark, and to honestly sit with who you are? To sit alongside me, and just be here, now? Can you try?'

*

And because it was her training, to give herself to his will, and because there was no one else there beneath the desert and because he was dying, surely he was dying, and because she had no idea if Samuel would come back or not, so maybe she was dying too, Laurie gave up fighting, she let herself be in the dark.

She was only open, vulnerable, wounded, and the parade of her shame, all those times she had not been the person she wanted to be, the little jealousies, the bitter thoughts, were just the surface of her deficiencies. Beneath were deeper and dirtier truths, how even now she wanted to fuck Samuel, not for the sex, but because she knew he wanted to fuck her, he still believed them covenanted, believed them destined, and that gave her a sense of power over him. And then admitting that desire for a devious power, built on manipulation. Desire and fear and shame of the desire, shame of her fear, all of it spinning in her guts. Laurie was no longer recounting past memories or dreaming future possibilities, she was just sitting in the meat and blood and bone and skin and sinew of herself, alive, for now, with no control beyond this one breath, then the next. Sitting in the shame of fully knowing herself. She tried to get up, to get away from what she was understanding, but her ankle hurt too much and she couldn't find the walls to hold and so she brought herself to the ground, on her knees on the ground, because there was nowhere left to fall, nothing to do but swim in the pain, in her truth. She gave herself to the earth.

Five small children in the children's room. A place of soft toys and silliness, where they were encouraged to be free, to enjoy themselves – although only there, only in this room. The adults were aware that these children, out of the toddlers' corral but not yet covenanted, not yet promised, still needed to let off steam somewhere, so a space was made where they could play. There were pale blue walls and red and green cushions, low chairs, hand-made like most of the furniture on the compound. At that age, six, seven, they were beginning to learn discipline. To be a disciple one must have discipline, they knew this to be a rule, and they longed to be disciples, chosen, beloved. And so, every day, they struggled against their wriggling toes, gurgling bellies, fidgety fingers. They laboured to temper themselves, base metal, becoming pure. Each day another ten seconds were added to the timed waiting. Each day they were getting better and better, closer to beloved.

Laurie was in the middle of five children, there was Samuel who was nearly ready to leave this group, and a girl a few months younger than him, Laurie was coming up to seven, and then there were two little ones, only just turned six, just come from the corral in the past week, struggling to learn that there were times to play and times to attend. Even so, they were often better than Laurie at holding, at being still.

The seconds were counted. The children of the community learned to count in ten-second lots. Later, with Dot and Henry, Laurie found that she could time an hour with her eyes closed and her ears blocked, that time was etched into her.

Teacher – which is what all of the adults supervising them were called, just Teacher, no matter who the adult – was counting seconds. The first ten. The second ten. The third. Fourth. They were doing so well, all five children holding themselves still in the moment, trying not to giggle. And then one of the smaller ones burped. She didn't mean to, and it was not the burp that set Laurie off, it was the new friend's little face, all ready to cry, all ready to crumple up, and Teacher's finger held up, Teacher still counting, ignoring the crying little one, daring them all to notice.

Abraham says: The body will do what it does, we do not have to attend to it. We are greater than body.

Laurie practised not attending, tried not to hear the farts in the dormitory at night, the burps and belches, the snuffles from someone crying, so often tears in the dark. She worked to rise above her flesh, but that day the noise was so funny and she saw Samuel's eyes crinkle, barely crinkle, saw him bite his lip to stop himself smiling, and then she couldn't help it, she laughed out loud. It was funny.

She was six years old.

And her laugh did what laughter often does, it sparked the others, all five, even though they had not yet finished the sixth ten seconds, they had not held a minute. They were shaking and giggling and the blue walls and the red and green cushions did not soak up their laughter, they amplified it and Teacher's face became red because she could do nothing until she had finished counting to sixty, because her counting was part of everyone's training, and Teacher also wanted to be special, desperately, and she too must follow the regime. She could not stop her counting even though she was getting redder and redder and then her red face was funny, her red face and the sweat patches under her arms and she reached sixty and they were five giggling, rolling bundles of silliness and joy and the silence was broken and Teacher must do what she must do.

It was a hot day, a huge, dry heat. All of the adult women combed and twisted and pinned their hair back, Teacher must have been no more than fifteen, though she seemed fully adult to the children, and her hair was long and red and frizzy. It must have been so hard for her to make it behave, to twist it into itself and keep those tempting curls under control. That day the poor girl had no control, five giggling children, a sweltering day and heavy storm clouds looming as they had since first light, her face red with upset and what Laurie later knew to be fear, her sweat showing the fear too, and her hair escaping as laughter escaped the children. No control.

Abraham says: Every action has a consequence, every consequence another. Nothing is inconsequential.

Laurie laughed and so she was lifted up and placed into the dark room, to consider her actions, to consider what she knew to be correct and what to be incorrect. It was one of the hottest days she had ever known in her short life and in the heat of the dark room she held herself to the ground, trying to find something cool in the dirt floor. The dark place was covered by burlap sacks and corrugated iron, and even though Laurie was small she could not stand up in there. The heat pushed her down, held her down, she was the heat's held moment.

Six hours in the heat, with her own waiting and the dark earth and the storm clouds above. Heated by her sorrow and her guilt, Laurie liked Teacher and she knew that Teacher must also be punished for her lack of control over the children. All of that time on the ground, embracing the dirt, burning with shame, and there was something else, something for which she did not yet have words, something she only understood years later. There was something small and squirming but also enjoyable about the shame – in public shame, there was attention.

Later, living with Dot and Henry, and when she was a parent herself, Laurie realised that she had been hungry for the attention that any child receives in a family; the nagging, loving, cuddling, cajoling, chastising, exalting attention that any child of any ordinary family becomes accustomed to, day in day out. But the community was not ordinary and it was only a family by choice. At six years old, Laurie did not yet know that she was hungry for attention.

When she emerged into the blinding light she was faint with heat and thirst. Even then, she had been to enough reckonings to know what to do. They led her to Abraham, leading because she could not see through eyes tight-shut against the fierce light after hours in the dark place. She stumbled when they pushed her in front of him, only knew it was him because she could smell the oil of roses, and Laurie laid herself down in the dust at his feet and she felt the full community around her, waiting to see his reaction.

She knew they would be standing in a circle, the cooks and kitchen hands clumped together, anxious that it not take too long, no one could leave the circle until Abraham was done and the meal might be spoiled. On the other side would be the gardeners and farm workers, called in from their work to witness. Some would be annoyed, the half dozen older men who rode day in day out beyond the compound, others would be relieved, back-breaking work to weed the dust-gardens, to coax life from the parched earth of the compound's land, a reckoning might also be a rest for those who witnessed.

Laurie lay in the dust, shamed and – part of the shame, a deep core of it – excited to be there, to be in the centre, to be noticed. In the strange, hot place deep in her belly there was also pleasure, and she was confused.

She lay face down and Abraham recited the pledge of community, everyone echoed his words a moment after.

When the pledge was done – *I maintain this to be my truth and am ready to sacrifice all for this truth* – there was a silence, the held moment. Held into minutes, maybe as long as an hour, Abraham could always wait longer than any of them.

Then Laurie felt a cool hand on her dusty, sweaty head. His soft and cool hand, he was touching her, anointing her. She knew what to do. Came to her knees the better for him to hold one hand under her chin, to lift her face to his, and then she would open her eyes and see his tears. Abraham's tears born of her transgression.

Fighting the urge to rub the hours of dust and dirt from her lashes, Laurie looked up, ready to be embraced, held, forgiven. She saw his face smiling in pain at her wickedness and yet ready, as ever, to take back one who might yet be a disciple. She opened her eyes and everything she had craved in every other reckoning she had been called to witness – a dozen at least, even in her short life – was hers.

Abraham picked her up and rocked back on his feet and lifted her above him and pulled her to his chest. Rare laughter rumbled from his belly to his shoulders, roared from his mouth. He rolled in the dust and rolled little Laurie with him. He was so happy to have her back from the dark place, from individuality into community. She was another who had fallen and had risen through her own penance and by the community's witnessing and, above all, by his own redeeming generosity.

A hot day, trees wilting in the sun's glare, chores left for an hour or more by a community called to serve, a community who would collectively pay if those chores were not done before the day was out, and a dirty, tear-stained, giggling child welcomed back into the fold.

Abraham says: Suffer little children.

Abraham said, 'Suffer little children.'

Laurie woke at the sound of his voice. She woke shivering, the ground beneath her was freezing cold now.

'It's just after three, he's been gone several hours, you've been asleep.'

Abraham's voice was slow, strangled, and Laurie was finding it harder to work out where the sound came from. She must have been somewhere near the centre of the room, she remembered falling here, falling into the depth of where she was and what this was.

'I thought, perhaps, you were dead,' she said.

'You wished?'

'No,' she answered quickly and then, because they were here, because she knew he was tied too tight to move, she said, 'Maybe, yes.'

'Then your wish will come true.'

'What?'

'I'm dying. He kicked me in the chest, many times. There is something affecting my heart, or perhaps my lungs, a broken rib I think. It's hard to breathe, getting harder.'

'I don't know what to do.'

'I'm not afraid of dying. I've been afraid of pain in my life, dying in pain, but being dead doesn't worry me at all.'

Being dead worried Laurie very much, and being alive in here, alongside a dead Abraham, terrified her.

'Maybe he's gone to get help.'

Abraham started to laugh, but it caught in his cracked throat, ripped along his broken ribs, 'Christ.'

'What?'

'There's stuff, coming out of me.'

'Blood?' she asked, scared to ask.

'It doesn't taste like blood,' he sounded different, he sounded worried, 'OK,' he was speaking into the dark, ragged speech and even more ragged breath, 'I can do this. I can do this too.'

She wondered if he was talking to her or to himself, 'Abraham?'

'It's funny, you know,' he said, 'out here, on the land . . . ' a break while he collected his breath, some breath, any breath, 'I was always hurting myself at first, forever cutting myself or dislocating a thumb, a finger. I got good at putting them back.'

'Yes.'

'I had to teach myself to take care of my own body, my flesh, on the land. I got good at it all, but the inside-out part,' he took a deep breath, coughed and groaned as he coughed, spat, 'I hated that. I'm glad I can't see this, maybe I'd hate it still.'

'Inside out?' she asked.

'The bones, the meat of us. The pus when the body is trying, failing, to heal.'

'I don't—'

'Understand? No. You're young. You will. When you get hurt and don't recover for months, when you split your skin and it takes weeks to heal, when a bone,' he groaned again, 'when a bone sticks out of your flesh, and the liquid leaking from your wound is not blood.'

He was silent then, for a long while, silent but for impossibly broken breaths. Laurie waited, finding herself holding her breath in time with his.

'We are disgusting, underneath,' he said, 'we disgust ourselves. That's why we cover it up with clothes and hair and artifice, the shame of being meat and bone. But in the end, we're just blood and piss and crap, we are liquid in a sac of skin.'

Laurie lay on the ground, crying into the dusty floor, listening to Abraham die.

A while later, an hour or more, he began to groan again, differently this time, his breath faster and harsher.

'I wanted him to call you, in the night, from my office,' Abraham said, 'I wanted him to get you back. You belong here, I brought you here for him.'

Then silence again and another long, dark while. Laurie thought she was cried out, dried out.

'Laurie,' his voice was so faint, almost all breath yet no whisper, 'It's close. Can you hold me?'

'You must be too broken to touch.'

'I'm past that now. Will you hold me?'

It took her several minutes to find him, scrabbling around the dirt floor of the bunker, and when she did she was both relieved to feel another's skin, and horrified at how cold he was, how dying. She followed the line of his spine to his head and, in the dark, she carefully stroked his hair. It was sticky with matted blood, or worse.

Abraham grabbed her hand, squeezing it tight, suddenly strong, 'I don't want to ...'

Now he was hurting her, dragging on her hand, squeezing against her still-aching thumb, writhing and then rolling on top of her wrenched ankle and she retched in pain, nothing to bring up but bile.

'I don't want this,' he whimpered.

'You said you weren't afraid, you said, all my life, you said ...'

'Stupid girl,' grabbing at her, reaching for her face with dirty hands that were tight claws, bringing her face to his so they could stare at each other with sightless eyes in the bitter darkness of the bunker, 'Everyone is afraid of death.'

She was looking into his eyes, she thought, when he stopped. She struggled out from underneath him, crawling backwards until she felt the opposite wall, not far enough away, a wall to lean against, rock to hold her up.

Only then, finally, was she truly able to give in to the dark and the cold, and all that was left to do was howl, her jaw wrenching itself apart, her mouth so wide it ripped at the corners of her lips, a silent scream because there was nothing to see and no one to hear.

It was hours later that Samuel returned and Laurie found herself crawling into his arms, relieved, grateful, shaking, freezing cold. He told her not to look behind and he helped her up the stairs and outside into a starlight that, even so, felt blinding after all that time beneath the earth. She suck- led the water he gave her, breathing in the air of the desert night, breathing in air that did not stink of blood and pain and death.

He had brought a bandage for her ankle and driven one of the four-wheel-drive vehicles out as far as he could, even with the pain of her ankle, the walk back towards the jeep felt much shorter than the walk out. After a while her voice came back, her words were less jumbled.

'What are we going to tell them?'

'Not you, me. I'll deal with this. You're going back to your adopted parents tonight. You'll call them, they'll arrange a ticket, they'll make it happen. They'll be glad.'

'What about you? I'm not leaving without you.'

Samuel was very quiet, very cool, 'It's not safe for you to go back to the compound.'

'What?'

'They think you kidnapped Abraham. They're going to think you killed him.'

'Why? How?'

'Someone saw you going to Abraham's office. When I went back there were two of the women going through your stuff. I told them I was heading out to find you, but someone will come here eventually, and when they do, you have to be gone.'

Laurie knew he was right, if they thought she had killed Abraham they would attack her. There would be no coming back from it. And if she and Samuel told the community the truth, told them that Samuel had beaten Abraham, and she had let him, it would be even worse, a transgressive act and a transgressive witnessing.

'Will you come with me?'

'No,' he said, 'if we both leave they'll work it out. It doesn't matter, this will pass, there will be a different time. We are covenanted, Laurie, destined. One day we will lead the people here on this land. It will happen. I promise you.'

She left that night. Samuel had a little cash, he took her out to the stop on the main road and she caught the bus into town, and then called Dot and Henry to come get her. It was weeks before she felt warm again.

Thirty-Seven

Hope had given up thinking that perhaps it would be all right if only she could dance well enough. Samuel had been very clear that it had nothing to do with her. He explained as he told her to get changed into new dance clothes, he explained as he told her to brush the mud and leaves out of her hair, he explained as he laid out the small glass of water and the apple he was about to allow her to eat and drink, the first thing she'd had in hours.

'This isn't about you, Hope, this is about your mother and I, we knew each other a long time ago.'

'In America?'

'A different America, a different world. There is a great deal she hasn't told you.'

'I know she was in a cult.'

'A cult? She said that?' He looked hurt, 'The community was no cult, and we were both privileged to be a part of it.'

'So what happened?'

Samuel rubbed the apple on a cloth, shining the deep red skin, 'My father was a visionary.'

'What's his connection?'

Hope was stalling for time, trying to engage, trying to get Samuel to talk to her, and they both knew it. Samuel decided to indulge her and he explained.

'My father founded the community, he uprooted his life in order to make a difference for people he didn't even know yet. People like your mother.'

'But she was a baby when the—' Hope stopped herself at his look, 'the community?'

He nodded.

She took her chance and went on, the more he chose to answer, to talk to her, the less he was shouting at her, the less he was playing with that sharp knife.

'When they took her in, she was just a baby, isn't that right?'

'Yes.'

'So did your father adopt my mom? Was she your sister?'

'No,' his response was sharp, 'not in the way you mean, not like you and your sister, your brother. We were all children of the community. And she and I had a much stronger connection than mere blood ties, we were covenanted, promised to each other. The reason they brought her from China was for me. Your mother was destined to be my partner in the future of the vision. She broke her promise.'

Hope looked at the glass of water he had set down, at the apple he was holding still, the sharp paring knife alongside. She wanted them so much, and she knew she needed to wait until she had his permission.

Samuel was still speaking, 'He who cannot remember the past is condemned to repeat it. And none of us want to repeat the past, do we, Hope?' He looked at her, but it felt as if he was looking through her, 'I'm here to help your mother remember her promise, live up to her promise.'

'But she was a child when she lived there, you can't hold her to anything she promised as a kid.'

'Are you a kid, Hope?'

'No. Yes. I don't know. I'm eighteen,' Hope said, wishing she wasn't, wishing she had never had the party, never run away.

'Yes you are, and your promises now are adult promises. Your mother made adult promises too. And she knows that no one can escape reckoning.'

He smiled, slowly and carefully peeling and coring the apple, cutting it into fine slices, 'Come and eat.'

He was pointing at the apple with his knife and Hope was too scared of him to move closer.

'Come on,' he said evenly, 'eat the apple, drink the water.'

'I'm not hungry.'

'I'm going to call your mother, and I want you to have the apple and the water so that when I tell her you're just fine, I'm telling the truth. Fed, watered, exercised, all good.'

She took a deep breath and spoke quietly, 'No.'

Samuel frowned, 'No. Interesting. And why not?'

'I want to go home. I don't care about your past with my mother.'

'With your mom, Laurie, not your mother, not the mousey one, what's her name?'

'Martha, and she's not mousey. You don't know her and you don't know me as well as you think you do. You need to take me home, I've had enough. This is stupid.'

It took all of Hope's courage to stand then, to face him, keeping the tremor from her voice, her body.

Samuel shook his head, 'Seriously? You've spent the past five months doing pretty much anything I asked, like a desperate puppy, happy even to be kicked, and you have to beg me to drag you out of a disgusting swamp and now you work out how to say "no"? Now?'

He was laughing at her and Hope wanted to laugh too, she wanted to laugh it all off. He was right, she was ridiculous, she'd been an idiot, there was nothing attractive about him and nothing rebellious or exciting about hanging around in a cold old hall, playing an absurd game that was only in his head, but she wasn't stupid and she wasn't going to be his victim any more.

'Take me home, Samuel.'

Before she even realised he was coming towards her, Samuel had grabbed her by the hair hard enough to wrench her off balance, and then he was pushing her round to the table, jamming her into the chair, the knife so close to her eye that she thought he was going to blind her.

'Eat. The. Fucking. Apple.'

The front door banged open and slammed closed and Jack came running into the sitting room where Martha and Laurie were waiting for Samuel's call, Ana ran downstairs, her phone in her hand, Jack must have called her on his way back in, they were speaking at the same time,

'I think I know where she is, where they are.'

'Jack thinks he knows where they've gone.'

Laurie held out her phone and showed them both the photo of Hope, 'He sent a photo.'

'Like a fucking kidnapper?' Jack asked.

Martha winced and Laurie shook her head, 'We don't know. It's only him who's been in touch, not her.'

Ana grabbed the phone for a closer look, 'She looks exhausted.'

'Let me look,' Jack said, clicking on the photo and squinting past the image of Hope to what little showed of the space she was in, 'It's hard to tell what's in the background, but I think it might be – Ana?'

Ana nodded, 'Maybe.'

'What?' Martha asked, 'where?'

Jack looked shamefaced but he answered anyway, 'It's where I thought. A place we sometimes go to, the kids from our team. Hope knows about it from swimming parties. It looks like the hall at that old boarding school.'

'You guys use it?' Laurie asked.

'It's been boarded up for years, and it's all covered in ivy and weeds and shit, the river has burst its banks loads of times,' Jack said, 'they keep saying they're going to develop it but nothing happens and—'

'Jack,' Laurie said, 'I'm not telling you off, just tell me exactly where it is.'

'Not far, and there's a shortcut. Twelve miles maybe, fifteen at most.'

Laurie was already looking for her car keys.

Martha stood in front of her, 'You can't go.'

'What?'

'The kids and I will go. You have to stay here. He said he's going to call again, he only wants to speak to you and you need to be able to answer the phone.'

'Then you drive,' Laurie handed the keys to Martha.

Martha was already heading down the passage to the front door, 'Reception is shit out here, you know that. If he hears the sound of the engine, if the phone signal cuts out, he'll know you're not at home. He said to wait and he'd tell you what to do. If Jack's right and they're at this hall, they must have parked somewhere, we'll see his car or lights or something, we'll call the police, straight away. I promise. But if that's not where they are, you need to be here when he calls.'

Hope ate the apple and drank the water, slowly, trying to work out what to do next, while Samuel paced and looked at his phone and paced some more.

When she was finished she set down the water glass, leaving everything on the table as neatly as Samuel had laid it out.

'Samuel?'

'Yes?'

'My mom has a hidden room in our house. Do you want to see it?'

Two cars passed each other on a long, flat road, slippery with rain that had been falling all day, watery land and low storm clouds above. One speeding to a derelict hall, the other going home.

Thirty-Eight

Left alone, Laurie at first stood still in the old sitting room at the heart of the house. Then she went up to Hope's room, sat on her bed, stroked her pillow, prayed non-believer prayers to bring her daughter home and safe. She climbed more stairs to her office, pulled back the bookshelf and stared into the tiny room she had made for herself. The wind and rain outside sounded higher here, harder, and the room offered no solace. Her phone was in her hand, resolutely silent.

She sat on the floor in her small room, facing the open bookshelf door. This was the problem, this was her fault. She had brought this upon them through her secrecy and there would be a reckoning. She walked back down to the ground floor and waited. It was coming.

'Laurie? Let me in.'

It was Samuel's voice, Laurie smacked her shoulder on the hall wall as she raced to the door. She wrenched it open and he strode inside, but no Hope.

'Where is she? Where the fuck is Hope?'

'She's having a little rest, she's earned it.'

'They're on their way to find her, they know you were at that school hall.'

He shrugged, 'Good, then they'll find her. I'm here for you, not the happy family.'

'They'll call the cops, they'll come straight here.'

Samuel, wet from the rain that still beat against the house, shivering with cold and joy at his plan almost completed, stood very close to her face, 'Jesus, Laurie, you think I care about police? I'm here for you.'

'I have a new life now.'

'One life, all joined up.'

'I'm not interested.'

'You have no choice. We were promised.'

Samuel reached out to her, simply, calmly, his face coming close to hers as if he might kiss her, she reached out to push him away, and then, very quickly, he had his arms around her, tight, pinning not holding, and there was a sharp blade against her ribs, she felt the point of the knife through the fabric of her top.

'Hope says you have a secret room. Let's go take a look at it.'

Laurie was backed into the corner of her room, tied up with the tape Samuel had taken from her desk.

He had bundled her in, gleeful at the idea of a hidden space.

'Hope will tell the others if she told you, we can't hide here.'

He closed the door behind him and sat back against it, 'We're not hiding Laurie, we're reckoning. And how terrific that you made a perfect space for it, your own little bunker. So, let's start again. You killed Abraham.'

'You killed him, I was with him when he died, I held him.'

'You were down there for hours, Laurie, you were dehydrated and disoriented.'

'I had been locked up with a dead man, I was terrified that you weren't coming back, that I was next.'

'You thought you were going to die?'

'If you didn't come back, yes.'

'And you were scared of his ghost?'

'No. Yes.'

Samuel shrugged, 'There are no ghosts.'

'You're a fucking ghost, Samuel, a malevolent spirit. He'd been beaten senseless by you, you beat the crap out of your own father. Twice.'

'If I did "beat the crap out of him", you stood by and let me.'

'You think I don't know that?' she asked, 'That I've ever forgotten?'

He stared at her, forcing her to look away because it was so hard to look at him and hear this, 'I believe you know it, but do I believe you remember it truly? Oh Laurie, your head is full of so much else, your lovely home and your lovely wife, your great kids. You think about work and how successful you are now – so successful that you're in the press, lauded, interviewed, so that someone who has searched for you for years stumbles across your story one day when he had almost given up hope.' He stopped and smiled, 'Hope. You must have been scared when you started to get all that attention? Worried I'd find you?'

'I assumed you'd started a life of your own, Samuel. It genuinely didn't occur to me you would be so pathetic as to have done nothing but wait for me.'

She watched him flinch and his hand grow tighter on the knife, thought perhaps she'd gone too far, but he was too concerned with the reckoning he had promised himself, recounting her faults.

'Most people would have gone to the authorities, once they got away, would have gone and told what they'd seen, the behaviour on the compound, what happened in the bunker. But not you, you wanted it too, didn't you? You wanted me to kill my father. You'd have stopped me otherwise. You didn't tell the truth afterwards because you wanted Abraham dead as well.'

'I couldn't tell the truth, about any of it. You'd made me complicit.'

'You were complicit.'

'I tried to stop you,' Laurie wasn't even sure she believed herself.

Samuel laughed at her, 'Laurie, you remember me back then, I was weak, confused. Sure, I wanted to be amazing and strong and passionate but mostly I was just scared, I was fucked up by Abraham and the community and everything else.'

'I thought you were lovely.'

He was almost gentle in return, 'Because I was kind to you? Because I gave you attention?'

'Both,' Laurie acceded.

'And I could never have done what I did without you by my side. I needed you by my side and you left me.'

Laurie stared at him, 'That's not what happened, you told me to go. The community thought I'd kidnapped Abraham. You let them think that, you wanted them to.'

'I had no choice.'

'Neither did I.'

'We were destined, and you believed we were, that's why you came back from your adopted parents.'

'I can't remember what I believed – but I watched you kill your own father, was that destined too?'

Samuel was as angry as Laurie, 'It happened, so it must have been. And now the community needs us, both of us. Marshall has done enough, too much, he's been modernising the community, and it's not right. We can go back, help them find the original path. They'll welcome us home, they need us, both of us.'

'I have a family, Samuel, a life. I'm not going anywhere with you, you stole my daughter,' Laurie said.

'Hope is an adult, she made up her own mind.'

'You brainwashed her.'

He groaned and stretched his arms high above his head, 'You don't think much of her, do you? "Brainwashed"? I expect that's what you've told people about our childhood too?'

'It's true.'

'Except for the part where you came back at seventeen, willingly. The part where you stayed, willingly. The part where you and I took Abraham into the desert, willingly. We were good together, you and I, and there's much we have to do, to repair. We can fight against these stories that are coming out now, people talking about indiscretions from so long ago.'

'Like the women who left the community and are speaking out now, saying we were sent off as sex slaves when we were special ones? Or like Abraham abusing us as children? Which indiscretions do you mean, Samuel?'

'You know those are lies made up by angry, bitter women. You and I can right all those wrongs. We were covenanted.'

'Is that what you really want, you want me to give up my life and come back there with you, and live out some fantasy made up by your mad father?'

He smiled, 'Yes. All of that. And I want to hurt you, Laurie. You remember what happens to runaways?'

She did. She couldn't speak. She did remember.

'I don't have a branding iron, I guess this knife will have to do.'

Thirty-Nine

Abraham reaching out to her, a child, just covenanted, in the hot room, his office door closed, blinds pulled. The scent of rose oil on his skin.

Feet taped together at the ankles, wrists bound at her back, there was no way for Laurie to fight back when Samuel came to kneel beside her, when he began to stroke her face in her hidden room, exposed room. She tried to bite, tried to push him away with her head, her jaw, but she was bound and he was free, and then he taped up her mouth because he couldn't bear the words she was saying, and anyway, he didn't believe them. Rain drumming against the old window, the ropes of wisteria holding tight to the house in the high winds.

Abraham in the almost-dark, stroking her skin, promising Laurie that this too was a privilege, Abraham's time, Abraham's attention, Abraham's touch.

*

Laurie felt Samuel kissing her face, her bound hands, as from a distance. She felt it as they had trained themselves to do as special ones. The body that was being kissed, the body that was touched, it was not her, not Laurie, not really. It was just flesh, just body, real Laurie was far inside. Though she did wish it had not been in this room, she did wish that her one safety had not been desecrated, was not being desecrated.

Laurie is small, not yet out of the toddlers' corral and she is raised up by the big man's hands, raised up high, lifted above all the other children, and Abraham, who smells of sweat and prayer and rose oil, whispers how precious she is, how sweet, his dear little predestined daughter. She is three years old.

Samuel kept repeating how beautiful she was, that he had always loved her, loved her above all others, and Abraham had chosen her for him.

In the bunker and Laurie remembering those times, the memories she had forced away, hidden away, all those memories clear and bright in the underground room that was only dark. Glad Abraham was dead, happy to have witnessed his last breath, and then she was getting up from the ground, struggling up and beyond that main room, there had always been rumours of another way, a hidden exit, there must be another way.

The things Laurie had never spoken, the things she did not remember if she could help it. The reason words had left her, the reason it took months of Dot and Henry's kindness before she attempted to speak again. The reason it had been so easy for Samuel to call her back to the compound, to persuade her to help him rid the place of Abraham. Laurie did not say the words and did not remember the occasions, the specifics, but she could never get that smell out of her head, rose oil and stale whiskey on Abraham's breath. When she began to find some ease living with Dot and Henry, they tried to help. There were several therapists, and each time, Laurie found it impossible to explain, to speak what had happened, and after a while she realised that retelling the story was simply rehearsing how it had been, how hard it had been, compared to this new, messy, laid-back life with Dot and Henry. Yet she missed some of her old life on the compound anyway, and then everyone behaved as if she had been saved when they took her from the community, which made her feel bad for missing any of it, and so there was a backlog, a growing dam, built of all the things that were never said. The more they were not said, the more impossible it became to ever say them. Martha had always understood that Laurie's life would not be given to her in shared confidences about bad teachers and childhood crushes and long summer holidays. Just once, when she was living with Dot and Henry and seeing a therapist that she began to trust, Laurie told a little more, she said that Abraham had always been drunk, that he only hurt them, Laurie and the other children, she was not alone, she explained that she was not special, at least not in this – he only hurt them when he was drunk. The therapist asked, was it perhaps possible, that Abraham became drunk in order to hurt them, that he did not become abusive when he was drunk, but that he drank in order to abuse. Laurie couldn't bear the calculation in that possibility and so she did not think it again, did not speak to that therapist again.

*

Samuel was kissing Laurie, and her face was covered in his kisses and her tears, and Laurie was straining hard, trying to get away, to pull herself away from him, but her hands and feet were hog-tied with office tape, simple office tape, and there was nowhere she could go.

Laurie slowly, laboriously, agonisingly making her way through the rubble in the hidden passageway, searching for the secret door that no one had ever been able to find, another way out, a way out that did not have dead Abraham or living Samuel. There was no way. She did find bones though, thought it was more rubble at first, thought it was still more dirt and dust and rubble and then she realised there was some light, grey light, that there was an exit after all, high up, too far up to reach. And that grey light lit the dry bones of the runaways. Just as they had always whispered.

Laurie did not want to be in her body, in her room, in her home. She was trying not to be there at all. But with the cut of the knife into her skin she came back to the room, wrenched back. There was exultation on his face when he demanded she open her eyes and look at him, witness him witnessing her. He would not let her be anywhere else, and it was his pleasure in her pain that made her hate him the most.

Laurie lying in the grey light among the old bones, Samuel taking her back to the dark, this exit impossible, too broken. The only way out was the way in. Back through the broken tunnel, back past dead Abraham, back up into the light of sacrifice.

Laurie was still tied up in the small room when Martha quietly let herself into the house and found her wife, freed her wife, whispered that Hope was safe. Laurie was forcing herself back to the here and now when Martha took her sharpest knife from the kitchen. Laurie was waiting when Martha found Samuel washing himself in the little bathroom off their small bedroom.

He saw the knife and he smiled at her, 'You're not like that, Martha. Laurie is, and Hope will be, one day, but you're the quiet, dependable one, aren't you?'

'You know nothing about me.'

He smiled again, lightly, still not worried, 'I know your wife though.'

'Did you rape my daughter?'

He shook his head, 'Little girls were my father's thing, not mine.' He held out his hand, 'Come on, you're the nice one, Martha. Everyone thinks so, the nice mother, the sensible one. You're good. And good girls don't—'

'This one does.'

Laurie was watching from their bedroom door when Martha killed Samuel. Witnessing. Samuel wasn't expecting Martha to leap on him, to roll him, he didn't expect to be knocked sideways and leaned over the bath, and the cut to his throat was so well executed, almost kind, far kinder than he had been to Laurie. A sharp hiss of air, and Martha held the head back just enough for the blood to rush out fast and easy, pouring down the drain. He didn't take long to bleed out and, for once, Martha was glad of the skills her father had insisted she learn.

She waited a minute, two, three, four, until she was sure Samuel was dead, then she hoisted the rest of his body into the tub and, having washed her hands thoroughly, she held her wife.

Forty

They didn't waste time with explanations or reasons. Martha had long known about Laurie's room, Hope had found it a few years back, and asked Martha about it, Martha told her that Laurie's childhood in that difficult place meant that she always needed secrets. It was fine for a mother to have a place of her own.

They held each other for a short while and then Martha phoned their children.

She spoke to Ana, trusting her to be the most calm, the most likely to obey, and said she would come back to fetch them, she needed to sort a few things at home, but she would be there very soon. She was clear that they should not, under any circumstances, walk home themselves.

'Samuel is leaving, Laurie and I have persuaded him he had to go, he's leaving here, going back to America. But I don't want Hope to come back and find him anywhere near if he's stalling. You need to give us a couple of hours at least.'

Ana relayed the message and Jack agreed, 'Fair enough,' he said, wanting to protect Hope from any more pain, wanting to be the big little brother. Anyway, the storm was even worse now, it was dark and it was freezing cold, they could wait.

Laurie and Martha rinsed the blood away from the body and the bath, and then wrapped it in heavy plastic bags and carefully carried it outside. They said 'body' and they said 'it'. They did not say the body's name. They laid it in the foundations for the new office and, standing in the pit in the bitter rain, Laurie pulled down the dirt and rubble from the old shed, covering the body, scraping and cutting her hands on chunks of brick and stone. Martha did not stop her.

'The storm will be gone by morning,' Laurie said. 'It will be dry enough come afternoon and I'll lay the concrete, put the steels in. Later on I can get the kids to help me begin the frame. It will be a project.'

'Good.'

'We can't ever sell this house.'

'No.'

'We'll be here until we die, one of us, then the other.'

'I'm sorry,' Martha said, 'you've always wanted to go back to the city.'

Laurie looked up from where she knelt on the ground, her hands raw, her body aching, the cut on her back bleeding into her shirt, 'And you always wanted to stay here, but I'm sorry you got your wish this way.'

'I'm not. He hurt our girl, he hurt you. I have no sorry at all. None.'

And then they were both crying and Martha helped Laurie up and they threw rubble on the pile as the cold rain fell down. Then Laurie said they had done enough, it was safe from foxes for the night, they laid the tarpaulin back over the space that had been empty, replacing the barriers so that none of their children would notice.

'The kids pay no attention to the garden anyway,' said Laurie.

'Good. I want them to never pay attention to the garden.'

They washed in the stream before they went back into the house, washed away dirt and blood and the night, and Martha cried because they had a house with a stream and now the stream had another purpose.

Martha left to pick up their children and Laurie went into the house. She showered in the bathtub that Martha had already sluiced down and washed and sprayed with chemical cleaners, and as she scrubbed at herself she scrubbed again the tiles and the glass and the bath. The room was steaming and sodden when she stopped. She was not finished washing, but she stopped anyway, Martha would be back with the children, Hope had been through a horrible time, it was important to give her attention to the three of them. Laurie knew that the cuts and scratches on her hands would heal, even the deep wound cut into her back, she knew that the sick horror in her stomach would recede, ebb away. None of it would ever disappear, and she would keep going anyway, because she was skilled in keeping going, had a lifetime of practising, and because she had three children and a wife and a life that wanted living. She cried as she dried herself and dressed, then she went upstairs and closed the door on her hidden room. Tomorrow she would take off the book-shelf door. She would open up that space, they would stay in the house, she would build herself a beautiful office in the garden and they would live under that flat high sky on this wide watery land for ever. For now there were curtains to be drawn and lights to be turned on, a kettle to boil and pizzas to find in the freezer. She was surprised to realise that she was hungry.

Forty-One

Once Laurie had finished building her office, she decided she wanted to remodel the whole of the outside space around their house, they were never moving back to London, she would make the flat land her own. On wet days she worked on her old office in the house and the hidden room, turning it into a studio for Hope. Once the wisteria was removed, the light through the old window was perfect for Hope's new-found interest in painting and drawing, in line and movement on the page. She had chosen not to go to university yet, it was all too hard, so she had taken time to help Laurie with the building and landscaping work and discovered she enjoyed the design part of it. In the spring she went to a sixth form college to study design, and her mothers were happy that she was learning and she was enjoying it.

The twins were swimming and studying, Martha had a full list of clients and plenty of work. Like Hope, Laurie had taken some time away from work to concentrate on the land-scaping, the indoor and outdoor builds. She had also taken the time so that she never had to sleep away from home, away from Martha. Both women still had the nightmares, nights when one would wake sweating and shaking, and the other would hold her into calm, into slow, soft breathing again. Neither shared what she had dreamed, there was no reason for the other to have those images in her head as well, they each had enough to contend with.

The year turned and summer came and the children went to stay with Dot and Henry for three weeks while Laurie and Martha gutted their little bathroom, and repainted most of the house. Then Dot and Henry came back for a fortnight and there was a noisy time of extended family, Martha's father came to stay, Jack slept in a tent in the garden, the girls made a summerhouse bedroom of Laurie's new outdoor office – how could the mothers say no when they suggested it, it was a lovely light space, perfect to sleep through the hot nights, resting on flat land. There was one warm evening when they ate outside, lights strung between the trees, the newly fashioned garden soft in shadow. Hope was going away at the beginning of autumn, the meal was a farewell and a celebration of her new start. She was moving to London, to study design and, perhaps, follow in both of her mothers' footsteps.

Laurie and Martha dropped Hope off at her halls of residence, a bland modern building in north London, they saw other students who were just as young, as hopeful, nervous, excited. They met her course tutor who seemed too young himself, but warm, friendly, serious. They assured themselves, as much as any parents of a child leaving home could do, that Hope would be happy and that she would be safe.

They took her out for a drink and then left her to make friends with the other young people on her floor. Martha drove Laurie through city streets they used to know well, then to the motorway, then out to the long, low land that would always now be home. The twins had dinner waiting, the house seemed much less full, and it was right that Hope was making her own life, a new life.

That night, while Jack and Ana were sleeping, ready for training early in the morning, when Laurie and Martha lay in each other's arms, Martha's sleep deep, Laurie's as fitful as ever, Hope was thinking of home. She was dancing, five steps forward, three back, and again, five steps forward, three back, up and down the narrow space of her little single room. Hope was not dancing alone. There, on her laptop screen, was another dancer and another. Laurie would have been surprised to see how technologically adept the community had become, and how they used that technology to reach out to the world, welcoming the world to the joy of community. Hope was glad the community had no idea she had known Samuel, that he had left the community before she met him, she never wanted to have anything to do with him again, wherever he was. Even so, she would always be grateful for the dance, and for the connection he had helped her make, showing her the hidden site, the unlisted access. In retrospect, he must have been mad, or at least very sad, but he had given her this, and this was a good thing. Hope was learning, with the community's online help, their chatrooms, their forums, that there was value in every experience, as long as she worked to find it.

The dance shifted on screen and Hope allowed herself to shift with it, into a faster pace, wilder, the steps less formalised, the dance more her own, their own.

A voice came through her little speakers, distant but warm, 'That's great, Hope, really beautiful. Let your pain go in the movement that we create together, as one. We're so glad you have joined us. You are indeed a special one.'

The man called Marshall smiled at her from the edge of the screen, she waved briefly, and then as the low musical note came from Marshall and from the others dancing behind him, Hope gave herself to the dance, gave herself to the community.